Wedded Bliss (Lancaster)

The Reluctant Bride

The Ruthless Groom

The Reckless Union

The Arranged Marriage box set

College Years

The Freshman

The Sophomore

The Junior

The Senior

Dating Series

Save the Date

Fake Date

Holidate

Hate to Date You

Rate a Date

Wedding Date

Blind Date

The Callahans

Close to Me

Falling for Her

Addicted to Him

Meant to Be

Fighting for You

Making Her Mine

A Callahan Wedding

Forever Yours

You Promised Me Forever

Thinking about You

Nothing without You

Damaged Hearts

Her Defiant Heart

His Wasted Heart

Damaged Hearts

Friends

Just Friends

PRAISE FOR MONICA MURPHY

Lonely for You Only

"Monica Murphy has the uncanny ability to yank at your heartstrings and leave them in tatters. Angsty, sexy, funny, and delicious—this is another slam dunk straight into my top three books this year!"

—L.J. Shen, *Wall Street Journal* and *USA Today* bestselling author

"Monica Murphy books are guaranteed five-star reads. With addictive writing and lovable characters, her stories hold you captive from the first page to the last."

—Devney Perry, *Wall Street Journal* and *USA Today* bestselling author

A Million Kisses in Your Lifetime

"I loved everything about this book. From the storyline to pacing, the characters . . . everything. It was so romantic. Crew is by far the BEST hero Murphy has ever written."

—Jessica, The Lovely Books

Close to Me

"This book is like a sexy, angst-filled treat that readers will absolutely devour. I can't wait for the next!"

—Rachel Van Dyken, #1 *New York Times* bestselling author

"As a longtime fan of Monica Murphy, I have to say *Close to Me* is one of her best books! Autumn and Ash scorched my Kindle with their chemistry, sexual tension, and the perfect amount of angst. I devoured this in one sitting! An engrossing coming-of-age, enemies-to-lovers tale, *Close to Me* is a definite one-click! Fans of Drew and Fable from *One Week Girlfriend* won't want to miss this next-generation story."

—Lex Martin, *USA Today* bestselling author

END
GAME

ALSO BY MONICA MURPHY

Lonely for You Only

The Liar's Club

Lancaster Prep

Things I Wanted to Say

A Million Kisses in Your Lifetime

Birthday Kisses

Promises We Meant to Keep

I'll Always Be with You

You Said I Was Your Favorite

Lancaster Prep Next Generation

All My Kisses for You

The Players

Playing Hard to Get

Playing by the Rules

Playing to Win

Billionaire Bachelors

Crave

Torn

Savor

Intoxicated

One Week Girlfriend

One Week Girlfriend

Second Chance Boyfriend

Three Broken Promises

Drew + Fable Forever

Four Years Later

Five Days until You

A Drew + Fable Christmas

Stand-Alone YA Titles

Daring the Bad Boy

Saving It

Pretty Dead Girls

END GAME

MONICA MURPHY

Published by Montlake, Seattle

www.apub.com

Amazon, the Amazon logo, and Montlake are trademarks of Amazon.com, Inc., or its affiliates.

ISBN-13: 9781662522796 (paperback)
ISBN-13: 9781662522789 (digital)

Cover design by Hang Le
Cover photography by Wander Aguiar
Cover image: © EFKS / Shutterstock

Printed in the United States of America

To the paramedic who responded to my daughter's car accident—your charming smile put her at complete ease (me too). When I asked your name and you said, "Nico," I thought, Of course that's your name. Straight out of a romance novel, this guy. Thanks for the inspiration, Nico.

Chapter One

Everleigh

The text comes through after I've been waiting for a response for over an hour. Picture it: Me sitting on imaginary pins and needles, anticipating the answer. Throwing one single thought out into the universe and hoping I'll receive the news I desperately need.

Only for my hopeful anticipation to be tossed into the trash with the ding of a text notification.

Sorry, the room has already been rented.

An actual frustrated growl escapes me, and I glance up quickly, wondering if anyone heard me in the busy coffee shop where I'm currently sitting. But no one is paying attention to me.

Not the moms clad from head to toe in Lululemon who are clustered around a small table not too far from me, a total of four baby strollers beside them.

Not the girls who basically remind me of . . . me, sitting at another table, all of them watching as their friend taps out a response to someone I assume is a guy she met on a dating app. She said his response to her reaching out was "I like your tits. And your face."

Was I listening in on their conversation? Yes. Do I regret it?

No.

By the way, that guy sounds like a douche. She should move on.

The three dude bros sitting at the table directly next to mine are definitely not paying attention to me. Two out of three of them have their hats on backward, and they're all massively broad in the shoulder and chest area. Like impressively so. Athletes, I would assume, consuming breakfast sandwiches at a breakneck speed and not saying much save for the occasional grunt. Football players, maybe?

I have no clue. I don't watch sports. And I definitely don't keep up with the athletic teams at this new college I'm supposed to be attending in less than a week.

Well, there's no *supposed to* about it. I'm registered. I've picked out my classes, and my schedule is so perfect I could almost cry. I'm a transfer student starting at UC Santa Mira as a junior, and only a few days ago, I was beyond stoked to be coming here. Excited to move into my new apartment with my three other roommates. Eager to make new friends, have new experiences, and just be . . . free.

Only for one of those new roommates to reach out the literal day I arrived in this gorgeous beach town with an overly apologetic email (God, I hate email) saying that my new room—well, essentially my new bed because I was sharing a room—had been rented out to someone else. That I was mistakenly offered the room/bed when it was already taken.

Reading that email, my vision blurred with unshed tears. I wanted to cry. Took everything within me not to just break down and sob. But I didn't.

Chin up, Everleigh Bailey Olmstead. You won't let this setback get you down. You need to press forward.

My grandmother's inspirational words are the only thing keeping me going in this life, I swear.

I used some of the precious money I'd saved over the last two years for this new adventure to stay at the cheapest motel I could find, only to be scared and unable to sleep because of the rather nefarious things going on through the night. Like the woman who knocked on my door at one in the morning insisting she was room service. Trust me, there was no room service at this motel. I didn't open the door, too freaked out to even move as I pressed my back against the headboard, curled into a ball as the insistent knocking went on for far too long.

Now here I am, dragging ass and needing this coffee to rejuvenate me. Student housing in Santa Mira is sparse. I should know. I wrote a paper about the student housing crisis my first year of college, and now I'm a victim of it. I'm homeless.

Homeless.

I can't adjust my schedule to online only and go back home. I will never hear the end of it if I do. My mother will give me that look and say, "I told you so. Getting too big for your britches gets you nowhere."

I can literally hear that particular tone in her voice ringing in my mind. The judgmental one. There is no way I can return to the small town I grew up in with my tail tucked between my legs and pretend it's okay that I'm taking online courses. Because it's not okay. First, I can't stand the idea of going back to the place where I grew up, just knowing everyone is watching and waiting for me to fail. And I can't justify taking courses at UCSM and paying those UC prices while living at home. I wanted an actual experience when I went away to college.

Looks like I'm definitely getting one. Just not the one I'd hoped.

"Fucking Sampson. He's such a loser," I hear one of the dude bros mutter before he shoves the remaining half of his breakfast sandwich into his mouth.

My stomach growls, and I take a sip of my scalding-hot coffee, wincing when I burn my tongue. I came in here to feel normal and wake up and bought the cheapest item on the menu, delusional in thinking that a cup of coffee will be a good enough breakfast.

It's not. I'm starving. And jealous of everyone currently consuming those breakfast sandwiches.

"I knew he'd walk," another one says, and takes a noisy slurp of his iced whatever. It's practically white, so I imagine it's full of sugar and not much caffeine. If these guys are athletes, they're not taking very good care of their bodies with this meal. "He can't cut it."

"Doesn't help that you gave him so much shit," says yet another one.

"If he can't take my shit, how is he going to be able to handle Coach?"

I'm about to tune out this very sports-heavy and boring conversation when one of them says something that has my ears perking up big time.

"Now we'll have to find someone else to move into his room." This is said with an exasperated groan. I even catch the guy tossing the rest of his muffin onto a napkin on the table, and I swear I see steam rise from the broken bits.

Oh my God, I am so hungry.

The one who gave poor old Sampson endless shit—I slide my gaze over to check him out, and holy wow, his freaking face makes my breath catch—is glowering at his friend the muffin destroyer. "That shouldn't be a problem. Empty rooms are a commodity around here."

"I don't want to live with someone else," the muffin man practically whines before he snatches up a chunk of the muffin—looks like blueberry—and shoves it in his mouth. "We had a good thing going."

"We still do," Mr. Handsome pretty much growls, and be still my rapidly beating heart. The voice matches the face, and the face is like whoa. Dark hair. Dark eyes. High cheekbones and a strong chin. Even frustrated with his friend and teammate and roommate, there's a faint smile curling his lips, and it's a good one.

Mad understatement. It's a *great* one.

"Right." Muffin Man shakes his head, and the other guy at their table just laughs. "I'm going to let you take care of finding a roommate to rent out that room, then. I don't have time for that shit."

"I don't have time for it, either, but I'm sure it won't be difficult." Mr. Handsome chooses that moment to glance around the café, and for the briefest moment, our gazes meet. Lock. He doesn't look away, and neither do I, and on his face appears this slow, downright panty-melting smile that has me dropping my gaze, my cheeks going hot.

Holy hell, this guy is way too good looking. And he knows it.

I keep my focus strictly on the table while I listen to them discuss roommate options as they finish eating. Then all three of them stand, impressively towering above everyone else as they move as one unit toward the door, tossing their trash on the way out.

Within seconds I'm on my feet, following them at a discreet distance, my earlier hunger forgotten. The great thing about Santa Mira is that the college campus is literally in the center of town, and most everything a student needs to get to is within walking or biking distance.

My suspicions are confirmed when they don't jump into a car and take off. They amble at a leisurely pace down the sidewalk, chatting loudly and gesturing with their hands until they eventually make a left onto a side street that is lined with apartment buildings and the occasional house.

"Should we mention the open room on one of those Facebook groups?" the muffin man asks, his voice ringing loudly.

The handsome one makes a dismissive noise. "Who's on Facebook anymore besides people as old as our parents?"

"I have a Facebook profile." Muffin Man sounds offended.

"So do I, but I'm never on it," Handsome retorts as they all slow in front of a cute older white clapboard house trimmed with black. And there's an actual porch with a saggy couch that's definitely seen better days, but I could live with that.

"Then what do you suggest we do to find a new roommate?" asks the other guy, who apparently doesn't talk much. He's bigger and broader than the other two, his bulky arms covered in tattoos.

"Ask around, I guess." Handsome shrugs as they head up the path that leads to the porch, and then all three of them practically run up the stairs. "We'll find someone. I'm not worried about it."

He glances over his shoulder as if he can feel my presence, his gaze snagging on mine, and he comes to a stop, turning to fully face me. I start backing up out of pure instinct at being caught.

"Can we help you?" He doesn't sound hostile. No, he seems downright open. Definitely friendly.

Deliberately charming.

His roommates turn to check me out, the three of them imposing as they stand shoulder to shoulder on their porch.

"Um." I stop walking, the rest of my words getting caught in my throat. How do I approach this without sounding like a stalker who listens in on their private conversations? "I was in the café earlier—"

"Right." Handsome interrupts me. "I remember."

Oh. Did I make an impression?

Probably not.

"And I couldn't help but . . . overhear your conversation?" I wince, feeling bad. My heart is racing and my palms are sweating. I shake them out, and the guys share a look.

One that definitely says *What is this girl's problem?*

"What conversation?" the muffin man asks warily.

"About needing a roommate?" I clear my throat. Take a few steps forward, curious to see the inside of the house. Are there enough bedrooms? A decent-size kitchen? I'll take a sleeping bag on the bathroom floor if I have to. I can't be picky right now. "I, um, I happen to know someone who needs a room."

"Who?"

"Me."

Chapter Two

EVERLEIGH

They're quiet, all three of them sharing a quick look before Handsome steps forward, that gorgeous smile appearing on his face once more. Pretty sure he's trying to disarm me with it. "A pretty girl like you doesn't want to room with us. What would your boyfriend think?"

"I don't have a boyfriend." I cross my arms in front of my chest, vaguely offended he called me a pretty girl. It almost seems patronizing there for a minute and definitely not like a compliment.

"Oh." He shares a look with his friends before returning his attention to me. "We've never roomed with a woman before, so maybe it's a bad idea."

"Why is it a bad idea?" I raise a single brow, resting my hands on my hips. Trying to appear braver than I feel. "From what I heard, it sounds like you need a roommate, and I need a room."

"You do realize school starts in four days." He tilts his head, watching me carefully. "Move-in officially started yesterday. And you don't have a room arranged already?"

I get why he's asking questions. I probably look like a dumbass to these guys, and maybe I am, but it's not my fault everything fell apart on me. I'm just having a serious bout of bad luck.

Like . . . really bad luck. But they could turn everything around for me if we can make this work.

"I had a room rented, but it all fell through yesterday." I lift my chin, swallowing hard when I notice the way his observant gaze skims over me from head to toe. "So now I'm on the hunt for whatever I can find. A room, a bed, a couch. One roommate, twenty roommates. I just need somewhere to live. Whatever it takes."

"Whatever it takes?" Now it's his turn to raise his eyebrows.

I'm blushing. I can feel the heat warm my cheeks. "I don't mean it like that . . ."

"Like what?" His smile grows, if that's even possible, and now I realize he's teasing me. At my expense.

I sort of hate that.

"Can you cook?" asks the muffin guy with a hopeful expression on his face.

Handsome sends him a scathing look. "We're not hiring her to cook for us."

"What if she can, though? That would be kind of nice, right? None of us can cook for shit." Muffin Man smiles at me, his brows lifting. He's not as charming as the other one, but he seems pleasant enough. My heart rate doesn't ratchet up when he aims that smile at me, not like with the other guy. "Can you?"

I nod slowly, not about to give away all my cards yet. I've been cooking dinner for my mom and grandma for years. Grandma taught me everything she knew and gave me a bunch of her recipes. "I can."

I'm not a gourmet chef, but I doubt that's what these guys are looking for. And if cooking meals is a part of the deal, my class schedule allows for it. I have no night classes this semester. They're all on Tuesday and Thursday afternoons, giving me ample time to find a job, which I need to do ASAP.

After finding a place to live first, of course.

"Then the room is yours," Muffin Man says firmly, earning a slap in the chest from Handsome. "Come on. Why wouldn't you want her to live here?"

They form a huddle right there on the porch, with me standing on the sidewalk watching them, and I wish I could hear what they were saying. The coffee in my stomach sloshes around, reminding me I didn't eat anything beyond a quick, cheap hamburger—not a cheeseburger, which I prefer, but I'm trying to save money here—from McDonald's for dinner last night, and I'm starting to feel a little queasy.

"Want to come look inside?" the quietest one finally asks me, and the relief that floods my system nearly has me stumbling over my own feet as I head toward the porch of what could possibly be my future home.

"Sure." I keep my voice purposely nonchalant, entering the house as he holds the front door open for me.

They all follow me inside, crowding behind me as I stop and take in the living room. There's a brown leather couch with a matching love seat, and they're both a little worn, as is the beat-up coffee table and the end table, which has a basic lamp sitting on top of it. The giant TV hanging on the wall looks brand new, though, and there's a game console on the stand just below it, along with a couple of controllers.

I can see what their priorities are. Not a surprise.

There is nothing hanging on the white walls. No curtains on the windows, just basic white blinds. There's nothing in here to make this place very homey. But it appears relatively clean, so that's a bonus.

"I'm Cooper." The quietest one offers his hand to me, and I shake it, startled by his strong grip. "That's Dollar." He points at the muffin man.

"Dollar?" I ask, my voice weak. What kind of name is that?

"Frank Dollar," the guy formerly known as Muffin Man clarifies. "I go by either name."

"Dollar, Dollar Bills, yo," Cooper says with a smile, and I paste on a polite one, my gaze sliding to the only guy whose name I don't know yet.

He's watching me carefully, his gaze skeptical. I don't think he's 100 percent on board with the idea of me moving into their house, so I choose to ignore him, allowing the other two guys to take me on a complete tour.

"The kitchen is small," Cooper says as he waves his hand toward the narrow space. "But it's got everything you could need, and the fridge is pretty big."

"We need the space since we're growing boys," Dollar adds, patting his stomach.

If that's another hint he wants me to cook for him, I don't know what to say. It's best I remain quiet, pasting on a smile and nodding politely.

We make our way down the hallway, pausing to pop our heads into each open doorway.

"There's four bedrooms total, which is pretty rare in this neighborhood," Cooper explains as he points toward one of the rooms. "And there are two bathrooms. One of them is attached to the primary, though."

"Which means you'll have to share a bathroom with these assholes." Mr. No-Name jerks his thumb in Cooper and Dollar's direction. "Don't know if you're ready for that."

I can't help but wrinkle my nose at the idea. "I'm guessing you've got the primary bathroom?"

"Yep, I sure do." There's that smile again. The one that most likely makes women all over this campus drop their panties for him. "But I also pay a little more rent for the privilege."

"How much are you renting the room for, anyway?" I mentally brace myself for the amount, heading for the last bedroom, which they haven't shown me yet. I peek inside to find there's a bed already in there, as well as a desk and a chair. But that's it.

No problem. That's good enough. The other room I rented had a similar setup.

I enter the room and check out the closet, which isn't very big. But I don't have a lot of stuff, so I can make it work. The bed is stripped and isn't covered in gross stains, so that's a good sign. There's no dresser, but I could buy those cheap storage-bin drawers at Target or Walmart.

This has tremendous possibilities. Living with three guys, though? Will that be an issue?

I can't worry about that. I need to take my opportunities where I can, and this one basically landed in my lap.

Moving away from the bed, I walk over to the window and push back the vertical blinds, making them clack noisily against each other. My breath catches when I take in the view.

It's nothing but the ocean. The Pacific is right there, seemingly only a few feet away since the house sits close to a cliff. Which might be a little disconcerting if I think about it too hard, but beggars can't be choosers in this moment.

"Rent for the room is fourteen hundred a month," Cooper says, and I whirl around, shock coursing through me at the amount.

"But I was only paying eight hundred at the other place," I protest weakly.

"That was just a bed," Cooper reminds me. "Here you get an entire room."

"I have to share the bathroom." With two big burly men who probably aren't very clean.

Ew.

"Maybe you can convince Nico to share his bathroom with you." Dollar waves a hand in Handsome's direction, and I turn to look at him, frowning a little at the revelation.

Of course his name would be Nico. Sounds and looks like he walked right out of a rom-com or a romance novel. I mean, look at him.

Tall, dark, and handsome barely covers it. He's also broad and muscular, with a disarming smile and eyes that seem to see right through me. It's a little disconcerting, if I'm being real with myself.

"Yeah, that's never going to happen. I'm not big on sharing." Nico crosses his arms in front of him, his expression turning stern, his biceps bulging. I don't know what's more distracting, his face or his muscles. "It's why I pay extra rent."

"Would you guys take a thousand a month?" My brain is scrambling, trying to process if I can even cover that much.

All three shake their heads, and I can feel it.

I'm losing them.

"What if I cleaned the house once a week?" Ugh, I hate to make that offer, but I'm getting desperate.

They share a look, one that says *Who cares.*

Men.

"I could cook too," I add, a little reluctantly.

Dollar's eyes light up. "You already know I love that idea."

"But it means we'd all have to pay more rent," Nico reminds him, sounding all growly and sexy.

Ugh, scratch the sexy part. Just growly. Grumpy.

"I don't mind if she cooks for us. I'm so sick of fast food, bro. And pizza. We go there all the damn time," Dollar practically whines. I'm sure he's referring to the Woodstock's Pizza that's down the street.

"I mean, maybe not every meal, but a couple of dinners a week?" I offer, trying my best to remain calm. Like I don't have everything on the line.

But I do. I'm desperately in need of a place to live, and this would work out great—only if I can get my rent down to a more manageable cost.

"We need to discuss this, if you don't mind waiting?" Before I can respond, Nico is dragging the other two into his bedroom, the door slamming shut.

Oh God. It feels like my fate is in their hands, and I hate it.

I scurry back into the living room and perch my butt on the edge of the couch, fighting the anxiety that wants to sweep over me. I remind myself there have to be other options. They're not the only place with a room/bed for rent.

Hopefully?

Eager to prove it, I grab my phone and google "rooms for rent Santa Mira."

I scroll through the meager options, frowning. My heart sinks into my stomach. There's not much offered, at least online. One of them is a bed for rent for $1,500—more than what they're asking me now. There are also a couple of listings that sound super sketchy.

Sighing in utter frustration, I exit the Google search and hang my head, closing my eyes.

This is looking grim.

Chapter Three

Nico

"This is a crazy idea," I announce the moment I shut my bedroom door.

"What's so crazy about it?" Cooper leans against the wall, crossing his bulky arms. "She seems nice enough."

"But do you really think we should rent the room to a girl?" I sound like an asshole. I feel like an asshole for even saying it, but damn.

I've never lived with a woman before, beyond a relative, and that doesn't count. Wouldn't she encroach on our stuff? Our personal lives? Would she try to turn this place into a pink palace? Would she have all her friends over under the guise of a study session, but really they're all there trying to check us out? What if they're boring or nerdy or flat-out awful or worse . . . active fangirls who won't leave us alone?

Yeah. I'm a complete asshole sometimes. I can admit it.

"What's the problem? You think she can't handle us?" Cooper's brows lift.

"Handle us how?" Dollar asks, sounding confused.

Typical. The guy can be kind of clueless.

"I mean, do you think she's aware of . . . who we are exactly?" I sound like a jackass, but come on.

We're on the Dolphins football team, and for the last couple of seasons, we've been the hottest shit alive. The love and adoration we get from everyone on campus and in town is fucking crazy. Last season they had to hire security guards just for us to safely exit the stadium after games. It was completely out of hand.

While it freaked us out some, truly?

We pretty much loved every minute of it.

This season is predicted to be even wilder, and I'm ready for it. National championship, here we come. I'm tired of the South or the Midwest always seeming to have the advantage. We're bringing the trophy back to California again. We have to. It's my senior year.

I'm ready to go out with a bang—and plan on finding plenty of women to bang along the way.

Cheesy segue, but I made it work, I think.

"Give me three reasons why you think this idea is crazy," Dollar retorts, looking pissed—specifically at me. This guy. He always seems frustrated with me since we moved in with each other over the summer. Even a little on edge, though I know why. He's been dealing with a shoulder injury that keeps him from playing, and he hates it.

"One, we don't even know her name." I hold out my hand, my index finger up. "Two, we should probably run a credit check on her. She freaked out over the rent amount. What if she stiffs us and we can't kick her out because the laws are so crazy here?"

I watched that nineties movie with my mom back in the day where this couple fixed up their house in San Francisco and rented out the rooms. One of the tenants was a nightmare, and they couldn't evict him. It was like a legit horror movie.

I'm not about to get us caught up in something like that.

"She wouldn't do that," Dollar says with a finality that makes me wonder if he's hot for her.

I mean, I'd get it if he was. She's cute. Great legs that are on full display thanks to the denim shorts she's wearing. Long dark hair that's pulled into a high ponytail, and big blue eyes that seem to eat me up every time we look at each other.

But yeah. I can't think of her like that because if she was to move in with us, I wouldn't mess around with her. I'm the type who hooks up and moves on fast. I don't have to keep facing them days or weeks or months later. The one time I did that—and it was only last spring, so not too long ago—it ended in utter disaster.

If I hooked up with this girl *and* we lived together? I wouldn't be able to escape her.

"You don't know that," Coop says, sounding levelheaded, as usual. "Nico's right. We don't know her."

"What's your third reason?" Dollar asks me, completely ignoring Coop.

Here's where I reveal my biggest fear.

"What if she's a secret fangirl who'll make our lives absolutely miserable?" They're out there, the secret—and not-so-secret—fangirls who try to chase us down every chance they get. Last season we had a few who sneaked into our apartment. Gav found one naked in his bed. They get a little wild at bars and try to get us to sign their tits after games, and their antics are . . .

A lot.

It's a little calmer around town since school hasn't officially started yet. Orientation for the incoming freshmen is being held early next week, so things are pretty quiet around campus and Santa Mira in general.

But the majority of students are moving in over the weekend, and come Monday? It's balls to the wall. Students everywhere. Fangirls lurking at every corner.

All right, maybe not every corner. Not every woman on campus cares about the football team, but a lot of them do, and some of them come on really strong. Too strong.

"Oh, what, you'll be miserable because some cute girl wants to suck your dick on the regular? What a hardship." Dollar shakes his head. "I'm not even interested in her like that. I just want someone around to cook us meals on occasion. Like I said, I'm tired of the fast-food runs or DoorDashing everything. It gets expensive. I want a home-cooked meal."

"She could be lying."

"I don't think so." We both swivel our heads in Cooper's direction when he speaks up. "She seems . . . nice."

"But you don't know her," I remind him. "Anyone can seem nice when you first meet them. Jeffrey Dahmer's neighbors always said he was a nice, quiet dude."

"Bro, they said that but also complained about his place stinking. They just didn't know he was cooking up body parts." Dollar mock shivers. "She's not a serial killer, Nico. She seems like a girl who's in a shit situation and desperately needs a room. We have a room. Why wouldn't we help her?"

"What sort of discount should we give her for the cooking deal?" Cooper asks, changing the subject. "Four hundred off? Five hundred?"

"Five hundred? That's a lot." I got almost a complete full ride when I came to UC Santa Mira, but I still have some minor expenses. And since football and school don't allow us much time to have a job, I'm lucky that my parents help me out with those expenses.

"Split three ways it's not so bad. Like a hundred and sixty bucks or so." Dollar shrugs. "The money we save from not going out to eat all the time will pay off in the long run."

"He's right," Coop adds quietly. I turn to look at him, remaining quiet because I want to hear his opinion, which I respect more than Dollar's. "If she feeds us three days out of the week, in the end, we'll be better off, money-wise."

"We'll have to pay for the food," I point out.

"And it'll still be a significant savings over going out all the time."

"How do we run a credit check on her?" Dollar asks.

"If we're going to do this, we should at least ask her for a deposit. Like five hundred bucks. She can Venmo us," Cooper says. "And we charge her nine hundred dollars for rent up front. What do you think?"

This is crazy is what I want to say. Again. We don't know this woman. What if she's a complete psycho? Unfair of me to think, but hey. It could happen. The idea of having a stranger move in with us—a female stranger—and change the dynamic in this house . . .

Can't lie. It makes me uncomfortable.

"I don't know—"

Cooper cuts me off. "I'm all for it." I send him a questioning look, and he shrugs. "I'm tired of rooming with dickfaces who bail on us like Sampson just did. I agree with Dollar. Let's rent her the room."

"We don't know her—"

"We can get to know her," he says, interrupting me again. "Maybe she prefers to keep to herself. We won't be around much, anyway. Football is going to keep us busy the entire semester."

"Think she'll lose her shit over us being on the team?" I'm repeating myself, but I don't care. We need to make sure we're not getting tricked. "Or maybe she already knows we're on the team and this is all a ruse for her to move in? She could be a clout chaser." Saying it out loud sounds ridiculous, but hey. Weirder shit has happened.

"Doubtful. She seems pretty oblivious about who we are. Even a little naive." Cooper shrugs. "I'm thinking she's probably a transfer student from who knows where and has no clue who we are."

"I don't care if she knows who we are or not. I say we just do it," Dollar says.

A ragged exhale leaves me as I scrub my hand along my jaw, rubbing the stubble that's already growing there. "I'm getting outvoted on this one, huh?"

"Yes," Dollar and Cooper say at the same time.

"Fine." I drop my hand. "Let's go tell her."

We exit the bedroom, entering the living room to find her—Jesus, we should at the very least know her name—perched on the edge of the couch, wringing her hands together with a stressed-out expression on her pretty face.

The chick is clearly sweating over our decision.

"Before we give you an answer, we need to know one thing," I say, making her sit up straight, her wide blue eyes meeting mine.

I immediately feel like a shit for doubting her. For thinking she's a psycho or a clout chaser or anything like that. Her expression is downright angelic, with an ounce of fear added for good measure.

That's the part I don't like. The fear. I'm a big guy. So are all my friends—and teammates. But she has nothing to fear from any of us. Well, Dollar always crushes on random girls, so that might become an issue, but he'd never harm a fly. He's a little too persistent and annoying about it, but that's it.

"What is it?" she finally whispers.

I flash her what I hope is my most disarming smile. "What's your name?"

Chapter Four

EVERLEIGH

"Oh." My shoulders sag with relief. I thought they wanted to run a criminal background check on me or something. They might still want to do that. I don't know. "It's Everleigh."

"Everleigh?" Nico frowns and I sit up straighter. "Interesting name."

"Everleigh Olmstead." I jump to my feet, catch myself wringing my hands, and immediately make myself stop. "So did you guys discuss it?"

"We did." Nico nods, that captivating smile still on his face. He really needs to stop looking at me like that. I might start believing he cares or something. "We'd like to make you an offer."

"Okay." I draw the word out slowly, my gaze going to the other two, who both have unreadable expressions on their faces. Which is totally disconcerting. "What's the offer?"

"Nine hundred a month for the room, plus three meals a week," he says.

"Dinners," Dollar adds.

I do quick calculations in my head. That's close enough to the previous rent I was going to pay, and for one hundred dollars more, I get my own room, which is even better. Making three dinners a week for three giant starving men is a daunting task, but I'm pretty sure I can make this work.

"With a five-hundred-dollar deposit to put down before you move in. Plus the first month's rent," Cooper adds. "As a sign of good faith."

Ouch. I hate to just hand over five hundred bucks for it to sit there and do nothing but pad their bank accounts, but I get it. I'm a stranger to them, and for all they know, I could be a complete nightmare.

I'm not. Well, I don't think I am. I'm not that outwardly social, and I prefer keeping to myself.

"Is that a problem?" Nico asks when I still haven't responded.

My gaze locks with his, and I fall into it for a moment, mentally reminding myself I need to withstand his natural charm if I want to make rational decisions about my future.

I need this room. I can't worry if I can make it work financially or not. I'll figure something out.

"I can do that," I say without hesitation, not wanting them to think I'm unsure. "I'll take it."

"Can you grocery shop for us too?" Dollar asks hopefully.

"Maybe." I have no idea how my schedule is going to be once I add a job to it. "I'm going to find a job as soon as possible, so I'm sure I'll be busy."

"Too busy to cook us dinners?" The devastation on Dollar's face is obvious.

"No, not at all. If I'm agreeing to that, then I'll do it." This boy must be fixated on his appetite at all times. "Are we good then? Is the room mine?"

"What about the bathroom situation?" Cooper rubs his chin, contemplating me. "You sure you want to share a bathroom with me and Dollar Bills?"

No. I'm not sure about it at all. In fact, I'm fairly certain it's going to be a disgusting experience and I'll be scrubbing the bathroom at least three times a week. Maybe more. But I'll do what I have to do to ensure I have somewhere to live. "I can—"

Nico's deep voice interrupts my answer. "She can share my bathroom."

Dollar appears surprised. Cooper covers his mouth with his fist and coughs into it. Did he utter something into that cough?

If he did, I couldn't quite understand what he said.

"You don't mind?" I ask, chewing on my lower lip. This means I have to go into his bedroom—his personal space—to use the bathroom, and that's kind of . . . weird.

Right?

"I won't be home much, anyway. I get up extra early for practice and sometimes don't come home at all. I don't think we'll get in each other's way," he says.

Why doesn't he come home at all? Maybe he's staying the night with his girlfriend?

Oh God. I didn't even think of that. Do these guys have girlfriends? And if they do, will those girlfriends have a problem with me living with them? If one of them was my boyfriend, I don't think I'd love it if they were living with a woman they didn't know.

"Are any of you . . . steadily dating anyone at the moment?" I ask tentatively.

They all share a look once more, just before they erupt into sharp laughter.

I stand there watching them, hoping I'm not the butt of the joke.

"No," Cooper is the first to say. "I prefer to remain single. Dollar can't get a steady girl to save his life, and Nico doesn't believe in monogamy."

"Hey," Dollar and Nico both say at the same time.

"Okay. Cool." I shove my hands in my pockets, feeling silly. "I was just checking in case any of you have a girlfriend who wouldn't approve of you sharing a house with another woman."

"Do you have a boyfriend?" Dollar asks me.

"She already answered that question. Right, Everleigh?" Nico's gaze sears straight into me.

"Right," I say softly. "I don't have one."

I think of the ties I cut to my old life. I broke up with my high school boyfriend at the beginning of summer. We'd been together since the end of our junior year, and it was clear our relationship wasn't going anywhere, but Brad didn't get it.

When I broke up with him, he actually admitted to me that he believed we would end up getting married. I knew right then I was making the best decision. Didn't he sense my unhappiness? I didn't expect him to be a mind reader, but I told him more than once that we needed to work on our relationship.

He never got the hint. Truthfully, Brad didn't pay much attention to me—not really. Especially over the last year. Oh, he wanted me around and treated me like his possession, but he didn't care about my wants or needs. Not really. And I'm not surprised he was clueless about my dissatisfaction. It totally tracks.

He didn't listen to me. Most people in my life don't. Not my mom, and definitely not Brad.

I needed a fresh start. There was nothing left to save. My grandma died the year after I graduated, and there was no point sticking around any longer.

"Do you guys have parties?" I ask.

"Sometimes," Nico says, sounding wary. "Why do you ask?"

"I just want to be prepared. I'm not much of a partier." I wrinkle my nose. All the parties Brad would drag me to consisted of his friends sitting around eating Domino's pizza, playing video games, and getting high. It was boring.

"Uh-huh." Nico sounds like he doubts me, which is vaguely irritating, but I decide to ignore his comment and change the subject.

"When can I move in?"

"Venmo us the deposit and you can move in right now," Coop says.

Once I've got everyone added, I send them each their share, then head for the front door. "I'll go get my car."

"You have a car?" Dollar asks as he rushes toward the door and holds it open for me.

What a gentleman. Though I catch the other two rolling their eyes.

"Well, that's how I got to Santa Mira, so yeah." And all my worldly possessions are currently sitting in my car, so I should probably check on it soon.

"Parking around here is tough," Cooper says, rubbing his chin again. "Like . . . really tough."

"How bad can it be?" I laugh, but their expressions remain somber, causing the laughter to die on my lips. "That bad?"

"Like drive-around-the-neighborhood-for-an-hour-and-hopefully-find-an-open-spot bad. Nico has the driveway since he's the only one with an actual vehicle out of the three of us," Cooper explains.

I'm shocked the others don't have a car, but I suppose it makes sense considering everything here is in walkable distance. Or you can take the city bus, which is free for college students with proof of student ID. This town is very centered around the university and the students, which is cool.

This was exactly the sort of experience I was seeking. Living in a college town, making new friends, doing new things. Maybe go to a party or two if I feel daring enough. Get a new job and make even more new friends there. I have high hopes.

Big dreams.

"I better go get my car, then, and start looking for a parking spot." I offer them a wave before I turn toward the door. "I'll be back."

"Need help moving your stuff in?" Dollar asks me as I walk through the front door.

"Definitely!" I flash him a smile from over my shoulder and wave before I head down the steps, excitement bubbling in my veins.

This isn't going to be so bad, I think as I head down the sidewalk and back to the café. Living with three big, burly guys? I mean, they seem nice enough. I'll definitely feel safe knowing that they're sleeping in the same house as me.

Maybe my living situation didn't start out like I planned it, but I'm sure everything's going to be fine.

Just fine.

◆　◆　◆

"Oh my God." I stare in horror at my 2015 Honda Civic and the broken window on the driver's side, my stomach twisting into knots. I open the door carefully, shattered glass falling to the ground as I peer inside to find . . .

The back seats are devoid of the boxes I had in there earlier. The boxes full of everything I wanted to bring to Santa Mira.

My heart lurches, and it suddenly becomes difficult to breathe.

Leaving the door open, I rush to the trunk and open it, crying out when I see that it's empty too.

All my stuff is . . . gone.

Glancing up, I see two blonde girls exit the coffee shop. They're about to walk by my car, and they're talking and laughing, their outfits cute, their attitude carefree. I envy the sound of their laughter, the joy that they're radiating while it feels like my life has just imploded.

"Hey." They both come to a stop when I speak, their expressions open and friendly. "Did you see anyone near this car in the last few minutes?"

"No," one of them says, while the other one shakes her head. "Just you."

"Okay," I say weakly, unable to even smile at them. "Thank you."

I watch them go and then return my attention to the car, swallowing hard. I should probably call the police and file a report. I have car insurance, so I'll be able to get the window fixed, but how long will that take? I can't lock up my car at night if there's no window.

And what am I going to do about all my stuff?

Thank God I had my backpack with me, which also has my wallet, my laptop, and my favorite hoodie. But all my other clothes and personal belongings? Like even my toothbrush?

Gone.

Leaning against the side of my car, I cover my face with my hands and close my eyes, trying not to lose it. I want to cry, but what will tears get me? I'm even tempted to call Brad and ask for help. I know he'd rush over here to do whatever he could to support me. He's three hours away, but he'd drop everything and come to my rescue in the hopes that we might get back together.

He's not mine to depend on anymore. I need to learn how to stand on my own two feet.

I take a deep breath and drop my hands, reaching for my phone in the back pocket of my denim shorts, when I see a black-and-white police car approach. I step off the sidewalk and wave at him, and the officer pulls over, putting the car in park before he gets out.

"Everything all right?" He reminds me of what a good dad should look like. He's a little older, his dark-brown hair graying at the temples, his expression one of genuine concern.

My dad was never around. Not that I can remember. He left when I was young, barely a toddler, and never came back. My mom resented him for leaving, and I can't blame her. But she also resented me too. Like I was that constant reminder of the man who bailed on her, and it didn't help that I resembled him.

"Miss? You okay?"

I jerk my gaze to the officer, who is watching me with a slight frown pulling at his brows.

"No. No, I'm not." I shake my head, my lips trembling from holding back the tears. "My car was broken into. I'd like to file a report."

Chapter Five

Nico

"You're such a schmuck," I tell Dollar the moment Everleigh leaves the house.

"What are you talking about?" He acts like he has no idea what I'm talking about, but come on.

He has to.

"You wouldn't let up on her about making you dinners. You even want her to grocery shop for us," I remind him.

Poor girl. Look, I can't lie. I'll take some home-cooked meals a couple of times a week, but I don't want her to be our mama. Dollar is taking it too far.

"Yeah, and that's because I don't have a lot of time, and might I remind you that you don't either. Who's going to shop for these gourmet meals she'll prepare for us?" Dollar sounds so damn logical, he's almost got me convinced.

"She never once mentioned anything about the meals being gourmet," Coop points out, the true logical one of us three.

We're all in the kitchen, crowded around the tiny table that sits in the dining area. We barely fit around it, it's so small, and I hope when our new roomie makes us these supposed dinners that she doesn't expect to sit with us, because I don't know how we'll make it happen. She's a little thing, but I don't know where she'll fit.

Seriously, I'm just as much of a schmuck as Dollar is because I'm already anticipating those home-cooked meals too.

"True," I say, but Dollar is shaking his head.

"They might be. We don't know. I have faith in her. She seems cool." Dollar's voice is purposely nonchalant. "And she's cute."

Ah. There it is. He falls hard for pretty much any girl who looks at him twice, even if they're just being polite. And when they are into him, he comes on so strong, his behavior sends most of them packing, which sucks for poor old Dollar. He just wants to find a woman who loves him, unlike the rest of us, who are searching for something a little more casual.

"Don't get any wild ideas," Coop warns him.

"What do you mean?" Now Dollar is perplexed. Funny how he never seems to get it.

"He's basically saying don't shit where you eat," I explain.

Dollar grimaces. "That's disgusting."

"What Nico means is don't fuck around with our new roommate, Frank." Cooper sends him a look. "You can't think she's cute. Or pretty. Or beautiful. And you definitely can't flirt with her. That's just . . ."

"Dangerous," I finish for Coop.

"Exactly." Coop nods.

"That's some bullshit. If I want to flirt with her, I will. If I want to fuck around with her, I will." Dollar glares at both of us. "You can't tell me what to do."

I roll my eyes at Cooper before I say, "We're not telling you what to do, Dollar. We're just trying to help your ass."

"Yet you never listen to us," Coop mutters.

"Because you guys are full of shit most of the time." Dollar leaps to his feet, jabbing his index finger in our direction. "I'm gonna go check on her. I promised I would help her move her stuff in."

"You don't even know where she went," I remind him.

"I'll wait outside for her then. Better than being in here getting shit from you two."

He's gone in seconds, the front door slamming behind him and making the entire house rattle.

"Maybe we're too hard on him," Coop says, looking guilty.

He's probably right, but come on.

"Nah. He does this sort of thing all the time." Falling head over ass for some hottie who plays along because he's eager to please and will do whatever she asks him to do until she eventually finds someone better.

Frank Dollar is a nice guy. Not a bad-looking guy, I suppose. But he tries too damn hard, and some of the women he tries for know it. They use him, and he lets it happen every damn time.

I've never admitted this to either of my roommates, but I used to be the Frank Dollar of my high school. My confidence was for shit back then. I was kind of scrawny but still managed to play damn good ball out on the field because I was fast, but I never caught the attention of the girls.

Until I started laying it on thick with the ones I was interested in, just like Dollar does. They used me up and spit me out, and when I got burned by a girl I was interested in, forget it.

Commitment is for idiots, especially at our age. I'm too young for a serious relationship. Too busy to take the time to even contemplate one. I'm not interested. And it's like women sense that, are attracted to that sort of attitude. They know I'm not serious, and all they want to do is convert me. Change me into a relationship type of guy.

No thanks.

There was only one who interested me enough to see her on a semiregular basis this past spring, but it went sour fast. She got a little too possessive and placed way too many expectations upon me. I bailed out quick because I could see if I stuck with her for any length of time, it would become harder and harder to get away from her.

Again, no thank you. I'm done dating women until I at least graduate from college.

Done.

"Think she's going to work out as our roommate?" Coop asks, changing the subject.

Everleigh's pretty face pops into my brain, but I banish it quickly. I need to follow the same advice I gave Dollar. "Sure. Why wouldn't she?"

"She's cute. Seems nice enough. Plus she's in a tough situation. That's always appealing. The damsel in distress or whatever." Cooper chuckles. "Looking forward to someone cooking for us, though. Maybe not as much as Dollar is, but still."

"Right. That's not a bad deal." I shrug.

"Still can't believe you offered to share your bathroom with her. What were you thinking?" He bursts out laughing while I scowl at him. "All her girlie shit is going to be spread out on your counter."

Hell, I didn't even think about that. "It's a pretty big counter."

"What if she hand-washes her lacy bras and dries them by draping them over the shower rod? Then you gotta stare at her sexy underwear every time you take a piss." He's still laughing, and I know he's enjoying giving me shit. "And what if you're fucking some hot girl and right when she's about to scream your name, in walks our new roomie, eager to get to her nightly bathroom routine?"

"You know that won't fly," I retort. Coop smothers his laughter with a big hand while I toss a packet of parmesan cheese left over from the pizza we ate for dinner last night at him. "Not like I have girls over that often, anyway."

"Not after the last one," Coop oh-so-kindly reminds me.

"She cured me from having anyone over ever again." The problem with inviting women into your home is they start imagining it as their home. Next thing you know, she's getting a few bright ideas about decorating it. Burning a candle and shit. Starts leaving her things "accidentally." Her clothes are on top of your dresser, and there are tampons in the bathroom . . .

Well, shit. There's going to be tampons in my bathroom for the next nine months, thanks to me sharing it with Everleigh.

"What if you're like . . . jerking off in bed and she comes into the room in the middle of the night to pee? What are you going to do then?" Cooper raises his brows, clearly enjoying this.

My mind immediately goes to Everleigh offering to help when she catches me jerking off, and I banish that idea completely. "I don't jerk off in the middle of the night."

"If you tell me right now that you get so much pussy, you don't need to jerk off, I'm calling bullshit," Coop says with a laugh.

"If you have to know, I prefer jerking off in the shower," I tell him, which only makes Coop laugh harder. To the point that I'm laughing with him because I can't stay mad at the guy for too long.

And he's making valid points. I offered Everleigh my bathroom because I felt sorry for her. The look of pure horror on her face at the idea of sharing a bathroom with Coop and Dollar—yeah, gross, they're complete slobs—had me piping up without even thinking.

The utter relief I saw on her face once I did was worth saying it.

Maybe.

Shit, I don't know. I can't get too caught up in her looks, because she is definitely attractive, with the shoulder-length dark hair and bright-blue eyes and lush pink lips. Nice body, long legs that looked damn good in those denim shorts she was wearing. A little shyer than what I'm usually drawn to, but she's dealing with a lot at the moment, so I can get that.

But I'm not interested in that. In her. I can't be.

It's my turn to change the subject.

"Look, I kind of like that we can help her out," I tell Coop, who sobers up immediately. "But we should probably establish some rules with her, don't you think?"

"Like what?"

"I don't know." I shrug. "It's just—I've never lived with a woman before."

"We were in the coed dorms." Cooper knows this because this was how we became close our freshman year. We were in the same dorm building.

"Big difference. I didn't share a room with a girl, and neither did you."

"You have a sister."

"Who's much older than I am. By the time I was ten, she'd moved out." We're not close. She lives in Manhattan and works for a big PR firm. She doesn't have time for her little brother. Too busy living her fast-paced life. Much like our dad.

My mom, though? She's got all the time in the world for me. Maybe too much time. Once my parents got divorced, she funneled all her energy into me and my football success. While I appreciate her and love that she's so supportive and proud, sometimes she can smother me.

Gotta love her for it, though.

"So you've never lived with a woman before beyond your mother and your sister when you were basically an infant?" Cooper shakes his head. I don't bother protesting the infant comment. He's just being a jerk. "Trust me. It's . . . different."

He has two sisters around our age, so he knows of what he speaks. "It can't be that bad."

"Oh, it isn't bad. It's just like I said—it's different. They girlify everything."

"Girlify?"

"Yeah. They want things to look pretty and aesthetically pleasing." He grimaces. I don't even know what *aesthetically pleasing* means, and I think he hates himself for saying those words out loud. "Next thing you know we'll have cute kitchen towels and a candle burning every night, which isn't necessarily a bad thing."

Just what I suspected about the candle-burning thing, only worse because she's going to actually live here.

Not sure what we just opened ourselves up to, but hopefully it'll work out fine.

It has to.

"And she might take a photo of us and hang it on the wall. She'll put a wreath on the door for Christmas. She might even do that for Halloween, or some sort of fall thing that's made out of fake leaves and shit. She'll probably clean up around the house, which is always a bonus. Women hate it when shit is messy."

"Then they'd hate you because you're the messiest person I know," I throw back at Cooper.

Now it's his turn to toss a parmesan packet at me. I catch it with one hand and throw it back at him, laughing when it bounces off his big forehead.

The door suddenly swings open, and Dollar is leading a shaken-looking Everleigh into the house, his arm around her shoulders as he guides her toward the couch, settling her in. Coop and I watch from where we're sitting at the table, sharing a quiet look before Coop finally speaks up.

"What happened? Everything okay?"

"Ever's car got broken into," Dollar says, sitting on the couch next to her and slipping his arm around her shoulders once more.

For whatever reason, I don't like seeing that. This guy. He's going to try to make something happen with her, and she hasn't even moved in yet. Hopefully his behavior doesn't send her running.

Coop leaps to his feet. "Her car got broken into? What do you mean?"

"Someone busted the driver's side window, got into her car, and stole all of her stuff," Dollar explains. "Now she's got nothing."

Everleigh remains quiet, bending her head so her dark hair falls around her face.

His words actually seep into my brain, and I stand, too, moving quietly so I'm in front of them in seconds. *"Everything?"*

She lifts her head, her glassy eyes meeting mine as she gives a little nod. "All I have left is what was in my backpack. I have my phone and laptop, thankfully. But everything else? Gone."

"All of your clothes?" Coop asks.

"I have my favorite hoodie in here, but that's it." She pats the backpack that I only just now notice sitting at her feet.

"You have nothing else." I'm not asking her a question. I've already concluded this is it.

"Like I already said, everything Ever owned is gone," Dollar says to me, talking slowly like I'm an idiot.

I ignore him, hating how he calls her Ever. Like they're already great friends. "Did you call the cops?"

"Yes. I already made a police report." She presses her lips together, and I swear the lower one trembles a little bit. Like she might break down in tears at any moment. "I need to fix my window."

"Where's your car right now?" Coop asks.

"Parked down the street."

I speak before I can think. Something I'm afraid is becoming a habit. "You can't park on the street with a busted window. I'll share my spot with you until you get it fixed."

Dollar frowns. I can feel the surprise radiate off Coop at my offer, but I ignore them both.

I can't be a callous asshole toward women all the time.

This girl needs our help.

Chapter Six

Everleigh

After I told my new roommates the depressing news, Frank—I prefer calling him by his first name because calling him Dollar feels silly to me—was kind enough to go with me to Walmart so I can pick up a few things to see me through the next couple of nights. The cheapest sheets I could find, a toothbrush, some towels. Toiletries and a couple of tank tops. A pair of black sweats. Basic items that'll get me through until I figure out exactly how much I can afford—not much, I already know that—to spend on what I need to actually live.

Which is like . . . everything. When I said I wanted a fresh start, I didn't mean something this extreme.

Now I'm in my new bedroom, putting the freshly washed yet slightly scratchy sheets on the double mattress that was left behind. They didn't even mention that they have a washer and dryer in the house, which is a total bonus.

It's only when I'm holding up the empty pillowcase that I realize I forgot to buy a pillow. Maybe I could bunch up my hoodie and use it as a pillow or . . .

"I have one to spare if you need it."

I whirl around to find Nico filling my doorway with his impossibly broad shoulders. How tall is he, anyway? I clutch the empty pillowcase to my chest like a shield, ready to ask him what he means, when he continues talking.

"I was talking about a pillow. I saw you looking around with the empty pillowcase you're holding." He waves a big hand in my direction.

"Oh, right." I glance down at the slightly wrinkled pillowcase. The sheets are a pale pink. I even bought a matching pale-pink comforter that's pretty thin, but it'll do the job. "It's hard to remember everything, I guess."

"I'm sure it is." He leans his shoulder against the doorjamb like he's making himself comfortable and staying for a while. "You can use my pillow until you get one. Though I always prefer to sleep with a couple—"

"Oh, I don't need to borrow yours, then. I don't want to take it from you," I say in a panic, wincing because I interrupted him, which is rude.

"I have a bunch," he says. "I can spare one. I don't mind."

"Okay. Thank you." I set the pillowcase on the mattress, feeling awkward. His presence seems to fill up my small bedroom, and he's not even actually standing in the room with me. But he's here. Filling up the space and reminding me that this was his territory first. I'm just lucky enough he's letting me stay here.

"You can use my stuff when you take a shower too. Bodywash. Shampoo. A towel," he offers.

"That's so nice of you." My smile is faint. I do appreciate how accommodating he's being. "I bought some towels, though."

"Well, set them up in the bathroom. I emptied a rack for you."

"I appreciate it."

He's quiet for a moment, and we just stare at each other, the air seeming to crackle between us. I spent a lot of one-on-one time with Frank earlier today, and it wasn't like that for us.

Not even close.

So weird.

"You settling in okay?" he finally asks.

"As best as I can considering most of my worldly possessions were stolen." My tone is wry. At least I can joke about it.

Sort of.

"I hate to say this to you, but they'll probably never catch who did it." He crosses his arms, his biceps bulging with the movement. "Petty crime can be pretty bad around here."

"I've heard that about Santa Mira," I say with a sigh. "And what sucks is there wasn't much in those boxes that was actually valuable, you know? Like, what are they going to do with my clothes and makeup? The knickknacks I brought with me?"

It's so depressing to think of all my things ending up in a dumpster somewhere. Tossed out and forgotten forever.

"Did they steal any candles?" His brows shift upward ever so slightly.

"No, no candles." What a strange question.

He almost seems to sigh with relief at my answer, which is also strange.

"But you know what I mean. They stole my favorite bedside table lamp my mom bought me for Christmas, and I had this cute little tray my grandma gave me a long time ago that I like to leave my jewelry on before I go to bed at night. Oh, my jewelry." I finger the necklace that I'm still wearing. The simple gold hoops that are in my ears.

None of it was worth much dollar-wise, but it was worth everything to me.

Do not cry. Do not cry.

"That might've had some value," he says.

"It was pretty much all costume." I settle onto the edge of the mattress, my shoulders drooping. After a long day of just trying to keep it together, I finally wallow in my misery, feeling defeated. "This sucks."

"When do you take the car in to be fixed?"

"Monday morning. I can drop it off whenever."

"Need a lift to the mechanic?" I send him a questioning look, which has him explaining himself more. "I offer because I'm the only one who has a car here besides you."

"Got it." I nod. He's being terribly nice, which wasn't the vibe I got from him earlier. He went from charming to annoyed rather quickly with the idea of me moving in. Now he's nice again, but definitely not as charming.

He's actually pretty confusing, but maybe that's more a me issue because I've had the worst, most stressful last couple of days of my life and I'm exhausted.

"I actually planned on taking the bus back over here." I need to test it out because despite having a car, I don't want to pay for an on-campus parking permit. I need to learn the public transit system in this town, and I'll be walking a lot too. No matter what, I'm definitely going to need to save money, especially now that I have some added expenses.

"Well, the offer still stands if you don't want to deal with the bus."

"Thank you." I smile at him. "I appreciate it."

"If you need a ride Monday morning, let me know." He pushes away from the doorjamb and is about to leave when I say something.

"I thought you had practice in the morning," I remind him.

He stops, glancing over his shoulder and flashing that devastating smile. "You're right. I do."

I say nothing else. It's like I can't. Seeing that smile steals brain cells, and I'm already feeling pretty depleted thanks to everything that's happened over the last couple of days.

He eventually walks away, and I slowly shut the door, sagging against it. Staring at my barren room.

It may be empty, and I don't own hardly anything, but at least this is mine.

At least this is home.

I wake up two hours later with a crick in my neck from sleeping without a pillow—I never did grab one from Nico's stash—and the room shrouded in darkness. I lie there for a moment, vaguely disoriented as my eyes slowly adjust. Then I hear it coming from the open window, the vertical blinds clacking against each other lightly as a breeze blows through.

The faint sound of the ocean.

When I roll over onto my phone, I grab it from beneath my thigh and check my notifications, not surprised at all to find I don't really have any beyond a couple of social media updates.

What did I expect? I dumped Brad. My mom didn't want me to leave home in the first place, so I'm sure she's mad at me. Holding a grudge like she's so good at doing. And the few friends I have back home I wasn't in contact with much the last year or so because Brad wanted all my time when I wasn't working. I let those friendships drift away, and now I regret it.

Right now, it feels like I have no one.

Eventually I climb out of bed and rotate my neck a few times, working out the stiffness. I can hear murmured conversation coming from the living room, and when I pop open my bedroom door, I realize there are a bunch of people here in the house. And not just my roommates.

There's music playing and a girl squealing about something, and Frank magically appears in the short hallway, a big grin on his face when he spots me.

"You're awake!" He gestures toward the living room. "You should come meet everyone."

I slowly shake my head. "I should probably take a shower first."

I feel grimy. Like I've been in these clothes for at least a week.

His smile fades the slightest bit. "Sure. Okay. Go take a shower, and then come out and hang with us. It'll be fun."

"Who's us?" I smile, trying to pretend I'm not intimidated by the idea of spending my first night here with a bunch of strangers.

Deep down, I'm terrified.

"Some of the guys from the team. A couple of their friends." He shrugs. "It's super casual."

He mentioned earlier when we were shopping that all three of them are on the college football team, but he didn't make a big deal about it. I know the football team does well here at Santa Mira, and I bet it's fun to go to the games.

I wonder if they'll give me free tickets. The perks of being their roomie, maybe?

"I'll come out in a bit, if that's okay," I say when I realize Frank is still waiting.

"Cool. Sounds good." He's nodding, walking backward toward the living room, and he almost trips over his own feet, which has me giggling. "Take your time."

He darts off, and I go back into my bedroom, shutting the door before I search through the shopping bag and pull out a pair of panties. They're a pale pink and basic cotton. Nothing special. I tear off the tags with my teeth, clutching the underwear in my fist as I continue searching through the bag with my other hand.

And realize I don't really have anything to wear to bed. I don't want to sleep in just my undies. What if one of the guys just barges into my room? I'm sure that wouldn't happen, but you never know.

Sighing, I grab my new pair of sweats and a tank top along with the panties and exit my bedroom, about to cross the hall into Nico's room to use the bathroom when I collide with something solid.

And warm.

"Whoa." Big hands clasp my upper arms and set me aside, my skin tingling where he touches me. I glance up, not surprised at all to find it's Nico smiling down at me with that charming grin, his eyes actually sparkling, putting me into a trance. "Where you headed to in such a hurry?"

"Um, the shower. If you don't mind," I tack on because I'm definitely not comfortable just entering his bedroom and using his shower whenever I want, even though he offered. Even though that's the deal we have now.

"Of course I don't mind. It's now your bathroom too," he says, slowly releasing his hold on me. I immediately miss his touch, which is weird. I don't even know this guy. "We'll just have to get used to sharing it."

"Thank you," I say, my voice soft. "And I guess we will."

"You going to hang out with us tonight?"

"I don't know." I shrug. "Frank asked me to."

"You should. Meet some new people. A few girls are out there. Coop's sister, for one." He pauses, studying me carefully. I almost start squirming, his gaze is so intense. "How old are you, anyway?"

"I just turned twenty-one last month. I'm a junior."

"Sienna is the same age as you then. You'll love her. She's the complete opposite of her brother." Nico is grinning again, and I find myself smiling, too, because his mood is contagious.

When he's a little grumpy, though? Not so contagious. But still appealing.

And that's so frustrating, ugh.

Chapter Seven

Nico

I've loved football my entire life. There are photos of me as a baby holding a mini blue football. I dressed up as a San Francisco 49er for Halloween when I was three. I started in youth football when I was five and have been playing ever since.

I've played a variety of positions. Defensive lineman. Offense. Hell, I was the quarterback my last two years in youth football before I started high school.

Despite helping get us to a league championship my eighth-grade year, that wasn't my favorite position. I much prefer being a wide receiver. Catching the ball and running it into the end zone? A total glory moment. Helps that I'm fast as fuck.

Hey, it's the truth. No point in being modest.

I'm tall and solid, but Coop has me beat size-wise. But he's an offensive lineman who protects our QB, so that makes sense. Dollar is shorter than me but bulkier. He's a defensive lineman but didn't get much play last season due to injuring his shoulder, which ended up requiring surgery. He's hopeful he can get back out on the field and play the regular season, but I don't know. He's not as quick as he used to be and a little tentative on blocking. I think the shoulder injury fucked with his head a little bit, making him wary on the field.

All these thoughts run through my mind as I sip a beer and pretend to listen to the multitude of conversations happening in our living room. Coop's sister is chatting a mile a minute with a couple of other girls who just magically showed up with some of the guys from the team. I don't even know who they are, but a few of their pretty faces are familiar.

Groupies. We've got them. That they're even in our house I'm sure feels like a major win to them.

I kind of hate that they know where we live, but too late to worry now. What's done is done.

"Where's Gav?" I ask when there's a lull in the conversation. I'm referring to our quarterback and one of the team captains, Gavin Maddox. One of my closest friends, and not just because we work so closely together on the field. He's also a good guy. A solid leader. Smart as hell and already being courted by a few NFL coaches, the lucky bastard. He almost dropped out of school at the beginning of the year to go into the NFL draft in the spring, but he decided to stick with the team one more season and try to win that championship.

We got so close last year and worked so hard for a repeat of what happened our sophomore year, when we won our first national championship. He was so incredibly frustrated at not winning this last season.

Can't blame the guy. Last season was frustrating as fuck. There were mistakes made. Injuries that couldn't be avoided, like Dollar's. Other teams were coming for us. Eager to destroy us so they could be the ones to say they took us down.

Fuck that. We're not going to let it happen again. This season we're making sure our heads are on straight and in the game. We're more focused than ever and doing everything it takes to ensure we'll meet our goal.

And gain another national championship before we graduate from college.

"Gav texted me earlier that he's coming over," Coop says with a nod, glancing over at Sienna. "God, she's loud."

I chuckle, watching Cooper's sister's mouth move about a hundred miles a second. "She never stops talking."

"Tell me all about it. She's driven me crazy since the day she was born." His voice is full of affection—he loves his little sister and is very protective of her too. They're pretty close, and I like Sienna a lot. Even contemplated hooking up with her once or twice a couple of years ago when she first arrived here on campus, but realized what a mistake that would be.

Mostly because if I ever unintentionally broke his sister's heart, I think Coop would destroy me with his bare hands. It's easier to just keep her in the friend zone.

Hell, all of us on the team keep her in the friend zone out of respect for Coop, who is one of our team captains. I'm a team captain as well, but not everyone loves me like they love Coop. Everyone also cares about Coop's hot sister.

But none of us touch her, much to her disappointment.

"She's not so bad," I finally drawl, shifting my gaze to the hallway, wondering when our new roommate is going to make an appearance. "You think she'll be friends with Everleigh?"

"I already told Sienna about her." That's Cooper. Always one step ahead of me. "She's eager to meet Everleigh and warn her about us."

"Is that what she said?"

Coop nodded. "I think she might be referring to Dollar."

"Right."

"And you," he adds on.

I glare at him, making him crack up.

"Face facts, my friend. You have a reputation that you consistently hold up," Coop says with a grin.

"Don't remind me." Player. Manwhore. Fuckboy. I've been called all those names and more, and I've never cared about it. What does it matter what people think about me when it comes to my sex life? Most of the rumors that swirl around me are not necessarily true, anyway. For some reason a threesome story always seems to spread like wildfire every season, and truth be told . . .

I've never been in a threesome in my life. That's just too much work. I'm more of a one-on-one-for-one-time type of guy.

"Girls are gonna flip the fuck out when they find out you have a female roomie," Cooper says conversationally.

My gaze slides back to Coop. "Won't they flip when they find out *you* have a female roommate?"

"Nah. No one talks about me like they talk about you. It's all that rizz you've got." He's smiling. Looking real pleased with himself for saying it too.

I roll my eyes. "Rizz. What the fuck ever."

"It's true and you know it. All the women go freaking crazy over you. All you gotta do is just stand there and smile that stupid smile of yours, and they lose it. Don't know if you've noticed, but there are three women standing in the kitchen right now with my sister, and they all look like they're barely holding back from launching themselves at you," Coop says.

Oh shit.

As discreetly as possible I glance over at the kitchen, where I spot Sienna standing with the three other women, who are listening to her carry on about . . . whatever. Every few seconds they glance in my direction. All three of them at various times. And all three of them look like they're practically vibrating with excitement, which is . . .

Kind of weird.

"No way," I mutter when my gaze meets Coop's once more, even though I know what he's saying is true. "Maybe they want you."

"Uh-uh. They didn't start acting like that until you showed up." Cooper leans over and bats the back of my head. "Which one you like the most?"

I don't even look at them. "They'd all do."

Cooper starts laughing. "You finally going to make that threesome rumor come true? Though if you like all of them, it'll end up being a foursome."

"Maybe." I'm grinning. Chuckling. "Think I could convince them?"

"My guess is yes."

This time I do glance over at them to find they're all three blatantly staring at me. One of them even licks her juicy red lips. "Wonder if they're into girl-on-girl action?"

I mean, that shit is hot. Again, I've never witnessed it live and with my own eyes, but I watch porn. Who doesn't?

"To get into your bed? They'd probably be up for anything," Coop drawls.

We're laughing together, and I'm about to finish off the rest of the beer when I catch sight of our new roommate emerging from the hallway, her expression unsure. She's even wringing her hands together like she's nervous, and I wonder if this is going to be a problem. Us having our teammates over for a casual hangout.

I sure as hell hope not.

I let my gaze roam over her for a moment as she stands there, taking her in. Admiring the view, even though she's obviously uncomfortable. If I was a nice guy, I'd run right over to her and introduce her to everyone.

But in this scenario, I'm not the nice guy. I'm the player. The manwhore.

The fuckboy.

I'll leave all that simp-nice-boy action to Dollar, who'll slobber all over her like an overeager puppy to the point that he'll start to annoy her. Because that's what he does.

That's who he is.

And that's not who I am.

"I'm going to go talk to the girls," I tell Cooper as I rise to my feet. "Watch and learn."

"Whatever, jackass," he calls to me as I start for the kitchen.

I'm about to pass Everleigh, and for a second, I'm tempted to say something. Check on her. I may have been reluctant to have her as our roommate, but I can play nice. And I meant what I said about her using my stuff when she's in the shower. She got herself into a shitty predicament, and I'm not a total asshole. I can be helpful when necessary.

But she's not my responsibility.

The moment I open my mouth to say something to her, Dollar magically appears, stepping in between us and placing his hand on her arm.

"Want to meet everyone?" he asks her, steering her away from me.

"Sure," she says, quickly glancing over her shoulder so that our gazes meet for the briefest moment.

Something unrecognizable passes between us. Quick as lightning. Hot as fire. Searing me where I stand, leaving me immobile and my mouth hanging open like a fucking dog.

I snap my jaw shut the moment she looks away, offering that pretty smile to Dollar instead of me. Yet again my gaze roams over the length of her. Her wet hair is in a knot on top of her head, and her face is devoid of any makeup. She's wearing baggy black sweats and a fitted, cropped black tank that shows off a slice of her flat, tanned stomach.

Simple outfit, yet somehow, she's the hottest thing in the room—

No.

That single word runs through my head, and I realize what's happening. It's what always happens.

I want the one I can't have. The one I shouldn't touch. I've always been tempted by the forbidden. I felt this way briefly about Sienna too. Like the rational part of my brain knows messing around with my new roommate would be a huge mistake—yet I want to.

Yeah. I really want to.

The problem? I can't fuck her and then kick her out of my bed, never to hear from her again. She'll still be here. Every single day, cooking us dinner and invading my private space. My freaking bathroom, for one.

Yeah. Can't do it. Big mistake.

Huge.

Instead of focusing on what I can't have, I pause in front of the three women staring at me hungrily and put on my best, most dazzling smile. The one that makes the panties fall off with a snap of my fingers.

"How's it goin', ladies?" I drawl.

They all giggle. Sienna rolls her eyes, but I ignore her. What she thinks doesn't really matter to me either. She knows what I am. Everyone does.

I'm just giving them all what they want from me.

Chapter Eight

Everleigh

"You need to meet Coop's sister," Frank says as he leads me into the kitchen, my hand clutched in his.

"Okay," I say, my head still spinning after all the introductions to the various guys filling my new living room. They're all big and burly and very attractive. Like, the entire room is overloaded with testosterone, and I swear it's having some sort of weird effect on me. Like I'm all frazzled and anxious, but that could also have to do with everything I've gone through in the last twenty-four hours too.

It's either from that or from the scorching look Nico gave me a few minutes ago, right when Frank wedged himself between us. The heat blasting from Nico's eyes. The blatant way he checked me out.

Not sure why, but I'm still a little shaky over it.

"Hey, Sienna, have you met our new roommate, Everleigh?" Frank asks a tall, striking redhead with a big smile on her face. I remove my hand from his, not wanting to give the wrong message. I definitely noticed the way she took in our linked hands, her brows shooting up for the briefest second.

"Not yet, but I've heard all about her from Coop. Hiiiii," she greets before pulling me into a crushing hug.

I have no choice but to hug her back, immediately put at ease by her welcoming presence. She pulls away, keeping her hands on my arms as she smiles down at me. "I'm so glad you moved in with them. Now I have a friend to hang out with here beyond my brother and his annoying roommates."

"Hey," Frank protests, but Sienna just laughs, slipping her arm around my shoulders and keeping me firmly planted at her side.

"Don't be so sensitive, Frankie. Now go hang out with your bros and let me and Everleigh get to know each other. Alone." Sienna makes a shooing gesture with her hand.

"Nico is right behind you," he points out.

Sienna barely looks in Nico's direction. "Oh, please. He's flirting with the blondes. He's not paying attention to us."

Frank leaves, albeit reluctantly, giving us both puppy dog eyes before he stomps off like a little kid who didn't get his way.

The moment he's out of hearing distance, Sienna is dipping her head closer to mine, her voice lowering. "Is he flirting with you?"

"Who?" I immediately think of Nico.

"Frank. He's a sweetheart and he means well, but he's desperate to find a girlfriend. All the guys give him endless shit about it too. Poor dude." Sienna mock pouts, her gaze going to where Frank currently sits on the couch next to Cooper. "I saw the way he was holding your hand."

"It was nothing." I smile, trying to dismiss it, because for me, it really was nothing.

"Not to him it wasn't. That's his problem. If he could learn how to play it cool for once, he'd have women chasing after him instead of the other way around," she explains. "I mean, look at Nico."

I don't want to. He's too pretty. "Right," I say weakly, making her laugh.

"He's hot, isn't he?" Sienna looks around me and right at Nico, fanning herself. "And I hear you two are sharing a bathroom?"

"Who told you that?"

"Cooper. He tells me everything. Well, mostly everything." Her eyes are sparkling with mischief. "By the way, if you catch Nico coming out of his bathroom naked, please, for the love of God, take a pic and send it to me. I hear his dick is ginormous."

She bursts out laughing, and I really hope she's joking.

"Oh my God." My cheeks are burning, and I shake my head, freaking out at the mere thought. "I really hope I never see his—dick."

A skeptical look crosses her face. "Come on, now. You've met him, right?"

"I can't let a guy distract me," I tell her, my tone earnest because it's the truth. "It's been one crisis after another since I got here. I need to get my car fixed. I have to find a job. I need to buy a whole new wardrobe—"

I clamp my lips shut, hating how on edge I feel just thinking about everything I need to do. It's overwhelming and I have no help. Well, it was my choice not to reach out to my mom and ask her for some advice or even a little money, but I know what she's going to say.

No.

And I don't want to hear it.

The skepticism switches to sympathy in an instant. "Aw, Coop mentioned all of your troubles to me too. I'm so sorry about . . . everything. I can give you some clothes if you need them. I have a couple of bags of things that don't fit me anymore—I was planning on asking my roommate if she wanted any of it before I donate it."

The dismissive noise leaves me before I can stop myself. "Please. You're at least five inches taller than me."

"I have bad luck when it comes to clothes. I buy something, wash it, and it shrinks on me more often than not. The laundry rooms at our apartment complex are the worst. So yes, I have a few things I can give you," Sienna says. "You can try them on, see if they'll work."

"I could pay you—"

"No way," she interrupts, shaking her head. "I'd just give it to my roommate, and she doesn't deserve it. That ho is so annoying."

I burst out laughing, my entire body seeming to relax. "She's a ho?"

"Not really. But she *is* annoying." Sienna tucks a few strands of hair behind her ear. "Look, I know we just met, but I mean it. If I can help you in any way, let me know. I'll bring over a bag of clothes tomorrow afternoon."

"I'm not sure if I'll be here." I grimace. "I have to go on a job hunt tomorrow."

"You should try the café down the street," she suggests.

"That's where my car got broken into."

"Oh. Well, maybe that's bad luck, but they're hiring. I saw the sign in the window. It's fast paced because, like, everyone goes there, but it should be fun too. I've known a few people who work there, and they say the owner is super accommodating to class schedules," Sienna explains.

"I'll have to check it out."

"What's your major?" Sienna asks.

"Nutrition. I think I want to be a nutritionist."

"Oh." Sienna makes a face. "That takes a lot of science, huh?"

"Yeah, it does." I'm nodding. Even laughing. I like her a lot. She's so friendly and welcoming.

"I'm a business-and-marketing major. I can't do science." She leans in closer, her expression serious. "Is that why you agreed to cook these guys meals? I told my brother it was completely sexist of them to put that expectation on you, but he reassured me you were okay with it."

"I'm fine with it. I would've agreed to almost anything to get this room," I tell her.

A devilish gleam lights Sienna's eyes. "Anything?"

Nico had the same reaction earlier. Does everyone around here have their minds in the gutter?

Maybe.

Probably.

"You know what I mean."

One of the blonde girls starts laughing outrageously, and when I glance around Sienna, I see she's standing extra close to Nico, her boobs practically resting on his arm. He doesn't seem to mind. When she tosses her head back, her laughter seems never ending, and I wince. Even the other girls standing with her appear annoyed, like they wish she would just shut up.

"It's always like this," Sienna says when I return my attention to her.

"Always like what?"

"Nico and Gavin. They flirt with the girls constantly." She rolls her eyes.

"Who's Gavin?"

"The team's quarterback. He should be here soon. Hopefully." Her gaze shifts to the door. "He's best friends with my brother and Nico. But he doesn't live with them because he comes from money, and he always gets his own apartment. Which is like . . . unheard of around here."

"Must be nice." I glance toward the door like I'm waiting for it to open too.

"Right? Gav hangs out here all the time, though, so prepare yourself." She lowers her voice. "He's really hot too."

"Great. They're all hot," I say with disgust, shaking my head.

Sienna laughs at my reaction. "Not Coop."

"You're only saying that because he's your brother." Coop is definitely attractive in that big, quiet way of his.

"Well, yeah. Duh."

"Nico isn't my type," I add, because it's true. I think of Brad. Little emo Brad and his faded band T-shirts and skinny jeans. The beat-up black Converse he always wore, and how he smoked cigarettes "ironically"—direct quote. He smoked too much weed, ate too much junk food, and had zero ambition. I don't know why I wasted so many years on him.

"Nico is everyone's type. Right, Nico?" Sienna calls to him.

"You talking to me, Annie?" He's grinning, and I realize he's got a blonde under each arm, the third one watching them with a massive pout on her face.

"Annie?" I ask Sienna.

"They used to call me Little Orphan Annie when I first came here, which is so stupid." She grabs a chunk of her red hair and waves it at me before turning to face him. "Come up with something more original, why don't you?"

"Aw, don't get your panties in a twist. You know I'm just teasing." He even winks at her, his gaze shifting to mine, but I look away quickly, not wanting to get caught staring.

The door swings open at that precise moment, and a guy walks in with the face of a Greek god—all chiseled angles and sharp lines, softened by his plush mouth and the way it curls into a one-sided smile.

The moment he's spotted, every guy in the room starts cheering, shouts of "QB!" ringing in the air.

"There's Gavin." Sienna's voice is wistful, her gaze locked on him and no one else.

The third blonde abandons Nico and runs over to Gavin, greeting him by wrapping her arms around his neck and delivering a smacking kiss to his cheek. He laughs, but the sound is uncomfortable as he places his hands on her waist and sets her away from him.

"Does that normally happen?" I ask Sienna, noting the subtle fury glimmering in her eyes.

"What, women throwing themselves at Gavin the moment he walks through the door?" She doesn't tear her gaze away from him and the blonde, who is still trying to talk to him. "Not usually, only because they don't have girls over that much."

"Really?" I find that hard to believe. "That's surprising."

"I think Frank invited the blondes so you'd have someone to talk to. But clearly, that's not happening. They're too busy trying to get with Nico." Sienna hooks her arm through mine. "At least you have me."

I glance around the room at the multitude of football players casually hanging out on the couches, the coffee table littered with empty beer bottles and cans, a football game playing on the TV without the sound on. There are no other women in this house besides me and Sienna and the blondes, and I'm starting to think she wasn't exaggerating when she said they don't have women over often.

"Is that why you're here?" I ask her. "To keep me company?"

"Coop did reach out and ask what I was doing. He knows I'm always down to meet someone new." She unhooks her arm from mine, her smile fading. "Look, it's hard for me to make friends."

I'm frowning so hard my face hurts. "Really? But you're so . . . friendly."

"Yeah, well, I don't trust that easily. Most people just want to be my friend because of who my brother is."

"What, is Cooper a big deal?" A little laugh escapes, but Sienna doesn't laugh along with me. At all.

In fact, her face is dead serious.

"Wait a minute. Is your brother really a big deal?" I whisper.

"Every single guy in this room is a big deal. The majority of them have won a national football championship."

I stare at her blankly, shaking my head like I don't know what she's talking about.

Because I actually don't know what she's talking about.

"Everleigh." She grabs hold of my shoulders, her gaze locking with mine. "You're roommates with some of the most popular guys on this entire campus. The UC Santa Mira Dolphins football team is a big deal. Huge. They're all elite athletes. Some of these guys are going to go on to become professional football players. My brother might, too, though he'll deny it every time you ask him."

I scan the room once more, noting the rippling arm muscles, since the majority of them are wearing T-shirts or tank tops. The thick thigh muscles on display. Their low, deep, masculine voices as they chat and laugh and give each other shit. How casually confident they all are.

Every single one of them.

"These guys are really elite athletes?" I ask, my voice weak when I return my gaze to Sienna. "But they look so normal."

It's a lie. None of them look like regular dudes. They're all tall and broad and muscular. It's clear they work on their bodies regularly. Maybe even obsessively.

"Please. They're not normal. Not even close. They're beasts on the field. I've heard some of them are beasts in bed, too, but I've never been lucky enough to test that theory out." Sienna's smile is wry when I give her a bug-eyed look. "Hey, I can't lie—there are a couple of them I wouldn't mind hooking up with, but I know they'd just break my heart."

"Right. I'm sure." I nod, my gaze returning to them. Trying to imagine them out on a football field, crushing the opposing team.

Sounds like I need to do some serious googling later tonight before I go to bed.

"You really didn't know they were a bunch of national-championship-winning football players, did you?" Sienna sounds surprised, and when I glance over at her, I notice that her eyebrows are up. "No wonder they were okay with you moving in."

"Why is that so surprising?"

"Every girl they encounter usually only wants one thing from them. The fame of knowing, of hanging out with, of having sex with one of the university's football players. It's the main reason why I'm allowed to hang out with them, besides being Coop's younger sister. I'm not an over-the-top fangirl. I don't view them like that." She nudges my side with her elbow. "Apparently, neither do you."

Chapter Nine

Everleigh

My first full week in Santa Mira goes by quickly and is busy in all the right ways. I got the window on my car fixed the same day I took it to the mechanic. I was offered a part-time job at the very café where fate delivered my new roommates, and I finally started school Thursday.

I don't understand why school started on a Thursday. Does that make sense? Not to me, but those are the rules, so I don't question them.

Since training for my new job doesn't begin until bright and early Friday morning, after I finish my first day of classes, I go shopping to get some new clothes and other items I still need. I ended up taking a few of Sienna's hand-me-downs, but not many. Everything was too long on me. She's so much taller than I am.

By the time I'm done and heading back home, I end up driving around the neighborhood for almost thirty minutes before I find a parking spot—one that's kind of far from the house, but I don't really have a choice.

Living in Santa Mira is a lot more difficult than I expected it to be.

The walk back to our house is long, especially when lugging all my shopping bags and my backpack. Feeling bitter as I trudge up the path toward the front porch, I send a scathing look toward Nico's pristine black truck sitting in the driveway. I wish he'd let me park there like he did when my car window was broken, but I get it. He pays more in rent, and our schedules aren't the same, so it would end up being a hassle, constantly moving our cars for each other.

Still hate having to park so far away, though.

The moment I walk inside the house, I spot Frank sitting on the couch, scrolling on his phone. His head pops up, a hopeful expression on his face when he sees me.

"Finally," he says, like I've been gone for days. "I'm starving."

I've made him dinner for the last three nights, which was our initial agreement, and I don't want to deviate from it. "Hate to break it to you, but I'm not cooking tonight, Frank."

"You're not?" The disappointment is clear in his voice—the look on his face.

"Give her a break. She's already sick of feeding your needy ass." This comes from Nico, who exits the kitchen clutching a giant foil-wrapped burrito in his hand.

"Fuck off," Frank mutters as he climbs off the couch, approaching me slowly. "You're really not making dinner tonight, Everleigh?"

I slowly shake my head, offering him an apologetic smile. "The deal was three meals a week."

"I didn't expect those three days to go by so fast." Frank pats his stomach.

"You're whining, Dollar." There's a warning to Nico's tone, one that surprises me. He sounds a little mean. I send him a questioning look, but he doesn't even glance in my direction.

What in the world is going on? Is he actually trying to watch out for me?

"Yeah, yeah. I think I'm gonna go grab a sandwich from the shop across the street. You wanna go with me, Ever?"

"Thanks, but no. I already got something when I was out." I offer him an apologetic smile, and his disappointment is clear.

I feel bad for lying. I'm starving. I just don't want to go out with Frank. He reads into everything I do with him. Everything I say. How am I supposed to blatantly tell him I'm not interested? It was one thing to break up with Brad. I knew him for a long time, and I wasn't that scared to tell him we were through.

Letting down Frank is going to be difficult. But if he keeps pushing, I'm eventually going to have to do something about it.

I'm not looking forward to it.

Sienna was right. He's nice enough, but he comes on way too strong and tries so, so hard to flirt with me. Act charming, though it's not effortless for him. More like it's a little off-putting, but I tolerate him because he's harmless. Plus, he's my roommate. I want to get along with all of them. Coop makes it easy. He's kind, doesn't talk much, and nothing seems to bother him.

Still a little unsure about Nico, though. We haven't spent enough time together, which is fine with me. I find his face distracting.

"Ah, okay. Well, see you guys later." He grabs his wallet from the table near the door and exits the house.

"Finally, some peace and quiet," Nico says once Frank is gone, taking a big bite from his burrito. It looks delicious and my stomach growls. Hopefully he doesn't hear it. "Doesn't he drive you crazy? He acts like a sad puppy dog around you."

"He's okay." I don't want to say anything bad about Frank to Nico. He's done the most for me out of the three of them, not that I'm judging them on that. It's just facts. "He means well."

"If you say so." The doubt in Nico's voice is obvious.

"Why do you live with him if you don't like him?"

He appears taken aback by my question, blinking at me a couple of times before he answers. "I don't dislike Dollar."

"You talk about him like you do."

"He's cool. Pays his rent on time. Is solid out on the field. Mostly." He grins.

I tear my gaze away from him, staring at a blank wall rather than falling into the trap that is his smile. Whereas Frank tries so damn hard, Nico doesn't have to try at all, and I find myself drawn to him.

It's annoying.

"He'll eventually take the hint and back off from you," Nico reassures me. "Give him time."

I shrug helplessly, sending him a quick look but not saying anything as I walk past him and head to my bedroom to drop off my bags before I fix myself something to eat. Weirdly enough, Nico follows me, hovering in my bedroom doorway and watching me set my bags on top of my bed.

"How was school?" he asks, like he actually wants to make conversation with me.

"Good." I keep my back to him as I slide my backpack off and drop it on the floor.

"And your classes?"

"They seem like they're going to be okay. Probably a little intense." I pause, turning to face him. He's still standing in the doorway, apparently not going anywhere anytime soon, so I keep up the conversation. "How were your classes?"

"They were all right. My load is a little lighter this quarter since I took summer classes. I only have fifteen units." He takes another bite from that delicious-looking burrito, and I swear my mouth waters.

"I'm jealous," I admit. "I'm taking eighteen."

"That's a big load. With football I couldn't handle it. Plus, I was here all summer, so it made sense to get some classes out of the way." He shrugs those impossibly broad shoulders, drawing my attention to just how big he is.

He towers over me. Feels like he's twice as wide as me and can probably crush me with his bare hands. I shouldn't find that hot, but there is something about him and all that contained strength that's a turn-on.

Or maybe I'm just warped and sex starved. It didn't help when Sienna described the football team as beasts in bed. Worse because the first one I thought of was Nico.

I can only imagine . . .

Shutting off my wayward thoughts, I ask, "Why were you here all summer?"

"Because of football. We have camp and then summer practice, and our season started a couple of weeks ago," he explains.

"Really? Before school started?"

He nods, holding his burrito out toward me. "Want a bite?"

"What? No." I shake my head, taking a step backward. More than a little confused by the sudden subject change.

"Oh. You were staring at the burrito like it was the hottest thing you've ever seen." He grins. "Figured you were hungry."

My stomach chooses that moment to growl, of course. I can feel my entire face get hot, and a knowing smile curls Nico's perfect lips. "Uhh . . ."

"You're definitely hungry," he says with a chuckle. "I'll share it with you."

"No. It's okay." I shake my head, embarrassed. "I couldn't take your dinner away from you. I'm sure I can find something here to eat."

There are plenty of things in the fridge, not that much of it appeals. I should know what's in there since I've been cooking dinner for these guys the last few nights. They're always appreciative of it too. Complimenting me on the meals I've made and offering to help clean up the kitchen, which I always let them do.

"This place makes the best burritos I've ever had." He's trying to tempt me. The seductive tone of his voice, the look on his face, the way he just took another bite of his burrito, his gaze never straying from mine . . .

No wonder women just fall into bed with him. He's working his magic on me over a freakin' burrito.

"I don't think—"

"Come on," he interrupts. "I'm taking you out and buying you one. Trust me, once you try it, you'll never look back."

"Do they sponsor you? Is that why you're pushing them on me so hard?"

He laughs, and the pleasant sound ripples over my skin, making me warm.

"Nah. I just like their food," he calls over his shoulder as he starts walking.

It's as if I have no choice but to follow him out of my room, trailing after him as he makes his way to the front door. "What about Frank? What if he spots us after I turned him down?"

"He just texted me asking if I wanted to meet up with him later at Charley's. A few of the guys are there already." Charley's is a bar not too far from campus—and our house—that also serves food. I applied for a job there but turned down their request for an interview when I got the position at the café.

"Oh." Nico's really got to be humoring me by offering to take me out for dinner. Wouldn't he rather be with his friends? "Did you want to meet up with them instead?"

"I'll hang out with them later." He faces me fully, his brows shooting up. "You ready to go?"

He's just being friendly, I remind myself as I follow him through the front door and watch as he locks it, shoving his keys in his pocket. I stare at the front of his sweatpants like some sort of deranged pervert, and when I jerk my gaze up to his, that knowing smile is back. Like he knows exactly what I was looking at.

Like he doesn't mind that I'm a deranged pervert. He might even like it.

This is nothing, I remind myself. It means nothing. Just two roommates grabbing food. That's it.

That's all it can ever be.

Chapter Ten

Nico

We walk side by side along the sidewalk, keeping up a steady stream of conversation, me dodging out of the way if someone approaches us. A few people say hello, calling out my name like I'm some sort of celebrity, and I realize it was pretty risky, coming out like this by myself.

It's not something I normally do. I'm taking a chance here. I could get swarmed by fans—and the rabid fangirls who just want to get in our pants—in a matter of minutes if word gets out.

Wild but true.

Everleigh, though? She's oblivious to my celebrity status. She doesn't treat me like a god, and I like it. To her I'm that guy she lives with who probably annoys her sometimes. I know I definitely embarrass her when I don't even mean to. It's awkward as fuck at night when we're both wanting to use the bathroom for a shower or to brush our teeth. One night, we even brushed our teeth together, which felt weirdly intimate especially since there's only one sink and we're both spitting into it.

Coop was right. Living with a woman is different.

Earlier she really couldn't stop staring at my burrito like it was the best thing she'd ever seen, and when her stomach growled?

That confirmed it. Girl was hungry. I was feeling generous, so I offered to feed her.

No big.

When we finally end up at Hector's, there's a line in front of the building. It's the kind of restaurant where you place your order at the counter and they call out your name when it's ready. They move pretty fast.

"There are a lot of people here," she observes.

I toss my wadded-up foil left over from the burrito I finished a few minutes ago in a nearby trash bin. "I'm not the only one who thinks this place is delicious."

"Clearly." She sends me a quick smile as she scans the area. There are a bunch of picnic tables to the left of the building where people can sit and eat, strings of lights hanging above them in a zigzag pattern. Every table is full of people our age, all of them talking and laughing while shoving food in their faces.

This town is a vibe, and I'm so fucking glad I live here. That I play football for this team. I grew up on the coast, but a little farther up north, in Atascadero. I could've gone to college near there, but their football team was for shit, and there was no way I could risk it. Plus I was eager to get away from my hometown and go somewhere new. I wanted to play for a D-1 school, and lucky for me, I got in.

Not without hard work both in class and on the field, that's for damn sure.

We're slowly approaching the inside of the restaurant, close enough for Everleigh to check out the menu board that sits above the order counter, when the hairs stand up on the back of my neck. Like someone's watching me.

Here's the deal. A lot of people watch me, and I'm normally unaffected by it because I'm used to it. But something is up. Whoever is watching me, I get the sense that it's not in a positive way.

When the hairs on my arms start to rise, I realize that someone is most definitely watching me. More like glaring at me.

Barely moving, I glance out of the corner of my eye, everything inside me seeming to sink when I see who it is.

Portia. The girl I fucked around with in the spring on a semiregular basis, which was my first mistake. The one who lost her mind on me when I told her I didn't want to see her anymore.

That pissed her off. Big time. From the look I just spotted on Portia's face, I'd say she's still pissed.

"Shit," I mutter, dropping my head so I can stare at my feet. I'm tempted to leave, but I'm not abandoning Everleigh. But I don't want Portia to make a scene either.

"What's wrong?" Everleigh asks, her voice full of alarm.

I must be giving off major shit's-about-to-go-down vibes. "There's a girl here who—"

"Nico Valente! I haven't seen you in *foreverrrrrr*."

I wince at the sound of Portia's grating voice.

What did I ever see in her again?

She magically appears in front of me, her glossy lips stretched into a smile, the scrap of a sundress she's wearing barely containing her voluptuous curves. The skirt's hem flirts around the top of her tanned thighs, and her tits look ready to bust out of the dress at any given moment.

Okay, that's what I saw in her. Portia has a bangin' bod, and she knows what she's doing when she's dressed like that. But she was too possessive, too mean . . . just too damn much. I was bailing on her all the time there near the end of it, trying my best to ghost her, but she still wouldn't take the hint. I finally had to tell her—to her face—that I didn't want to see her anymore.

And she lost it. Put on an ugly scene that had Cooper threatening to call the cops if she didn't leave our place. Back then it was just Coop and me living in a tiny apartment together. She doesn't know where we moved.

At least, I don't think she knows.

"Hey, Portia," I finally greet her, taking a step closer to Everleigh. Unfortunately, she shifts out of my way, and Portia notices because that chick sees everything.

"What are you up to, hmm? Grabbing one of your favorite burritos?" I've brought Portia to this place too. Hell, I wouldn't put it past her that she's hanging around here in the hopes that she'd spot me.

I'm not an arrogant ass by saying that either. This girl was flat-out obsessed with me, and not in a good way.

"Yeah," I tell her, taking another step closer to Everleigh. At least she doesn't move away this time.

"Who's your friend?" Portia sounds overly friendly and completely harmless, but I know the truth. She's digging for information and ready to say something shitty to Everleigh.

"Hi, I'm Everleigh." She extends her hand to Portia, who just stares at it like it's a dead rat, giving Everleigh no choice but to drop it, sending me a concerned look. "Uh, nice to meet you?"

"Likewise," Portia says breezily, lunging for me so she can wrap her arm around mine, pressing her tits against me. "You look good, Nico. I've missed you."

"Hey, whoa. Can't go grabbing at me like that, Portia. I've got someone else now." I pull away from her still-grasping hands and slip my arm around Everleigh's shoulders, tugging her close so she's practically lodged under my armpit.

I can feel her stiffen against me, and I send a silent plea to the universe that she cooperates.

Portia stares at us for a second, her mouth hanging open for a moment before she snaps her lips shut. "Really."

"Yep." I give Everleigh's shoulders a squeeze, the deliciously sweet scent of her flooding my senses.

"You told me you weren't the exclusive kind," Portia snottily reminds me.

"A man can change for the right woman." I flash Everleigh my best smile, and she just stands there, looking stunned. The deer-in-the-headlights look isn't what I'm going for. Hopefully Portia doesn't notice, but she sees all so . . .

"Oh my God, Nico, you are so full of shit right now. Text me when you eventually get bored with this one, because we so know that's going to happen, and soon." With a flip of her long blonde locks, Portia turns on her heel and stomps off.

The moment she's out of sight, I release my hold on Everleigh. "Sorry about that."

"Did you just tell her that I was your girlfriend or something?"

"Maybe?" I scratch the back of my head, glancing around to see if anyone is paying attention to us. Everyone acts like they're absorbed in their own thing, but I know what it's really like around here. Someone noticed.

More like a few someones.

Portia also has a huge mouth. I'm sure it's going to spread like wildfire that I told her I have somebody new in my life.

"Nico." The disappointment in Everleigh's voice is obvious, and I immediately feel like a shit. "Why did you lie to her?"

"Because she's a walking nightmare that I don't want to deal with," I answer truthfully.

Everleigh's shaking her head, wrapping her arms around herself like she's trying to ward off a chill—or my touch. Ouch. "I'm guessing you two used to be involved."

I nod. "She is a miserable human being. Possessive. A little mean."

Fine. She's a lot mean. Nothing made that girl happy. I gave her attention and she wasn't happy. I brought her around my friends and teammates, and she treated them like garbage. I couldn't please her—not even in bed.

And trust me when I say I put my all into everything I do—that includes sex. My top priority is making sure the woman I'm with always ends up pleased.

Sometimes multiple times.

"She's pretty" is all Everleigh says in response.

We remain quiet as we slowly make our way up to the counter, my brain turning over and over what Everleigh said about Portia. Calling her pretty.

She is. But all that beauty hides her shitty personality. If it had been a casual one-night fuck, that would've been one thing. But she sucked me in by acting like she was cool. She was down for whatever, always smiling and overly flirtatious. The moment she "got" me, she changed.

Turning sullen and downright angry.

"Just because someone is pretty doesn't mean that they're a good person," I finally say when we're next in line to order.

I can feel Everleigh's gaze on me, and when I finally turn to look at her, I see she has a small smile curling her lips. They're nice lips. Full and pink. Wonder what it would be like, kissing her.

Yeah. I need to push that thought straight out of my brain.

"Oh, I know," she reassures me. "I've met some beautiful people with ugly personalities."

"Exactly. That's Portia's problem." I shake my head. "I don't want to talk about her."

"Me either," Everleigh readily agrees. "I'd rather you help me figure out what I should order."

"That I can do," I say, relief coursing through me. "I usually go with asada when I get a burrito, but their carnitas is pretty good too."

"What about chicken?"

"I don't know—not my favorite."

"I'll go with the carnitas then." She offers me a smile, and I automatically smile back at her in return, wondering why she's not giving me endless shit over basically telling Portia she's my girl.

Maybe she doesn't mind, I think as she makes her order and I get another burrito because why not. I won't eat the whole thing now. I'll finish off the rest in the morning.

By the time our food is ready, I grab the bag and head outside with her, figuring we'd walk back to the house, where she can eat in peace.

"Want to sit down?" she asks, gesturing toward one of the now-empty tables with her drink.

"Only if you want to."

People still aren't paying too much attention to us, which is the only reason I agree to sit here. Most of the time my presence—especially when I'm with other teammates—causes a commotion. When I'm with my boys, I don't mind. We revel in it.

We settle in at a picnic table, and I watch Everleigh expectantly as she unwraps her burrito and takes a bite. A downright orgasmic sound escapes her when she begins to chew, and I watch her mouth move, staring at her like a dumbass.

"You weren't lying. This is delicious," she says once she's swallowed.

"Told you." My voice is a rasp, and I clear my throat, unwrapping my second burrito and taking a big bite. "Next time try the asada."

"Maybe," she says, her eyes sparkling. Like she's teasing me. "Just so you know, I'm not the type who does whatever my boyfriend says."

"Your boyfriend?" I raise my brows, starting to sweat.

There it is. Now she's going to let me have it for what I said to Portia.

"Isn't that what you told Portia?" Everleigh takes another bite, watching me thoughtfully. "No wonder you get yourself into trouble."

"What do you mean by that?"

"You say things you shouldn't." She smiles, ready to take a bite of her food, but I swipe it from her hand, quick as shit.

As per usual.

"Hey," she protests when I take a giant bite of her burrito like a complete asshat. "That's mine."

"Sorry, just taking advantage of my boyfriend privileges." I grin at her and she scowls.

Damn. She's really cute when she does that.

Chapter Eleven

Everleigh

This man has a lot of nerve, claiming me as his girlfriend to deter a woman who is clearly still not over him, only for him to steal my food and take a gargantuan bite, because these men I live with? These football-playing, elite athletes?

Their stomachs are endless pits, and they don't eat the best. I mean, we're young and all, but they need to treat their bodies better and give them the proper fuel to perform at their very best out on the field.

I've lived with them for almost a week, but I see what they consume. Too much alcohol, too much junk food. Considering I'm majoring in nutrition, I can't help but pay attention to what they eat and drink.

"You're not my boyfriend," I remind him pointedly. "Even if you tell other women that, it doesn't make it true."

"My bad," he says teasingly, handing my burrito back over to me. I take it from him, scooting down the bench some so I'm out of his reach, which only makes him laugh.

Dang it, I really love the way he laughs.

"I probably shouldn't have done that," he says.

"No, you probably shouldn't have." I take a sip from the water cup I got for free inside. "It didn't seem like that little fact stopped her either."

"She's pretty determined when she sets her mind to something."

I set my food down on the wrapper I have spread out on the table, staring at him intently. "How long were you two together?"

He grimaces. "Define *together*."

"Nico."

"Everleigh," he deadpans right back at me.

"Were you and Portia actually dating?" I wrinkle my nose. She may have been rude, but she was absolutely beautiful. I can see why he was with her.

Men. They're such simple creatures sometimes.

"Sort of? Kind of? It's not usually my thing, seeing a woman exclusively," he admits. "But I tried to with her, and it was an epic fail."

I would love to know what made this particular woman so special. Was it her looks?

Of course it was. She's gorgeous and exudes confidence, with no fear in showing off her curves in all the right places.

I am nothing like the curvy Portia, with her long blonde hair and perfect makeup. My hair is a boring brown, and most of the time I wear no makeup because I'm too busy to remember to put it on, and standing next to her earlier like that, having her refuse to shake my hand, she made me feel less than.

That kind of hurt.

"How long were you two seeing each other?" I'm repeating my question, but changing the way I say it to see if he'll actually answer me this time.

"A month? Maybe? Yeah, no. More like a couple of weeks. It didn't last long." He shrugs, staring off into the distance for a moment. The wind ruffles his dark hair, making pieces flutter around his forehead, and I have the sudden urge to push his hair out of his face.

Which is the dumbest idea ever, so I keep my hands clutched together in my lap.

"What happened? Why did you two break up?"

"There was nothing really to break up, but I ended things with her because she's not a nice person." He returns his gaze to mine, pinning me in place with all that intensity I see shining in his eyes. "And I realized it pretty quickly after we started seeing each other. She was the first girl I've actually dated in a long time, and now she's also the last girl I've been exclusive with."

At that last statement, a full-body shudder seems to take over him, and he's got a playful expression on his face. Like I'm supposed to find that funny.

"You have a hard time committing? Is that why? Is she mad at you because you might've—cheated or something?" I'm taking stabs in the dark. Meaning I have no idea if that's what he did or not.

Nico actually appears insulted. "What? No way. I'm not a cheater." He shakes his head.

"Sorry, I just—she was pretty hostile."

"Because no one ever told her no until I came along. That's it. Simple as that." His expression turns firm, his jaw tightening, and I remain quiet, his mood effectively shutting down the conversation.

It is obvious things didn't end well between them and Portia is still holding a grudge. And maybe Nico is holding a grudge too. Does he regret that they broke up? Does he miss her?

I have so many questions, yet I know I'm not going to get any answers.

"That's why you told her I'm your girlfriend?"

"I didn't call you my girlfriend."

"You implied it."

"Sort of."

"There's no *sort of* about it. You definitely implied that we're together." A thought hits me. "And we live together, Nico."

His smile is slow. "I really like it when you say my name. And you don't say it often enough."

I blink at him, annoyed that for the briefest second, I fell under his spell. Yet again. "You need to stop weaving your magic on me."

"Weaving my magic? What are you talking about?" He actually sounds confused.

"You know exactly what I'm talking about." I jab a finger at him. "You flirt. Excessively."

"Define *excessively*."

I roll my eyes. "All the time. Be real right now. You're very aware of the power you have with women."

"Power? You make it sound like I'm a total asshole who wields his supposed power over unsuspecting women." Now he sounds offended.

"I didn't mean it like that . . ." My voice drifts, and I throw my hands up, frustrated. "Now you're just twisting my words."

We're quiet for a moment, and I nibble on my burrito, my appetite disappearing. I feel like he just turned it on me and made me feel like the bad guy, which isn't cool.

"I shouldn't have told her we were together," he finally says, blowing out an obviously frustrated breath. "It was just a knee-jerk reaction on my part, pulling you close to me and making her think we're a couple. I haven't seen her in months, and I didn't want her getting any funny ideas."

"You definitely gave her a funny idea," I mumble. "Making her think we're together."

"Wait a second. Do you think that's a funny idea?"

"She definitely found it impossible to fathom." I roll my eyes, trying to play it off because I don't want him to know that it kind of hurt my feelings, how she reacted.

Like he'd never go for someone like me.

"She's just jealous. Portia can't stand the thought of me choosing someone else over her. That's all." He reaches out, settling his hand on my arm. "I'm sorry I put you into that position. I didn't mean to make you uncomfortable."

The moment his fingers connect with my skin, I feel it all the way in the pit of my stomach. Lower even. He streaks his thumb back and forth across my arm, and a shiver steals through me.

I think he felt it. That's probably why he removes his hand from my arm so quickly.

"It's fine," I tell him, desperate to brush this entire moment off. "Seriously. I hope Portia leaves you alone forever."

"Me too," he says, but his tone is full of doubt.

Matching the doubt that's churning inside me.

His phone buzzes, and he reaches for it, reading the text that's on his screen. "Coop's at Charley's. Everyone is. They want us to go there too."

"Us?"

"I told him we were together." Nico keeps tapping at his screen. "I let him know we'll be there when you finish dinner."

"I have to work tomorrow. It's my first day at the café," I protest.

He lifts his gaze to mine. "What time do you have to be there?"

"Five thirty in the morning." He winces at my answer. "They open at six."

"Damn, that's early."

"I know." But the pay is good, and I like the fact that the earlier hours mean I won't have to work late at night.

"Don't worry. We won't stay long," he reassures me.

I smile and nod but don't say anything. His using the word *we* is misleading. There is definitely no *we* going on.

There's just me.

We walk into the darkened bar fifteen minutes later, everyone greeting our appearance with a constant stream of "Nicooooooo" said in varying deep voices. I take a step back as people surround us, most of them his teammates and a few hangers-on. I shift to the side, eager to move out of the fray, when I feel a hand pulling on mine.

I look over my shoulder to see that it's Sienna wearing a friendly smile on her face. She tugs me into a quick hug, keeping me close as she murmurs in my ear, "Walking in with Nico, I see. Look at you moving fast."

I pull away from her to stare deep into her eyes, wanting her to see the sincerity in mine. "It means nothing, Sienna, I swear. He just took me to Hector's. Insisted I try their burritos."

"Oh, he loves that place, and I get why. The food is amazing," Sienna says with a reaffirming nod. "What else is going on between you two?"

"Like I said, that's it." I glance around the bar, ignoring the men who are carrying on around Nico like he's some sort of god. He's got that dazzling smile on his face, the one that makes everything inside me shiver, and I notice the various women on the fringe of the group are watching him carefully, all of them wearing hopeful expressions on their faces. Probably wishing one of those guys—specifically Nico—would notice them. "I desperately need a drink."

"Good thing you showed up at a bar." She hooks her arm through mine and leads me over to a tiny table she must've been sitting at. There are at least four empty glasses sitting on top of the table, meaning someone must've been sitting with her. "Have a seat."

I settle in, pushing some of the glasses away. "Did I interrupt you?"

"Not at all. I was sitting with Gavin." She arranges the glasses so they're all in a line in the center of the tiny table. "We were just catching up."

Uh-huh. I don't call her out on it, though, because I don't know her that well, and I don't know enough about the history between them either.

A server appears at our table, a woman about our age, and she smiles at Sienna. "You want another one?"

"Yes," Sienna says with a firm nod. "And my friend just showed up."

The server turns to me. "Hey, friend. What are you drinking tonight?"

"A rum and Coke, please. Heavy on the rum," I tell her.

"Coming right up." She takes off toward the bar.

Sienna leans across the table the moment the server is gone, her tone eager. "I want all the details."

"There are no details to share that are interesting." I hesitate. "Well, there was one thing that happened."

"Spill it."

I tell her the story about Portia showing up and Nico pulling me close and slipping his arm around my shoulders. How he told Portia that we were involved, and how rude she was toward me.

"Oh my God, I hate her so much," Sienna interjects at one point. "Like she is seriously the worst."

Her opinion about Portia doesn't surprise me. "You know her?"

"I remember her hanging around last spring. Nico and my brother were roommates but living in an apartment back then, and it was tiny. When I would come over, it seemed like she was always there. Sitting in Nico's lap. Trying to take all of his attention so he couldn't hang out with his friends like—ever. Plus she's freaking mean. I know she didn't like me being there, and the feeling was mutual." Sienna shakes her head. "She was awful."

"She was so incredibly rude toward me. Like I don't think I've ever had someone act that way toward me before." Her behavior was so blatant. She did not give a single crap about my feelings whatsoever.

"What did she do when she found out you and Nico are together?" Sienna bursts out laughing before I can even explain myself. "No offense, but that is truly the craziest thing, what he did. Like, why would he say that to her?"

"Right? He wasn't even thinking straight. He just—did it. Next thing I know, his arm is around my shoulders and he's pulling me into him." He is as solid as a rock. Firm and muscular, and as hot as a furnace.

"I'm sure that was a hardship." Sienna's mischievous smile has me rolling my eyes, but I'm also smiling along with her.

"It was terrible," I agree, both of us laughing. "When he did that, I'm pretty sure it only made her madder. Trust when I say she wasn't discouraged about this news." I'm startled when the server reappears

75

quickly, setting our fresh drinks on the table in front of us before she takes the old ones and stacks them on her tray.

"Need anything else?" she asks brightly, even though she's walking away from us.

"No thank you," Sienna answers, holding up her drink toward me. I do the same. "Cheers to the dumb things men say."

"Cheers." We clink glasses and both take a drink. It's strong, heavy on the rum just as I requested, and I take another drink, needing the liquor to mellow me out. I've been tense since the moment I walked into the house and Frank tried to get me to cook him dinner.

Speaking of Frank, I glance to my left to see him sitting at the bar with a couple of his teammates, his gaze stuck on me. The second I catch him staring, he looks away, his cheeks turning ruddy, and a sigh leaves me. Sienna notices, of course.

"What's wrong?" She glances over her shoulder, spotting Frank. Her expression is sympathetic when she faces me once more. "If it makes you feel any better, he used to have a raging crush on me too."

"Really?" Another sigh escapes. "He's so nice, but—"

"He tries too hard, and he's constantly up in your business. Right?" I nod at her assessment. "I finally had to tell him I wasn't interested in him like that, and from the way he reacted, you'd have thought I kicked his puppy repeatedly. He was so disappointed. I think he even used that exact wording. 'You disappoint me, Sienna.'"

"Yikes." I can't imagine having the balls to tell Frank to his face that I'm not interested. I don't like confrontation, and the last thing I ever want to do is hurt someone's feelings.

"He pushed me to it. He comes on so strong, and he wouldn't let up. Constantly turning him down or saying I was busy wasn't working. He didn't take the hint." She shakes her head, sipping from her drink. "He has a reputation. He's done this countless times before to other women. I just wish he'd find someone who was totally into him so they can fall in love and produce little Dollars together."

I start laughing at the image. "Little Dollars."

"Maybe we could call them fifty cent. When they're first born, they'd be quarters. Maybe dimes." Sienna is laughing too. "Seriously, I like him as a friend, but that's about it."

"Same."

"How do you feel about Nico?"

"He's just a friend too." No way can I tell her that I think he's hot. It's fairly obvious that he is, so there's no point in mentioning it. "That's all he can be."

"And why do you say that?"

"Because we're roommates. I can't mess around with a guy I live with."

Her smile is a little dirty. "So you've thought about messing around with him."

"No, I have definitely not." I clamp my lips shut, cutting myself off. I'm protesting too much. The bigger the reaction, the more she's going to think I most definitely have thought about it, and damn it . . .

I have.

"He's not forever material, anyway. None of them are." Her expression immediately turns glum, and she's watching someone from across the room. I don't even have to check on who it is. I already have my suspicions.

"Who are you crushing on?" My voice is gentle, and I take a huge gulp from my drink, wondering if the alcohol is making me braver. We're delving into private territory, and we barely know each other. Though sometimes isn't it easier to confess your truths to a virtual stranger?

"No one," she says way too quickly.

"Come on, now. You can tell me."

She blows out a frustrated breath. "Fine. I'm madly in love with Gavin, but he barely knows I exist."

This time I do look behind me to check on who she's staring at, and yep, there's Gavin, along with Nico and Coop. All three are standing by a table full of students, smiling and nodding as the students seem to gush over them.

"I'm sure he knows you exist," I tell her when I'm facing her once more.

"Only as Coop's little sister and nothing else." Oh, she sounds down in the dumps. "He doesn't really see me, you know?"

"Are you so sure about that?"

"Positive. I basically threw myself at him a couple of years ago when I first started here, and he turned me down. We've been 'just friends'"—she uses air quotes—"ever since."

"Ouch." I finish off my drink in one last swallow, realizing that Sienna has barely touched hers. Though she had a head start, so I shouldn't feel too bad. "That was kind of a long time ago, though."

"Yeah. I was eighteen and way too confident." Now she's the one gulping down her drink. "I was trashed that night and positive he could feel the vibes between us. I'm fairly certain that's how I phrased it to him."

"And I'm guessing he was kind and thoughtful and said he could never touch you because you're his friend's sister," I say.

"That's exactly what happened, and I was devastated. I essentially avoided him for a year. Then I started coming around to Coop's again when he was with his friends, and now I think we're at peace. Sort of."

"What do you mean by *sort of*?"

"He keeps talking to me. Like one on one. Seeking me out all the time. It's confusing."

"Men are confusing."

Sienna holds up her glass, and I clink mine against hers again. "Amen."

Chapter Twelve

NICO

"And . . . go!"

I'm running as fast as I can, 100 percent focused on getting nothing but mass yardage. I hear the heavy footfalls of the defensive line running after my ass, but I ignore them, turning at the very last second and holding my hands open.

The ball lands into my hands like that was supposed to happen. I run the ball into the end zone with fucking ease, a giant grin on my face.

The entire offensive coaching team is standing on the edge of the field by the goalpost, watching me. Head Coach Porter is blowing his whistle repeatedly.

"What the fuck, guys? You couldn't catch him?" His voice is a mixture of anger and incredulity.

"I'm just that fast," I tell him, keeping the grin on my face. The grin that I know irritates him most of the time because he thinks I'm too arrogant. He's told me that multiple times over the course of our relationship.

Then I pull a play like what just happened, and I want to tell him there's a reason I'm what I prefer to call *confident*: I'm fucking good. Gav's accuracy when he throws the ball, combined with the fact that I know when that ball is about to land in my hands, is something I can't describe. We're connected on the field. It's fucking magical.

Even the sports announcers call it that. Magic. They warn NFL teams considering drafting Gavin to consider me as well because we're a team within a team.

I would love to go anywhere with Gav. Together we would dominate, just like we do now. But there are no guarantees that's ever going to happen.

It most likely won't, which not going to lie, makes me a little sad.

Resting my hands on my hips, I scan the field, taking it all in. The stadium sits on a hill that overlooks the ocean, and we have the best damn view out of any university in this entire country. The sun is blazing down upon us, but there's a breeze coming off the water that cools the sweat on my skin. There is nowhere I'd rather be than right here, finishing out the season with this team. The majority of them I can call my friends, and some of them will be lifelong friends for sure. I'm a lucky man. My college football career has been amazing, and I couldn't ask for a better experience.

So why do I feel this gnawing in my gut? It started up late last week, when I ran into Portia and told her Everleigh and I were together. Everleigh wasn't too thrilled I did that, and I suppose I don't blame her, but we haven't really talked much since that stupid encounter happened, and that was a week ago.

Doesn't help that she took off with Sienna that night when we were at Charley's. She had to go to work early that Friday morning, and we left for an away game and were gone over the weekend. Since then we haven't run into each other again.

Which is fucking odd. I live with the chick—we share a bathroom—yet I never see her. Our schedules must be the total opposite, especially once she got the job at the café. She's gone most mornings, and sometimes I don't come home until late at night, and she's already locked away in her room.

I don't have the nerve to go knock on her door and ask her how it's going either. Like does she really want to have that conversation with me? Doubtful.

Instead, I leave her alone and deal with that hollow feeling on my own.

Why do I care what she thinks, anyway? Or what she's doing? She's just a girl I don't really know that well. She's pretty enough. She seems cool. She went along with my stupid scheme without calling me out in front of Portia, so that earned her points right there. I guess she's hanging with Coop more often, and he has nothing but nice things to say about her, though he's not interested in her like that.

Thank Christ. I don't want to resent one of my best friends.

I hear Frank has eased up with her, too, according to Coop. I think Dollar finally got the hint. I'm sure he's moved onto some other poor, unsuspecting woman. If he could just relax for two seconds and stop trying so damn hard, he could probably score a woman fast. He just wants to be loved.

That's all so many of us want—except for me.

That's what I tell myself.

"Hey, asshole." I turn to see Ralph Jones strutting toward me, a shit-eating grin on his face.

"What's up, Jonesie?" I watch him approach, dodging away from him when he acts like he's going to slap my ass.

"Thinking you're hot shit out on the field, always catching those balls," he drawls. "Someday we're going to get that ball first."

He's a defensive cornerback, which is one of the hardest positions to play, and he's really fucking good at it. His hands are huge, and when he splays his fingers and tries to bat that ball out of the way, watch out.

Jonesie is usually successful.

"Not if I have anything to say about it," I tell him. He's excellent practice for me in that he always makes me play harder. Run faster. I'm just lucky that instincts kick in and I can practically sense when Gav lets that ball go.

"You guys are on fire lately. You got some telepathic powers going on between you or what?" He's referring to me and Gav.

"We're in sync. Can't lie." Pretty sure it's four seasons of working together that'll do it.

"Hear you guys are having a party next weekend since it's a bye week," Jonesie says.

"Where'd you hear that?"

"Coop. He's going around telling everyone we're gonna get crunk." Jonesie laughs. "Who says crunk anymore, anyway?"

"Cooper does," I deadpan, making Jonesie laugh harder. "I guess if he says we're having a party, we're having a party."

"Excellent." He holds his hand up, and I give it a slap. "Please say there will be women there beyond Sienna."

Everyone knows Cooper's sister. We're all used to having her tag along, and most of the time when we get together, we want it to be chill. She's one of the only girls allowed to "chill" with us.

"I'm sure we can wrangle some up," I say. "And hey, you're a player. You can bring a few of your own if you want."

"I can do that. I know a couple of ladies who'd love to party with us." He rubs the side of his face with one of his big hands, tapping his long fingers on his cheek. "I hear you have a hottie living with you."

I stand up a little straighter. "I guess."

"You guess? Word on the street is she's gorgeous." He whistles under his breath. "And you're actually living with her? How do you avoid that when it's in your face on a daily basis?"

"I don't think of her like that," I say between gritted teeth.

He takes one look at me and starts laughing. "Uh-huh. Sure."

"I'm serious." I kick at the field like I'm a toddler having a tantrum. Fucking great. "I don't shit where I eat."

"Excuse me?"

"You know what I'm talking about. I live with her. I'm not about to hook up with her and then have to deal with her needy ass when we still live in the same house together." I sound like such a prick, but I don't want Jonesie thinking I'm into Everleigh or whatever.

I also don't want him to have a thing for her either. He needs to stay away from Everleigh. She's off-limits.

I'm frowning at the possessive thoughts currently running through my head. What the hell am I thinking? Like she's mine and no one else can touch her?

Please.

"Right," he drawls, that smug tone of his making irritation rise within me. "You keep telling yourself that."

He struts away, and I watch him, letting the anger simmer in my veins. Not even bothering to try to convince myself I'm overreacting.

There's no convincing. I know I'm overreacting. And I don't know why.

Practice is eventually over, but I don't go straight home. Instead, I take a quick shower in the locker room before I go to the library, where I finish up a paper that's due at midnight. Only once I've got that done and sent off do I head back to the house.

It's like I'm purposely trying to avoid Everleigh, and maybe I am. I don't like that she's invading my thoughts. Maybe I need to find someone to hook up with. Yeah, that sounds like a plan. Some nameless, faceless, willing woman who's down for some fun and nothing else.

That's freaking perfect.

I'm so pleased with my plan that I'm whistling as I enter the house, coming to a dead stop when I see what's happening in front of me.

Everleigh is bent over into what I assume is the downward-dog position or whatever you call it, leading the guys in a . . . yoga session?

What the actual fuck?

And it's not just Coop and Dollar who are doing it. There are a couple of other guys from the team here, too, their big bodies hunkered over, muscles straining, legs shaking. I swear I hear some of them grunting as they try to hold the position.

"Okay, and breathe out," she murmurs in this calm, downright sultry voice that has my entire body switching on to high alert.

"What the hell is going on here?" I ask, slamming the door.

Every single one of the guys jumps at my voice. Coop even falls over on his side with a grunt.

Only Everleigh remains calm, her blue eyes sweeping over me before she returns her focus to the guys in front of her. "We're having a yoga class."

"You're giving yoga classes in our house now?" I sound incredulous. I *am* incredulous. "When did this start?"

"A few days ago," Coop says as he climbs off the floor and repositions himself. "It's actually pretty relaxing."

"I sleep better at night," Dollar chimes in.

"Same," says another teammate.

Rolling my eyes, I push past all of them and head for the kitchen, opening and closing the cabinets with extra force, searching for something I will never find because I have no idea what I'm looking for.

What I want.

Everleigh's gentle voice continues to counsel them through the various positions, and I swear just hearing it also somehow calms me. I end up sitting at the counter eating a bag of chips, wondering why I never got an invitation to the yoga classes. I frickin' live here, for the love of God.

By the time I'm putting away the chips in our tiny pantry, the session is over, and I can hear all of them move about the living room, their steps seeming to shake the foundation. Everleigh laughs at something one of them says, and next thing I know she's entering the kitchen, her smile fading when she spots me.

I take her in, noting how much skin is on display. She's wearing hot-pink leggings and a matching sports bra with white sneakers on her feet, and holy shit. I can't stop staring at her. Her hair is pulled back into a tight ponytail that swings when she moves, and her skin is covered with a light sheen of sweat.

I'm trying not to focus on the fact that her body is fucking incredible but . . . it is. Jonesie was right.

She's hot.

Damn it.

"Haven't seen you in a while," she eventually says as she makes her way to the fridge, opening it and pulling her Stanley tumbler out. She keeps it in there sometimes to make the water colder.

"Been busy." My voice is gruff, and I clear my throat, not wanting to sound like an asshole. "Sorry I interrupted."

"No worries." She takes a sip, her lips wrapped around the straw making me think all sorts of dirty thoughts. "You should join us sometime."

"I don't do yoga."

"Have you ever tried it?"

I say nothing because she knows my answer.

No, I haven't.

"Neither had any of those guys in there." She waves a hand toward the living room. "But they love it. You might too."

"Didn't realize you were running a gym in here." I'm teasing but not.

I see a flash of emotion in her eye and wonder if I pissed her off.

"I'm just trying to help these guys out. Coop has been complaining about how he can't ever relax and that he feels stressed out all the time."

I frown. I complain about the same thing.

"He laughed at me when I suggested he should try yoga, but then when we worked on it together—and Frank joined us—he went to practice the next day praising my yoga skills." She smiles, looking amused. "I've taught yoga before, but I didn't mean to turn this into a class for others to join us. It just sort of happened."

Again, why didn't I hear about this? "That's uh . . . that's great."

"You really should join us sometime. You seem a little stressed." She tilts her head to the side, her ponytail swinging. I want to tug on it. Wrap it around my fist, and pull her into me. "You've been really busy. It might be getting to you."

"Yeah," I croak. I know what's getting to me, and it has nothing to do with stress.

It's her.

Chapter Thirteen

"I'm not going to look like a complete fool in the stands, am I?"

Sienna makes a scoffing noise at my question. "Please. You don't have enough spirit going on, if you ask me."

Is she serious right now?

I chance a glance in the mirror that we're currently sitting in front of, but I can't see much. Sienna has this nice vanity table in her bedroom with a three-way mirror and a cute pale-blue tufted-velvet bench seat that we can both fit on while she paints my face in the school colors.

It's Saturday. Game day. The Dolphins are playing at home this afternoon, and I'm attending my first ever football game at UCSM. I'm equal parts nervous and excited, and I don't quite get why I'm nervous.

Maybe it's because I get to watch the men I live with out on the field? I've heard all about their playing thanks to the conversations that flow at the dinner table. In the living room. Everywhere, really.

They're obsessed with football, and I get it. They live and breathe it and are really damn good at it.

Or so I hear.

"Okay." Sienna leans back some, her gaze roaming over my face, examining her work. "You look good. You want to see?"

"Please," I say, practically thrusting my face into the mirror so I can check out what Sienna did.

She dotted light-blue, white, and black face paint—our school colors—underneath one eye for it to swirl across the bridge of my nose and above my other eye in an S pattern. She also painted the number eighty on my right cheek.

"Whose number is this?" I point at it on my face when I turn toward her.

Her smile is downright devilish. "Nico's."

"Oh my God, really?" I turn to look at myself in the mirror again, noting the panic in my eyes. "Take it off."

"No way. It looks great! You're just supporting your roommate. It means nothing," Sienna reassures, knowing that it means more than what she's saying.

She's such a shithead.

"I have three roommates who are on the team," I remind her. "I can't just support one and not the others."

Plus it looks like I might have a thing for him, which I so do not. I don't want him getting any ideas. Not that he'll see me.

Will we see each other directly after the game? Probably not. I shouldn't get my hopes up.

Oh man, I need to stop thinking like this. Feeling like this. He is my friend and that's it. The guy I share a bathroom with. I didn't even bother telling Sienna that I caught him coming out of the bathroom last night wrapped in a towel and nothing else. His skin gleamed because he was still a little wet, and his hair hung around his face. And I swear . . . I swear I saw the imprint of his dick beneath that towel.

I can't tell Sienna because she'll want details, and I'm not ready to share them. I'm assuming what she told me about it being ginormous is the truth because it most definitely was impressive.

He didn't seem too bashful at being caught in just a towel either. Pretty sure he was about to whip it off right in front of me when I slammed the door and locked myself away in the still steamy bathroom, the scent of him lingering in the air.

This sharing-a-bathroom situation is getting harder by the day.

"Don't worry about it. You'll blend right in," Sienna reassures me.

"What do you mean, I'll blend right in?" I sound skeptical.

I am skeptical.

"Everyone wears Nico's number on their cheeks. Well, mostly everyone," she explains.

I'm groaning. "You mean mostly girls, am I right?"

She nods.

I groan again. "Wash it off. Please, I'm begging you."

"No way. Ooh, I know! I'll add Coop's number on your other cheek." She grabs the black color stick, reaching for me, and I dodge out of her way at the last second.

"What about Frank's number?"

"He's currently benched." Her gaze turns sympathetic. "His shoulder has been bothering him. They still won't let him play."

Oh no. "I feel so bad for him. I know he's been trying to get back on the field."

"Coop says the coaches don't want to risk it."

Not that Frank has mentioned any of that to me, considering we're not talking as much as we used to. He's been a little more standoffish since I told him as gently as possible that I only liked him as a friend. That wasn't an easy conversation for me, but I'm glad it's out there.

"I think that's the reason he's been so big on the yoga sessions. He focuses on his upper body, specifically his shoulders."

"Yeah. It sucks. He's definitely not playing today." Sienna's face visibly brightens. "But you can wear Cooper's number. He'll be out on the field."

"I won't look stupid with two numbers on my face?"

"Absolutely not. You'll fit right in. No one will really notice, because we're all going to be painted up like crazy." Sienna definitely is. She even drew a little dolphin on her cheek, and it turned out really good.

I borrow one of Sienna's shirts with a dolphin on it and do my hair into two braids, tying the ends with some ribbon she has. We are completely decked out in school colors, and she even drags me outside and makes us take photos that she posts to her stories.

"Okay, let's go," she says once the photo sesh is over.

We walk over to the stadium along with a big crowd of people that grows and grows as we get closer. The weather is perfect. The sky is crystal clear, and there's a breeze coming in off the ocean, making the air cool despite the intense sun. Anticipation ripples in the air, and as we enter the gates, I can hear the college band playing. I can feel the thundering drums deep inside me, ratcheting up my own excitement to the point that I'm clutching Sienna's arm as she drags me through the sea of people.

"Are we sitting in the student section?" I ask her.

"No. Coop hooks me up with better seats. It's called the friends-and-family section," she tells me.

She wasn't lying when she said the seats are better. We're in the lower section sitting right on the fifty-yard line on the home side. I glance around as we settle into our seats, both of us clutching giant UCSM-Dolphins-themed soda cups. Sienna sets hers carefully into the drink holder to her right, and I do the same.

"This stadium is nice."

"It's practically brand new. It opened up a few years ago, right when Coop started." She grabs her drink and takes a big sip. "It's actually pretty cool."

It's huge and filled with so many people. I can't believe how many there are here to watch this game.

"I haven't been to a football game since high school, and those were always no big deal. Our football team sucked."

"You haven't been to a college game? Or an NFL game?" When I shake my head, Sienna rests her hand against her chest, as if she's offended. Or shocked. "Well, you haven't lived then, have you, Everleigh Bailey Olmstead?"

I should never have told her my middle name. "That's a mouthful."

"Hey, it's your name," she teases.

As we wait for the game to start, we chat with the people sitting nearby. Sienna seems to know a lot of them, but she told me that it's her third season in this section, so it makes sense.

The announcer starts talking, his booming voice practically commanding us to watch the field, and then there's a blast of sound that makes me jump in my seat. Smoke fills the air from unseen fog machines, and then the team is running out onto the field, the roar of the crowd deafening as they make their appearance.

I jump up with Sienna and scream until my throat aches. She's grinning. I'm grinning. Caught up in the moment, and the game hasn't even started yet.

The team gets into formation out on the field and runs through some stretching exercises. I spot Nico immediately, thanks to now knowing his jersey number, and I watch him like some sort of salivating stalker. He looks good in the black uniform, but he looks good in almost everything he wears. This isn't a surprise.

"They look great," Sienna murmurs, and I realize she's staring at them much like I am. Now I don't feel so bad.

Right before the game begins, Sienna dashes off to buy popcorn, and I remain in my seat, soaking up the moment. Being here, the excitement for the game to start making the air practically vibrate, I feel like I'm a part of something real. Before I came to Santa Mira, I was just going through the motions. Living my life and taking it day by day, but not really paying attention. Working toward the moment when I could leave my old life and begin a new one.

I might've had a few roadblocks thrown at me in the beginning—and they were major problems, I'm not trying to downplay them—but everything is finally settling in. School is going well, I have a job I like and a place to live, and I'm slowly rebuilding my wardrobe. I've made a couple of friends. I'm hosting yoga classes at my new house, and I get along with my roommates.

I might even have a crush on one of my roommates.

Fine, there's no might about it. I do have a crush on Nico, and it's so dumb. But it's also kind of fun because I can't remember the last time I had a crush on someone. I'd been with Brad for so long, I forgot how that feels.

The nervous anticipation of seeing Nico and hoping he smiles at me. The butterflies in my stomach when he does actually smile just for me. The sound of his voice. It's low and deep, and sometimes when he says my name, or even better when he just calls me Ever, goose bumps rise on my skin.

I've got it bad. I play it off with Sienna because I have no idea if she'll run and go tell Nico I have the hots for him, which would be incredibly embarrassing. I'll just sit over here and savor my crush on my own, thank you very much. Because that's all it can ever be.

A silly crush.

As if he can read my mind, Nico looks in my direction from where he stands on the field, Gavin right next to him and Coop flanking him on the other side. Our gazes lock. Hold. His mouth curls into a small, closed-lip smile, and he lifts his hand in the subtlest of waves that has me positively giddy.

I smile in return, wiggling my fingers at him once. Just as subtle as he is, and he eventually looks away, getting caught up in conversation with his friends. His teammates.

While I'm sitting here squirming in my seat like I can barely contain myself.

"How do you know Nico?"

I turn toward the snide-sounding voice to find a beautiful blonde sitting behind me and to the left, her expression full of disbelief. Like she can't wrap her head around the idea of him knowing someone like me.

Maybe I'm taking this too personally. But she has a snotty expression on her face, and that makes me think I'm not overreacting.

"We're friends," I say, not about to confess that we're also roommates. No one needs to know that.

"Really?" She snorts in disbelief.

"You saw him wave at me, right?" I shrug, smiling. Reveling a little in my status. I guess it's a big deal to know Nico Valente, though I kind of already assumed that from just being here.

Sienna wasn't wrong. There are all sorts of women filling this stadium with his number painted on their cheeks. Or on their backs because they're wearing his jersey. Like the blonde I'm talking to. She's got eighty painted on her cheek just like I do.

"You're a Cooper fan too?" She nudges her friend with her elbow, both of them smiling, though they're not very friendly. "What do they do, pass you around?"

"Hey, blondie. Fuck right off." I glance up to see Sienna standing there with a giant bucket of popcorn in her hands. She's glaring at the blonde and her friend, and their smiles fade at the death look on Sienna's face.

"We weren't—" the blonde starts, but Sienna cuts her off.

"Cooper is my brother, so you better watch what you say." She sits in her seat, offering me the popcorn, and I take some, shoving it into my mouth. The blonde and her friend completely back down, wearing matching sulky expressions, and I'm relieved that it didn't turn into something more.

"Some women act like they own these guys. It's ridiculous," Sienna mutters.

I lean my head close to hers, lowering my voice. "She didn't believe I was friends with Nico even though he just waved at me from the field."

"He waved at you? Well, well, well." The sneaky smile on Sienna's face has me nudging her in the side.

"It was nothing." I refuse to let her get my hopes up even more. I already did that well enough on my own.

"Uh-huh." Sienna smirks.

I decide to change the subject. "Thanks for the popcorn." I lean my head against hers for the briefest moment. "And for rushing to my defense."

"These fangirls need to back off my new friend," Sienna says, her fierce voice warming my heart.

It feels good to be here, I think, as we settle more deeply into our seats, ready for the game to begin.

For once, I feel like I belong.

Chapter Fourteen

EVERLEIGH

We're in the fourth quarter of the game with only five minutes left and . . .

The Dolphins are freaking losing.

If they lose, it will be the first one of the season, and then they can't afford to lose another. Two losses and they're pretty much out of championship contention. Everything hinges on these final five minutes.

"I'm literally biting my nails," Sienna complains as she smooths the ragged edge of her nail with her thumb. "This is freaking stressful."

"I feel guilty." I refuse to look at her, keeping my gaze on the field. The other team currently has the ball, and they're doing everything they can to drive it down the field.

And the Dolphins are doing everything they can to stop it from happening.

"Why in the world do you feel guilty?"

"First game I come to watch and they're losing?" I shake my head. "I'm bad luck."

"You're being ridiculous."

"You can't stop biting your nails, and you look like you want to hurl. We're both being ridiculous." I'm literally sweating along my hairline, and I wonder if all the paint on my face is smeared. Great.

Sienna rolls her eyes, a horrified cry leaving her when the opposing team gains some major yardage. "If they score again, we're doomed."

My stomach is in knots, and I bet I look just like Sienna because I want to hurl too. This is awful.

We're both silent, never looking away from the field. One of the defensive linemen knocks the ball right out of the hands of the opposing team's receiver, and Sienna jumps to her feet, screaming her approval. And eventually, when the other team decides to try for a field goal, the kicker sends it spiraling into the air . . .

Only to hit the goalpost and fall to the right of it.

The referee makes it official—the field goal is no good.

Now we're both on our feet, jumping up and down. I can feel the blonde and her friend glaring at our show of enthusiasm—she's been doing that a lot this game, but I've learned to ignore her—and I laugh when Sienna yanks me into her arms, hugging me.

"We have a shot," she murmurs close to my ear. "A little over three minutes to go. If we score, we'll be up by a point."

"But what if the other team gets the ball and has time to score again?" Now I'm chewing on my fingernail, ruining the team-colors manicure I gave myself last night.

"We'll deal with that if the moment comes." I love how she talks like she's part of the team and out on that field playing the game with them.

We sit in agonizing anticipation as our offense runs onto the field and gets into position. Gavin calls out a bunch of words and things that don't make much sense to me, and then someone hikes him the ball. He stands there, arm cocked back, ball clutched in his hand as he surveys the field in front of him. He throws the ball, and it sails through the air in a perfect spiral.

I'm breathless watching that ball, Sienna clutching my arm so tightly it feels like she's cutting off circulation, and when it lands in Nico's hands, I exhale roughly in a loud scream.

Nico runs it down the field, defensive players trying their hardest to stop him, but they can't. He slithers out of their grasping hands, fast as lightning as he barrels down the field and straight into the end zone.

We're hopping up and down and clutching each other along with everyone else in the stadium. The crowd screams with joy, and Nico is doing a little dance in the end zone, Coop eventually joining him and slapping the back of his helmet.

I'm grinning and hollering at the same time, and when I glance over at Sienna, I find that she's smiling just as wide as me. This is a moment. One I probably will never forget.

"There's still ninety seconds left," Sienna says once we've all calmed down and our kicker got the extra point. "As long as they can't score, we'll be good."

I've paid enough attention to know that ninety seconds can stretch into five minutes, and that's dangerous. "Is that enough time for them to score?"

"Maybe." She's hedging. "Probably."

"Ugh." I slump in my seat. "This is so nerve racking. I don't know how you can stand watching these games."

"You're going to find out because I'm dragging you to every single game I go to," Sienna says.

I don't know if I'll be able to survive. Watching them play is stressful.

The first few seconds are good. Our defense blocks the other team, not allowing them much yardage. One of our guys even sacks the quarterback just as he's about to throw the ball, but there's still too much time on the clock.

And all that time, even if it's only seconds, makes me nervous.

The entire stadium is on edge. I can feel it in the air. Taste it even. I'm leaning forward in my seat, my gaze finding Nico standing on the sideline, Gavin and Coop beside him, their backs to me. I wish I could see their faces, but then again maybe I don't want to see them. They might look worried.

I'm worried enough.

The quarterback throws the ball, and Sienna grabs my arm, squeezing tight as the ball flies through the air, only to land in . . .

One of our defense players' hands.

He catches it, looking stunned for a brief second before he launches into action. He tucks the ball close to him and takes off in a run.

The crowd is going wild. So are our guys on the sideline, yelling their encouragement at their teammate as he makes it into the end zone with the other team far behind him. He made that touchdown look easy.

And just like that, we win.

◆　◆　◆

"Is this normal?" I ask Sienna as we linger outside the team's locker room. There aren't very many people out here, which is odd, but Sienna knew the guards blocking the path that led to the building, so I'm guessing we're just some of the select few who can wait for the team out here.

"Is what normal?"

"You waiting here for the team." We're leaning against a brick wall, Sienna scrolling through all the photos she took as she tries to make a social media post.

"Definitely. I'm here pretty much every home game."

"Who did you used to go to the games with?" I'm assuming she has other friends she went to games with. No way did she go to them alone.

Did she?

"Well, last season I always went with this one guy's wife."

"Wife?"

Sienna glances up at me with a nod. "Yeah, they got married when they were twenty. Wild, right? I think she wanted to lock that guy down because now he's a second-string lineman for the Broncos. Got picked up in the draft."

"Wow. That's amazing."

"Like I told you when I first met you, Gav and Coop and Nico—they all have the potential to get drafted and play professionally."

"I can't imagine it." I'm shaking my head, not because I don't think they can do it. More like I'm in awe of the fact that they most likely *will* do it.

And I know these guys. I live with two of them. It's crazy.

"Well, start imagining because I'm fairly certain it will happen for one of them. Or all of them. They're that good."

I glance around the courtyard, where people are standing around. There are a couple of reporter-looking types waiting not too far from where we're standing, as well as a group of older men and women who are giving off strong parental vibes. There are a couple of little kids rocking Dolphins T-shirts with autograph books clutched in their hands, and I find that completely adorable.

Guys start exiting the locker room, a few trickling out at a time. All of them with big ol' smiles on their faces and decked out from head to toe in brand-new Dolphins gear. I'm sure they wear this stuff and get photographed in it, only for it to sell out everywhere.

Smart move on the school's part.

We spot Frank exiting the locker room, and Sienna calls him over. He approaches us with a smile on his face and hugs Sienna first, and then me.

"Sorry you didn't get to play today," I tell him once he releases me.

He shrugs, then winces. "It's fine. I didn't want to mess up my shoulder any more than it already is. I might end up benched for the season again."

"Oh, that sucks, Frank." Sienna reaches out and pats him on the arm. "I'm so sorry."

"We can work on it during our next yoga session," I suggest. Frank's gaze swings to mine, his expression hopeful. "I can't promise miracles, but I know some stretching exercises that might help."

"That would be great. I hate missing out on this season. It's my last one." Oh, he sounds so sad.

"We'll definitely work on it Monday night," I tell him.

"You're the best, Everleigh. Seriously." He lunges for me, picking me up in his arms and swinging me around so fast, my legs swing out behind me.

I'm smacking his chest lightly. "Put me down! What if you hurt yourself?"

"Nah, that won't happen. You barely weigh anything." He eventually sets me on my feet, and I'm laughing, a little breathless, when suddenly I can feel someone staring at me.

At us.

I glance to my right to see Nico approaching us with his usual buddies and teammates flanking either side of him. His expression is somber, his lips pulled into a grim line, and I wonder why he looks angry when everyone else is grinning. Rightfully happy after their amazing win.

"Valente, why you so pissed off? We just won!" This comes from Frank.

Nico barely looks at him, his attention all for me. I stand as still as a statue as he heads straight for me, all the air lodged in my throat as I wait for him to say something.

Anything.

"I thought she asked you to back off," Nico says to Frank through tight lips, stopping directly in front of us.

Frank's frowning. "Are you talking about . . . Everleigh?" He sends me a look, but all I can do is just stand there, gaping like a fish. I'm sure I look like an idiot with my smeared face paint and my braids coming undone, little flyaway hairs everywhere.

"Yeah, I'm talking about Ever." Nico looks in my direction, his dark eyes flashing with an unrecognizable emotion. "Are you okay?"

"I'm fine," I reassure him, my voice faint. "Frank's just glad I offered to help him stretch his shoulder."

"Yeah, bro. Relax." Coop slaps Nico in the chest, and Nico's gaze flickers with irritation. "It was nothing. She's just trying to help the poor guy out."

"Oh." Nico visibly relaxes, all the strain that filled his every feature slowly disappearing. "Right."

"Why such a strong reaction, hmm, Nico?" Sienna's smile is naughty. There's no other word to describe it. "You jealous of their friendship?"

"I'm not jealous of anything," Nico practically spits out.

"Then what is it?" Sienna is goading him into having a reaction, and I send her a look. One that says . . .

Knock it off.

Totally curious about his answer, though.

Chapter Fifteen

NICO

How am I supposed to answer Sienna's question in front of everyone when I don't even know how to respond? Am I jealous of Frank fucking Dollar?

Absolutely not.

I feel sorry for the guy. His shoulder is still messed up, and he's missing out on a fantastic season. I'm on an absolute high after that win. I ran in a couple of touchdowns, but I'm not the one who saved this game. We were on track to lose.

Thank God we didn't.

I let my gaze roam over Everleigh, who's standing there with a perplexed expression on her face. Most likely confused by my reaction.

Hell, *I'm* confused by my reaction.

She's adorable even with the smeared face paint on her cheeks. I can tell one of the numbers is my own—my chest puffs up with pride like the egotistical jackass I am—and the other number is Coop's.

Pretty positive Sienna is responsible for painting those numbers on Ever's face. Equal opportunity, showing her support for both her roommates on the field. Nice touch.

"Hey, let's get the hell out of here and go to Charley's." This suggestion comes from Gavin, and I sag with relief when I hear it.

"Yeah, let's get out of here," Coop says in agreement while I just stand there and nod.

The stadium is empty, and there aren't too many people lingering around. It's late, and I'd guess most of the student attendees are already at the bars. Or at house parties. Frats.

It's a Saturday night and we won. People are in the mood to celebrate. I know I am.

We all start walking, the girls coming along with us, and Sienna forgets all about me. Instead she's walking beside Gav, chatting away at him while Ever is standing next to Frank and listening to him talk.

All while I glower like an asshole and try to come up with ways to keep Dollar away from her for . . .

Ever.

Yeah. That sounds just about perfect.

"We just had the most major win of the season, and you look like someone pissed in your beer." This disgusting description comes from my good friend and roommate Cooper. "What's going on with you?"

"Nothing," I bite out, because I still don't know how to explain myself. "I'm just—"

"Into our roommate? I can tell, considering how you can't stop staring at her. Pretty sure she's into you as well," Coop says conversationally. Like he just mentioned the sky is blue and today is Saturday.

In other words, like what he just said is no big deal.

"I'm not into her." The lie tastes bad.

Fuck it, I'm into her. What am I doing? Why am I attracted to her? Why do I imagine her naked in my shower and jerk off to the image? Why, why, why?

I have problems. Well, one singular problem.

And she's walking just ahead of me, unaware of my struggles.

"Whatever you say, man." Coop is chuckling because he knows I'm full of shit. "Don't be jealous of Dollar. She just feels bad for him. She already told him to back off, remember?"

What if she tells *me* to back off? What if she's not into me and I'm over here wasting my time, lusting after a woman who sees me as just her roommate.

Exactly how I told myself to feel about her, but here I am. Thinking about her all the time. It gets worse as every day passes and she does something sweet, like when she offered to wash my towels when she was doing hers. When she made us dinner all week instead of just the agreed-upon three meals. When she sends one of those shy smiles in my direction—those do me in. I can't lie. Caught her staring at me when I was out on the field before the game started earlier, and I couldn't help myself.

I waved at her.

She waved back, and my heart tripped over itself when she did.

Silly. That is not a word I use to describe myself, but she makes me feel silly and hopeful and unsure. Which is not normal for me.

Not even close.

"I feel like I'm in middle school," I mutter to no one in particular.

Coop laughs. "Want me to deliver a note from you to Ever that says 'I like you'? I can do it, no problem."

That is the most middle school thing I've ever heard. Might've done that a time or two when I was like . . . twelve. Ten years ago.

I'd like to think I've evolved since then.

"Shut up, asswipe." I shove him, but he doesn't even move because he's as big as a boulder.

My reaction just makes him laugh harder. "What are you going to do about this?"

I'm frowning. "Do about what?"

Is there anything I can do? I was just . . . dealing with my feelings. Hoping that they'd pass because this is pointless.

"How you feel about . . ." He inclines his head toward Everleigh walking in front of us, oblivious to our conversation. "Her."

I watch her, my gaze lingering on her ass. She has a good one. Of course she does.

"Nothing. I can do nothing. There's nothing between us and there never will be anything, so there's no point in trying."

"So reactive, damn." Coop throws his hands up in front of him in a defensive gesture. "Guess you won't care when guys are flirting with her at Charley's then."

"I can't do anything about it. She's free to talk to whoever she wants." Just the idea of someone approaching her, flirting with her, makes me see red.

Vicious, angry red.

"If you really like her, Nico, you can do something about it." Coop's voice is gentle, as if he knows he needs to change his approach with me.

"Like what? Tell her how I feel? I don't even know how to explain it to myself, let alone her." I shake my head. "And if she feels the same way about me, what can I do about it? Try to establish something with her, only for it to blow up in my face, and then I still have to live with her for the rest of the year? That sounds like a nightmare."

"She's cool. I don't think she'd cause you any problems like Portia."

I hate that Coop even brought up that chick's name. She's the absolute worst. "No one is like Portia."

"Thank God," Coop mutters.

"There's nothing I can do." I'm repeating myself, so I remain quiet. Coop isn't talking either. It's bad enough that I feel the need to fill the silence that's lingering between us. "I'm just going to let my—feelings for her die a hopefully fast death."

"Best way to get over someone is to get under someone. Isn't that how the saying goes?" Coop asks.

"I suppose. And there's no one I need to get over." I slap Coop on the back a couple of times. "It's just a harmless . . . fixation. I'll get over it."

"You don't get fixated on anything but football," Coop so kindly reminds me. "But okay. Keep telling yourself that."

As we move through campus, more and more people show up, swarming all around us. Shouting questions at us and taking photos or videos. It's a lot, but we're used to it.

Somewhat. We should probably call the security team and have them escort us around campus.

"Hey, who's the girl?" someone yells at us at one point, and I know they're talking about Everleigh. Most everyone knows Sienna is Coop's sister.

"My friend," Sienna answers, hooking her arm through Ever's.

"Oh, come on. I heard she lives with Cooper and Valente," someone else says.

Shit. This is what I didn't want to happen.

"She's our roommate," Cooper says, sending me a quick look. "Nothing more, nothing less."

The crowd explodes with chatter, shouting questions at us at a rapid-fire pace. We start walking faster, but it's impossible to shake any of them, considering we're surrounded.

"We need security," I tell Coop.

"Already on it," Gavin says, glancing over his shoulder at me. "They'll be here soon."

Going on pure instinct, I leave Coop and move forward, shoving myself in between Dollar and Everleigh, my attention only for her. "You all right?"

She glances up at me, her eyes wide, her smile fragile. "It's a little overwhelming."

"Gavin called security." We haven't had to use them this season save for away games, where they always escort us off the bus and into the stadium on game day in case the fans from the opposing teams get a little wild on us. Looks like that's changing, though.

"I heard him say that." She glances around, her unease obvious. "Is it always like this?"

"Want me to be real with you?"

She nods.

105

"Yeah. Most of the time it's great." I step closer to her like I can't help myself, resting my hand on her shoulder. "Right now, not so much."

"Nico, Nico! Are you and your new roomie more than friends?"

I glare in the general direction where the question came from. "Not at all," I say firmly, wanting to quash the rumors.

I hate that she's being questioned and that they're speculating on a possible relationship between us.

"What about you, Coop? Something going on between the two of you?"

"Definitely not," Coop answers. "We're all just roommates. That's it."

The crowd's focus changes when they realize we're not going to give them the answers they want, and they start questioning Gavin about the game.

"I'm actually offended," Dollar mutters. "No one asked if me and Everleigh are involved."

I want to roll my eyes but hold myself in check. "Are you serious right now? That's what you're upset about?"

He shrugs, and Everleigh and I share an amused look. My dick twitches at seeing that secret smile curving her lips, and damn it . . .

I've got it so fucking bad.

Chapter Sixteen

EVERLEIGH

Monday is my busiest day, and what's funny is it's not even a school day for me. I open at the café, so I'm up bright and early, and I work through most of the lunch shift. Once that's done I head home and work on any homework or projects that need to be wrapped up before I have class on Tuesday. Or I'm studying for a quiz.

By the late afternoon I'm prepping for dinner. I've kept up my part of the deal and make at least three meals a week for my always-hungry roommates. Sometimes I make four or five meals. Mostly dinner. I originally thought there might be leftovers that could see them through, but no. These guys eat every last crumb of what I prepare for them.

It's always shocking and just the tiniest bit satisfying that they enjoy my cooking so much.

Today I'm prepping a marinade for some chicken I'll bake in the oven. I put it all in a plastic bag and leave it in the fridge, where it'll sit for a couple of hours and absorb all those flavors. I've made this recipe for them before, and it was a hit.

Everything is a hit with them. They're not picky and always appreciative. They also trade off and help me clean the kitchen. Well, Coop and Nico always shove me out of the kitchen and clean it for me.

Frank likes to help me because that gives him an excuse to talk to me constantly.

He's backed off on pursuing me, but I'd like to think we've become friends. He tells me a lot, and I share plenty of my own stories with him in return. I consider Cooper a friend too. There's something so calming about him. He's steady and quiet, but every time he opens that mouth, he reveals just how smart he is too. And observant.

Sometimes too observant.

I think back on Saturday night when we were at Charley's after being escorted there by the team's security crew. The mob that initially swarmed us asked so many questions—even to me.

Who are you?

Heard you're the roommate.

Are you involved with any of them?

Nico?

Coop?

It was funny how offended Frank was that they didn't ask him if we were involved, and I wasn't about to remind him that he's been benched most of the season so he's not in the forefront of their minds.

He knows that's happening, and he's devastated by it. Poor Frank.

Nico was quick to quash the rumors, and I couldn't help but feel the slightest bit . . . offended by how fast he said no, we weren't together. Which is dumb. So dumb. Even though he did tell Portia we were together, and I wouldn't be surprised if she's spreading that around.

Though maybe she isn't. I have no clue.

But anyway, he was just telling the truth, and he doesn't need any rumors about him hooking up with his roommate to spread.

Not that it hurts him. The moment we got to the bar, he was surrounded by women, all of them calling his name and flashing their flirtatious smiles. Each of them beautiful and hanging all over him. I was jealous.

And Coop caught me in my feels.

It was late, and I was sitting alone at a small table. Sienna had abandoned me for Gavin—I don't blame her, but she's always chasing him. Coop approached me, catching me watching Nico laughing with his fan base over at the bar, and he said the weirdest thing.

"You know he's just fighting his feelings."

That was it. The only thing he said before he settled into the chair next to me. A teammate magically appeared and sat next to Coop, engaging him in football talk for the rest of the evening while I sat there and turned that one sentence over and over again in my mind.

You know he's just fighting his feelings.

What did Coop mean by that? I'm sure he was referring to Nico, considering he looked right at him when he said it. But what did he mean? Fighting his feelings for what?

For who?

He couldn't have been talking about . . .

Me?

I didn't want to put too much thought into it because it just seemed too fantastical to me. Nico is friendly and flirts with women. A lot. It's part of his nature.

The front door slams closed, startling me from my thoughts, and I smile when I see Frank enter the kitchen. "Hey."

"Hi." He sets his backpack on one of the dining room chairs. "They cut me loose from practice early."

"Is that a good thing or a bad thing?" I hope he says good because he's been so down lately.

"Coach literally said he didn't need me to stick around, so he let me go." Frank shrugs. "I take that as a bad thing."

"Aw, Frank. I'm so sorry."

"They never let anyone leave practice early. We're a team. If you're hurt, suspended, benched, what the fuck ever, you stay for every practice. Every meeting. Every game. We're together always, and if you're pissed that you can't play, too bad. You're sticking with your team. I've never had a problem with it. I'm in it for the long haul, but today I swear . . ." He presses his lips together, shaking his head. "It hurt, having him send me away. Like I don't matter anymore."

My heart hurts for him, and I don't even think about what I'm doing. I go to him and give him a big hug, wishing I could absorb his pain.

He returns the hug, his arms coming around me carefully, holding me close. We just stand there for a few minutes hugging each other in the middle of the kitchen when I hear a familiar voice.

"Oh. Hey."

We spring away from each other at the sound of the familiar deep voice, and everything inside me shrivels a little.

It's Nico.

And he doesn't look happy to catch me and Frank hugging. Though why should he care? After all, I'm just his roommate.

"What are you doing here already?" Frank asks, rubbing the back of his neck.

"We all got released early. It's a bye week," Nico bites out as he strides toward the fridge and opens it, grabbing an apple. God, they are seriously always hungry.

"Oh yeah. That's right." Frank sends me a look, and I swear it says, *Maybe I overreacted.*

Maybe he did, but I'm glad I could be there for him. He was feeling down, and he needed someone to lift him up.

I hope I was that someone, even if all I did was show him sympathy and give him a hug.

"Could we maybe start the yoga session early?" Frank asks me. "Looks like everyone will be available. Want me to text the rest of the guys?"

He's already got his phone in his hands, ready to send out the text.

"Sure. That's fine with me." I send a look in Nico's direction, but he's not even paying attention. Too busy munching on the apple and scrolling his phone.

The door slams, and Coop comes sauntering into the kitchen seconds later, sending a glare in Nico's direction. "Didn't even wait for me, bro."

"I didn't know you needed a personal escort into the house." Nico's attention never wavers from his screen, and he taps out what I can only assume is a response to someone.

Who's he talking to? Texting with? One of his fangirls? Ugh, I hate myself for wanting to know.

"Could we work on some of those poses that'll help with my shoulder?" Frank asks me, not even paying attention to the mini fight that's currently happening between our roommates.

"Absolutely." I nod, sending a questioning look in Coop's direction, but he appears unfazed. Good. I don't like an angry Coop. "I'll go get changed."

"You doing yoga right now?" Coop asks.

"Yes." I offer him a brief smile. I'm a certified yoga instructor and even led classes back at home. I worked for a year at the local senior center and had so much fun with my students there. My oldest one was ninety-three. "You're joining us?"

"Definitely." He smiles at me in return.

"Okay, everyone's coming," Frank says, setting his phone on the counter.

"Damn, that was fast," Nico mutters, shaking his head.

I ignore him. He's being rude, but he's always somewhat dismissive of my yoga sessions.

"You finally going to one of her classes?" Coop asks.

"No." Nico sends a fleeting glance in my direction. "I'm not interested."

And with that, he exits the kitchen.

"He's in a bad mood," Coop says the moment Nico is gone.

"He's always in a bad mood," I grumble, grabbing my phone and sending Sienna a text that I'm starting the yoga session soon. "Is Gavin coming?"

"Yep, everyone is," Frank says.

Me: Your boy will be here for yoga. Wear your hottest workout outfit.

She responds immediately.

Sienna: I'll be there in ten looking like a total hottie.

A string of fire emojis follows her text.

I'm headed to my room to change when I spot Nico in his bedroom, his head lifting when I walk past. Our gazes lock and he doesn't look away.

Neither do I.

"You and Dollar have a thing going on, or what?"

I blink at him, absorbing his question slowly. Shocked by it because is he for real right now?

"Um, no."

"Looked pretty friendly just now in the kitchen." His deep voice is extra low.

And sounds extra serious.

"He was feeling down, and I wanted to offer him support."

"Uh-huh." The doubt in his voice is strong.

"I'm telling you the truth."

Nico leaves his bedroom, walks across the short hall straight toward me. I have no choice but to walk backward into my bedroom, nearly tripping over my feet to stay out of his way. He shuts my bedroom door behind him, towering over me with an intimidating expression on his handsome face. He smells like fresh-cut grass and spicy male with the faintest hint of sweat, which might disgust the average woman, but me?

All I can think about is *How can I rub myself all over his muscular body so I can smell like him?*

"He had his hands on your ass, Ever." He bites each word out, and they hit me like pellets against glass.

Ping. Ping. Ping.

"No, he did not," I retort, indignant. I don't remember feeling Frank's hands on my butt. No way did he touch me there. As a matter of fact, I know those hands were on my lower back, but definitely not any lower.

"Yeah." Nico is nodding, his dark gaze full of fire. "He did. I saw them."

I ignore his statement. I think he's just—mad, and I don't understand why. "It was nothing."

"Looked like something to me."

"Why do you care?" I toss out at him.

He rears back, confusion in his features. "I don't."

"That's a mighty big reaction then, for someone who claims to not care." I take another step backward, needing the space. His presence eats up every bit of air in the room, and I'm suddenly finding it hard to breathe. "You need to leave. I have to change."

"What you two do is none of my business," he says, his voice deceptively soft. "I already warned you about Dollar."

"He's not as bad as you made him out to be. He's actually a really nice guy." I cross my arms in front of my chest. "And what's funny is that all sorts of people have warned me off of *you*."

He's frowning, his brows drawn together. "What do you mean? Who's warning you about me? And what do they tell you?"

"How you're a player and that you use women." I drop my arms at my sides. "And I'm not interested in you like that."

Oh, the lies are just flying from my lips with ease, aren't they?

"Fucking great." Why does he sound so disappointed?

"And I'm not interested in Frank like that either."

His anger seems to dissipate. "Really."

"Really," I repeat. "Why do you keep knocking my yoga sessions?"

"What?"

"You always seem to make snide remarks or little digs at what I do. Your teammates love it. You might, too, you know. You seem so stressed all the time. I think it'll do wonders for you."

His expression goes blank. "I'm not interested."

"You won't know unless you give it a try."

He stares at me.

I stare in return, not about to back down.

"Will you stop harping on me if I try it out?" he finally asks.

Triumph curls within me. "Yes."

"Fine." He sounds vaguely irritated, and I can't help it . . .

I smile.

"Don't look too pleased with yourself. I'm sure I'll hate it."

"You are so grumpy."

Nico actually seems offended. "I'm never grumpy."

"With me you always seem to be." Reaching out, I shove at his chest lightly, but he doesn't even budge. The guy is a solid wall of muscle. "Get out of my room. I need to get dressed."

"You're already dressed."

"Not in my yoga outfit. Get out." I shove him again, and this time he goes, flashing that devastating grin at me before he turns and exits my room.

I shut the door, leaning against it, hating how fast my heart is beating.

How breathless I suddenly am.

Ugh, this man. He's going to ruin me for anyone else if I don't watch it.

And I'm going to enjoy every single second of it.

Chapter Seventeen

I have eight giant men in my backyard, all of them wearing serious expressions on their faces as they watch me while I lead them through various yoga positions. I'm putting extra emphasis on shoulder stretching for Frank and a few others who seem to carry their stress in their upper body.

Some of them have brought their own yoga mats, which I encouraged them to get. I love that they listen to me and that they seem to enjoy the yoga sessions. I know Nico is reluctant to give them a try, like he's full of doubt this even works when it's a proven exercise and great for stress relief.

Feeling extra petty about his reluctance, I let him borrow one of my yoga mats, making sure I gave him the bright-pink one with stenciled black flowers all over it. All the others I own are a solid color and plain. I'm currently using a black one, which I could've loaned him. But I didn't.

I have to take my small satisfactions where I can.

Nico is in the very back row along with Cooper, and he's trying to play it cool despite having some difficulty contorting his body into each pose. It's almost amusing, and if we were the only ones out there, I would probably laugh at him because he's ridiculous.

Coop is trying to help him as best he can, and he never gets irritated with Nico, which is something I can't say for myself. Coop is definitely the most patient person I know, and I appreciate him so much. I think everyone in this yard feels the same way, including his sister.

And speaking of his sister, Sienna is in the front row right next to Gavin, contorting her body into a pretzel so she can keep her eyes on him at all times. Frank is on the other side of Gav, his attention never wavering.

Sometimes, in moments like this, I glance around and am shocked that this is my life. That I live in this cute house right by the ocean with these somewhat famous football players and I can consider them my friends. That I help by teaching them yoga and fixing them nutritious meals with plenty of protein. My grandma would love this. She'd think it was hilarious that I was taking care of all these men, and I know she'd be proud of me. Right now, I'm feeling like a proud mama too.

A proud mama who can see her "children's" faults, though. For instance, there's Sienna trying to openly flirt with Gavin, who's not even paying attention to her.

Typical.

I notice the determined look on Frank's face as he goes through the motions, and I know he's hoping against hope that his shoulder will miraculously heal and he'll be back on the football field before the season ends.

I hope that for him. I really, really do. But the deeper we get into the season, the more I'm afraid that's never going to happen.

And then there's Nico. He's watching me carefully as I shift into each new position, his gaze tracking my every movement. I'm definitely not having proud-mom feelings toward him at the moment. I tell myself he's watching me so closely because he's trying to figure out what I'm doing since he's never participated in my yoga classes before, but there's a small part of me that feels like it could be something more . . .

Intense.

I chose my clothes carefully because I'm shameless like Sienna, who was with me when I bought the outfit while we were out shopping last week. I didn't need anything new, and I'm trying to watch my money, but Sienna convinced me to try it on and basically wouldn't let me leave the store without buying the outfit.

It's a matching leggings-and-sports-bra set in dark brown. Nothing special, right? But the sports bra has extra straps in the back that make a crisscross pattern. The moment I walked out of the dressing room to show Sienna, she practically screamed, "Wow, your tits look fabulous!"

I was slightly embarrassed by her outburst, but I can't lie. Her comment made me feel confident.

I pulled my hair into a ponytail practically on top of my head and have zero makeup on because it's kind of warm out here and the sun is intense at this time of the day. I can feel sweat forming on my hairline, but I can't worry about it.

Whereas Sienna has a full face of makeup and a pale-pink sports bra on with matching booty shorts. Like her ass cheeks are practically hanging out, and when she stretches her legs, I catch Coop looking away quickly more than once. He doesn't want to see his sister like that.

Oh, Sienna is funny. What makes it even funnier is Gavin acts oblivious. Does he do it on purpose? I don't think so. She could remove all her clothes and dance in front of him for a solid five minutes, and he probably wouldn't give her even an ounce of the attention she'd love to have from him.

I admire her determination. I would've given up a long time ago. Maybe she should, too, but if I were to suggest that, I know what she would say.

I'm no quitter.

And I kind of love that about her.

But how is that different from what Frank does? I suppose it's because Sienna is stuck just on Gavin, while Frank tends to fall for almost every attractive woman who speaks to him.

Poor Frank. He's so nice. He just needs to find the right girl for him.

I wind us down after about forty minutes, leading the group through simple stretching exercises that help their muscles cool down. Once I'm finished, I even hit them with a "namaste" because Frank loves it when I do that, for some reason, and Sienna even giggles after I say it.

"Such a cliché, Ever," she teases, and I just roll my eyes at her.

No one protests. No one complains. All these big dudes seem to love my yoga classes, and that fills me with pride. It makes me happy that they enjoy them so much.

"Hey, you did really well," I tell her as I approach, drawing closer so I can murmur into her ear. "You weren't obvious when you were flirting with Gavin at all."

"You don't need to lie to me," she says with a laugh when I pull away. "He could walk into his bedroom and I'd be laid out on his bed naked, spread-eagle and greased up, and he wouldn't bat an eyelash."

I make a face. "Greased up?"

"You know what I mean." She waves a dismissive hand.

"Um, not really, but okay." We both look in Gavin's direction. He's currently drinking from his water bottle, and he's not wearing a shirt, showing off the gloriousness that is his naked chest. I totally get why Sienna is so into him. First of all, look at him. It also helps that he's so nice. "He should probably put a shirt on."

"No, he definitely should not." A lusty sigh escapes my friend. "I would give anything to lick his abs just once in my life."

Now I'm the one who's giggling, my gaze shifting to Nico, who is currently lifting the hem of his T-shirt and wiping his chin with it. Exposing the perfection that is his abs.

Okay. I can get on board with Sienna's wish to lick Gavin's abs. Though I'd much prefer to lick Nico's.

"His abs are good, too, aren't they?" Sienna's tone is knowing, and I shoot her a quick look. "I saw you checking him out."

I'm sighing, too, though I don't think it sounds as lust filled as Sienna's. "Fine, you caught me."

"You two just going to flirt for the entire school year but never actually do anything about it?"

"He doesn't flirt with me" is my immediate response. "He seems annoyed with me half the time."

"You are so blind." The disappointment in Sienna's voice is obvious.

I meet her gaze, vaguely confused. "What are you talking about?"

"Men do this. Instead of acting like they're into the women they're—into, they act mad at them instead. I think they're frustrated with their feelings."

"I frustrate him?"

"No. Well, maybe. But his feelings for you frustrate him even more," Sienna explains.

Okay, this all sounds strangely logical. Maybe that's my problem too. My feelings for him frustrate me as well. Which makes me think of the conversation with Coop at Charley's, when he told me Nico was fighting his feelings.

Hmm.

"I think you two just need to do it and see what happens," she continues.

I'm gaping at her. "We can't just do it."

"Why not?" She shrugs.

"I don't just do it with random men."

"He's not random. You *know* him. You like him. You're definitely attracted to him. I say just fuck him and see how it is. Maybe you two need to get each other out of your systems," Sienna says.

What she's suggesting is way too tempting, but come on. That would be a huge mistake, messing around with my roommate.

But here's my dirty little secret: I've never been with anyone else besides my ex, and lately I've been fantasizing what it might be like with . . .

Nico.

Of course I am. Because Sienna is right. I'm attracted to him. I like him. I like his easy smiles and the way he genuinely cares about his friends. Even when he gives Frank grief, he's worried about him and his shoulder. He's smart and he cares and I love the sound of his laughter, and when he touches me, it's electric. I can feel the jolt of his fingers on my skin to the depths of my core.

I don't remember feeling that way with Brad. I don't recall the dizziness or the tingles or the butterflies. The anxious sensation in the pit of my stomach when I first hear Nico enter the house. I always know it's him, just from the distinct sound of his footsteps.

Oh God, I have it so incredibly bad for this man. And there's nothing I can do about it.

"I don't know," I finally say, my voice hesitant. I ignore the skeptical look on my friend's face. "I'm not the kind of person who just . . . fucks someone to see what happens."

"Oh, right. Because you've only ever been with one guy, and he turned into a complete asshole." Sienna nods, clearly remembering what I told her.

"Brad wasn't so bad—"

"He was a douche who bored you," she interrupts. "It's okay to say that. You can be honest with me. You wasted years of your life with that guy, and now you deserve to have some fun. Am I right?"

I am so glad no one is nearby to overhear this conversation.

"I am having fun, and I don't need a man to do that. Coming to Santa Mira is just what I needed to change my life. I'm enjoying school, I like my job, I met you, and I like living with the guys," I explain. "Nothing turned out like I imagined it would before I came here, and that's okay. I actually think everything has turned out even better."

Sienna engulfs me in a hug, squeezing me tight before she releases me. "I'm seriously so happy for you. I couldn't ask for a better new bestie."

I smile at her, and I swear I can feel tears forming in my eyes, which is silly. I shouldn't be this emotional, but for the first time in like forever, I feel like I belong to something.

I'm a part of something.

"I heard you're making dinner," Sienna says once she releases me.

I burst out laughing. "You trying to score an invite?"

"Only if Gav is staying." Her eyebrows shoot up.

"I have a lot of chicken marinating because I always make more than I think we'll eat, but I don't know if I can feed everyone out here." I nibble on my lower lip, counting all the guys who are milling about my backyard. None of them have left yet.

"Maybe I'll suggest to Gav he should take me out." Sienna flutters her eyelashes at me. "Think he'll go for it?"

"Probably not," I say truthfully, not trying to crush her spirit. "But that's only because he's oblivious."

"Ugh, men." She rolls her eyes.

"Come inside and help me prep." I take her hand and drag her into the house, ignoring the guys who watch us as we walk past. Once we're inside, I go to the junk drawer and pull out the extra-long wand lighter we keep in there, handing it to Sienna. "Light the candles for me, please?"

"Ooh, yes. Look at you. Next thing you know, you'll have these boys completely domesticated!" Sienna does a little shimmy as she moves about the room, lighting the candle on the counter first before she lights two more on the dining table.

"There's a candle in the bathroom and in the living room," I tell her, and she takes off to light them as well.

I connect my phone to the small speaker we keep in the kitchen and turn on my favorite Spotify playlist that I like to cook to. A jazzy tune starts playing, and I feel like I'm living in one of those cooking videos I see on social media.

We move about the kitchen in sync, Sienna doing everything I ask her to without complaint. I get through all the meal prep that much faster since I have a helper with me, and within ten minutes, I've got everything in the oven.

"Smells good," Coop announces as he enters the house from the back sliding door. Frank, Gavin, and Nico follow right behind him. "Whatcha cooking?"

"We're having chicken and potatoes, plus a salad," I tell them with a smile. "And Gavin, you're more than welcome to stay for dinner. I've made plenty."

"You sure? I don't want to impose," Gavin says.

"Oh, you'll want to stay, bro. She's the best cook." This comes from Frank, who's always singing my praises to someone.

"That's wifey material right there," Gavin says, earning a laugh from Coop and Frank.

Nico's not laughing, though. And neither is Sienna.

In fact, the entire kitchen has gone quiet, and when I chance a look at Nico, I see him glowering in Gavin's direction. Is he mad Gav said that? Why should he care?

"Um, I hate to do this, but something has suddenly—come up." Sienna grabs her phone from where she left it on the counter, checking it for what I'm sure is a fake message. "I need to bail on dinner. Sorry about it."

My heart drops, and I follow after her as she abruptly leaves the kitchen, heading for the front door. "Sienna, wait."

"Hey." She whirls on me, and there are tears shining in her eyes. Oh God. "Please know I'm not mad at you. It's that—I do everything I can to gain his attention, and he says nothing to me that's even vaguely flirtatious. Like, absolutely nothing. You invite him to stay for dinner with the gang, and he's automatically calling you wifey material. I just—I can't with him sometimes."

"Sienna." My heart is breaking for her. "Please don't let Gav upset you. He didn't mean anything by that statement."

"I'm starting to believe I don't mean anything to him either, you know? Oh God, this is so incredibly stupid." A tear escapes, sliding down her cheek, and I can't take it anymore.

"I hate that he made you feel so bad." My voice is soft and my heart is aching.

I don't like seeing her hurt. Worse, I don't know if Gavin is even aware of how much she cares about him. Is he pretending he doesn't see it? If that's the case, he's cruel. He needs to tell her he's not interested at all. It'll break her heart, but she'll be better off in the long run.

"It's fine. Really." She hauls me in for a big hug, and we cling to each other for a moment before she finally pulls away, turning toward the door. "Give me the recipe for the chicken, okay? Someday I'm going to make it for him and knock his fucking socks off."

She leaves before I can say anything, the door quietly shutting behind her, and I twist the lock into place before I turn toward the kitchen. I can hear all the men chatting and laughing without a care in the world, even Nico, and I shake my head.

Men. They are the most oblivious creatures sometimes. But I can't say anything to them. I'm not going to call out Gavin or make Cooper aware of anything. They need to figure this all out on their own.

Which might never happen, but that's the chance we have to take.

"Yo, Ever! You got a fancy bottle of wine we can crack open stashed somewhere?" Cooper calls.

This is another thing I've introduced them to. Pairing wine with the meal versus just slamming down a beer or whatever. I know I shouldn't encourage these guys to drink—unnecessary calories—but when they kept having beers with their meals, I decided to change it up.

"I do! Hold on." I rush into the kitchen and head straight for the tiny pantry, rummaging around until I find the bottle I bought with their money. I hide them because I like to have them with dinner and not when they're partying. Though they never reach for wine, so I don't know why I bother hiding it.

"Found it," I say as I emerge from the pantry, the bottle clutched in my hand. "Can someone open it for me?"

"I will," Nico volunteers, approaching me slowly, his dark gaze roaming over me from head to toe.

I'm still in the sports bra and leggings, and his hot gaze seems to spark on my skin everywhere he looks. I go still, my mouth popping open, no words coming out as he takes the bottle from my hand, our fingers brushing. My heart skips a beat.

He did that on purpose. I know he did.

"Thank you," I murmur to his retreating back, wondering if Sienna is right after all.

Maybe we should do it and get each other out of our systems.

But would he be down?

Chapter Eighteen

NICO

I take a quick shower to get out of that goddamn kitchen and away from Ever. Ever in the sexy sports bra and the leggings that cling to her body like a second skin. With the snatched waist and long legs and flat stomach and perky tits. Saw her nipples poking against the fabric of her sports bra earlier when she was leading us through the yoga positions, and I wondered what they looked like naked. Haven't busted in on her in the shower yet, which is a damn shame. Not that I want to violate her privacy but . . .

I sort of want to violate her privacy. Just to get a glimpse of that hot body without any clothes on.

While in the shower, I jerk off because I can't seem to help myself when it comes to Ever. Once her pretty face and sweet voice start filling my head, forget it. I'm hard just thinking about her, and what am I supposed to do about it?

Old me would make a move on her, flirt with her. Convince her we'd be good together, which probably wouldn't take much. I think she's feeling it.

Feeling me.

But we're both wary, and with good reason. It might be fun at first, fucking around with the roommate, but then reality sets in. Shit gets real, and we might get sick of each other quickly. Then what do we do?

Ever could maybe go live with Sienna, but she's in a two-bedroom with a roommate, and I've been in Sienna's room. It's fucking tiny.

And no, it wasn't like that. I was in Sienna's bedroom helping her move in along with Coop. She's like a sister to me. Besides, she's in love with Gavin.

Who's a fucking idiot. Didn't help that he called Ever wifey material. I didn't like that.

At all.

By the time I'm coming out of the bathroom in only a pair of boxer briefs, I catch the person I just jerked off to opening my bedroom door, her wide-eyed gaze meeting mine before it drops to my crotch.

Shit. I can feel myself getting a semi by her looking at me, and I just blew my wad only minutes ago.

"I'm so sorry!" She closes her eyes and reaches for the door but keeps missing the handle. "I just wanted to tell you dinner is ready."

"You've seen me in my boxers before," I drawl, enjoying the way she's scrambling. "And thanks for letting me know."

Her eyes pop open, and she remains in the doorway, her fingers now grasping the handle. "You're welcome."

We both watch each other as I grab the T-shirt I left on top of my dresser and tug it on, making her disappear from view for a brief second. She's still there once I pull the shirt into place, and I wonder what she's waiting for. It's like she wants to say something but doesn't know how to.

"Did you enjoy it?" she asks.

That is a loaded question. "Enjoy what?"

"The yoga class."

"Oh." I nod, rubbing my jaw. I need to shave. Should've done it when I was in the shower, but I was too busy playing with my dick.

When was the last time I fucked around with someone? I can't even remember anymore. "Yeah. It was good."

It actually was. Coop was a patient motherfucker, helping me get into position, and some of those moves were difficult. My muscles were straining at one point, and I regretted ever saying that yoga is for wimps.

Because I did say that. But not in front of Ever.

Her smile lights up her entire face, and I've never seen her look prettier, I swear. "I knew you would enjoy it. Okay, hurry up and get dressed. You don't want the chicken to get cold."

She's gone before I can say anything, slamming the door behind her, and I finish getting dressed, sauntering out of my bedroom only minutes later and walking through the living room.

There's a candle burning on the coffee table. When I enter the kitchen, I see there's also one burning on the counter, and two are sitting in the middle of the dining table with flickering wicks. There's jazz playing on the small speaker that sits on the counter, and Coop, Frank, and Gav are sitting at the table with Ever. There's one empty seat to the right of her, and I slip into it, noting how the table is properly set with silverware flanking my plate—not paper plates either. She went to a local thrift shop and bought a set for cheap. Said it was better for the environment, and none of us protested, though we're not huge fans of washing the dishes.

But we do it for her. We do a lot of things for her.

We make small talk, but we're mostly concentrating on the meal. Gavin can't stop complimenting Everleigh's cooking skills, and I keep sending him irritated looks. Every time I do this, I see Coop's amused expression, and it's annoying. They're all annoying me tonight. Even Ever, who's extra beautiful with the candlelight flickering on her face, casting her in shadows. The sound of her voice, how pleased she is by Gavin's constant flattery, and the way Coop laughs every time Gavin says something nice to her.

"Best damn meal I've had in a long time," Gav says minutes later, pushing his plate away from him as he leans back in his chair. If he pats his belly and burps, I'm going to kick him out of the house. "Thank you, Everleigh. That was delicious."

"You're welcome." She's blushing, her gaze stuck on Gav's stupid face, and the words leave me before I can stop myself.

"If you want to marry her, just propose right now, asshole. We get it. You like the way she cooks."

Coop starts laughing all over again, and I kick him under the table, making him start to cough instead. Frank's frowning, his gaze switching between me and Gav like he's at a tennis match. And Gavin is staring at me like I've sprouted two heads.

"What the hell is your problem, Valente? Can't I tell your room-mate that she's a damn good cook?" Gavin's brows shoot up. His voice is like a challenge. One I'm ready to meet.

"You won't stop gushing about her."

"I don't gush about anyone."

"You're gushing about her." I tip my head in Ever's direction, but she remains blessedly silent.

The tension grows between us, swirling. Making me angrier. I'm not backing down. Once I'm in it, I'm completing it, and wow, I sound like a total asshole even in my own thoughts.

"You're being a dick," Gav finally says.

"You're always a dick," I throw back, which is a lie, but I'm pissed.

"Hey, you guys." This comes from Frank, who sounds nervous as fuck. Gavin and I don't argue. Like ever. "Ease up, okay?"

"Shut the fuck up, Dollar." Gavin's voice is low. I can tell he's as pissed as I am.

I finally ask the question that's been on the tip of my tongue since Gav called Everleigh wifey material. "You into her?"

Gavin blinks, obviously confused. "Into who? Sienna?"

"What the fuck?" Coop mutters, shaking his head. "We're not talking about my sister, dipshit. She's not even here."

"I'm talking about Everleigh," I bite out.

"What? No." Gavin turns his attention to Ever. "No offense. You're cute. You're a great cook, but I'm not like . . . attracted to you or anything like that. And damn, that sounded awful but . . ."

"I know what you mean," Ever says, her voice soft. "I'm not offended."

"Why would you even bring up my sister?" Coop asks Gav.

Frank groans. "I don't think this is the right conversation to have over dinner."

Is Coop really so oblivious that he doesn't realize his sister is madly in love with one of his best friends?

Yeah. I think he is.

"Dinner is done," I announce, glancing quickly at my empty plate. "And I think it's a great conversation to have."

"You need to chill the hell out." Gav thrusts his index finger in my direction. "Why are you trying to start a fight with me?"

"Because he's hot for Ever and doesn't want you sniffing around her," Coop observes, sounding amused.

"Well, your sister is hot for Gavin, and he acts like he has no idea," I throw at Coop, angry that he exposed my ass.

"She is?" Coop and Gavin ask at the same time.

Ever leaps to her feet and starts reaching for our dishes, stacking them on top of each other. "All of you are ignorant jerks. Except for you, Frank."

"Hey, thanks, Ever." He sounds pleased by her comment, and that just makes me madder.

I pound my fist on the edge of the table, making everything shake, including the candles. The liquid wax even sloshes over one of the wicks and snuffs it out, thanks to me. "Ever is right. You're both idiots."

"She called us jerks," Gav corrects.

"And I was referring to you too," Everleigh says to me in the haughtiest voice I've ever heard. "Like I told you earlier, you're always grumpy around me."

"I am not." Am I?

She rolls her eyes. "And you definitely don't need to start a fight with Gavin. He was just being nice."

With that, she takes the stack of plates into her arms and stomps over to the sink, setting them inside noisily. She turns on the water and starts rinsing them off, and I almost want to correct her and say she should scrape off the plates into the trash first, like we always do, but I realize it's not smart to mess with an angry woman.

Instead I say nothing at all. Neither do the rest of the guys, with the exception of Gav, who is now standing, stretching his arms above his head.

"Hate to eat and run, but I've gotta go. Thank you again, Everleigh. That was delicious. One of the best meals I've had in forever."

"Anytime, Gavin," she calls, her back still to us as the dishes clank against each other extra loud.

He sends us a faintly amused, slightly sympathetic look before he hightails his ass out of our house.

"Want some help?" Frank calls to Ever.

"No thank you," she sing-songs.

"I need to study for a test. And by the way, you guys are mean as snakes." Frank leaves, slamming his bedroom door a few seconds later.

Coop is watching me, rubbing his jaw. Doesn't look so amused anymore, I'll say that. Now he appears confused. "Are you serious about my sister? She's crushing on Gavin?"

My exhale is ragged. "Yes. And you're just as blind to it as Gav is if you're trying to tell me you had no clue. She's liked him since her freshman year."

"How do you know this?"

"She might've hinted around to me once or twice," I hedge, feeling like a shit that I never told him this.

But he's Sienna's brother, and I didn't want to break her trust. Besides, she confessed her undying devotion for Gavin to me one drunken night, never to bring it up again. Once someone tells you that, though, you can't help but see it in their every little interaction with the person they're crushing on. It became really obvious to me that Sienna has a total thing for Gav.

"Damn." Coop sounds truly mystified. "I mean, I know she likes the guy, but I didn't think it was like that."

"Oh, it's definitely like that," Ever calls from her post at the sink. She's now started loading the dishwasher.

"You want some help?" Coop asks her, but she's shaking her head, that ponytail whipping around.

"No thank you."

Coop sends me a look. One that says *I wouldn't want to be you right now.*

"I'll leave you two alone then." He pushes his chair back, rises to his feet, and mouths to me, *Be nice.*

Then he's out.

What, like I'm not nice to Ever? Please.

With only Ever and me in the room, the tension grows. Thicker than it was between Gavin and me only moments ago. I'm going to have to reach out to him and apologize later. I was a complete dick to him for no reason.

Everleigh still isn't speaking. She's too busy slamming plates and glasses into the dishwasher like she's intent on breaking everything, and after a few minutes of this, she makes an irritated noise and shuts off the water. "Why did you start that fight?"

"What fight?" I am playing dumb on purpose.

"With Gavin. About me." She won't look in my direction, and it irritates the shit out of me.

"It was nothing."

She actually snorts. "Oh, it was something. What's your problem, anyway?"

I open my mouth and say the first thing that comes to mind. The God's honest truth.

"You are."

Chapter Nineteen

Everleigh

Nico's answer leaves me breathless.

A little angry.

A lot confused.

He's still sitting at the table, though his chair is pushed back and he's leaning forward, his forearms resting on his thighs, his hands hanging between his spread knees. Watching me with those dark eyes.

"Why?" I ask, my voice hoarse. My throat aches from holding back everything I want to say to him, and in that moment, I decide to unleash on this man who's driven me crazy from pretty much day one. "You don't like it that I cook you guys dinner? That I keep the house nice? That it doesn't smell like feet anymore since I'm constantly burning candles and I make you all keep your shoes outside? Am I the problem for finally getting rid of the mold in our bathroom? You're welcome for all of that, by the way."

"Thank you," he murmurs, his deep voice rippling along my nerve endings.

Making me shiver.

"Come here," he says after a few seconds of silence, and like a fool—like the stupid, gone-for-him fool that I am—I walk toward him, anticipation dancing along my skin. Coursing through my blood. My heart is racing, and when I stop directly in front of him, he glances up at me, sitting up fully, reaching out his hand to grab mine.

His reflexes are quick. Somehow, he yanks on my hand, and next thing I know, I'm pressed against the table, my butt right at the edge of it and Nico standing in front of me. Towering over me. Reminding me yet again how tall and powerful he is. His broad shoulders block everything else so I can see nothing but him, a shuddery breath escaping me when he shifts even closer.

"You're—you're invading my personal space," I warn, my voice weak.

He laughs—actually laughs, the jerk. "Seriously?"

I barely nod.

"Well, guess what? You invade my personal space all the damn time. In the morning when I wake up, you're in the kitchen making us coffee. Your late-afternoon yoga sessions and how you make us dinner practically every night with a smile on your face. Like you get off on feeding us."

I don't . . . *get off* on feeding them, but I do love seeing them looking pleased while they eat and how they always, always clean their plates after every meal. I also try my best to make sure the meals don't consist of wasted calories and that they include plenty of protein to keep their bodies fueled. They appreciate it. I know they do, thanks to all the compliments I receive from them after they eat dinner.

Does that go against every feminist feeling I have? I'm not here to serve the men, absolutely not. But I do enjoy cooking and doing yoga and helping people. I always have. My grandma told me a long time ago that I should lean into what makes me happy and make it my life's work if I could. That's why I'm majoring in nutrition and hope to help people as a career.

It just comes naturally to me.

"And you're especially right here," he continues, tapping the side of his head. "You invade this personal space of mine all the fucking time."

Shock washes over me, rendering me speechless.

"I can't stop thinking about you," Nico admits, his gaze never wavering from mine. "Because you're always right here." He taps his head again.

I remain silent, unable to come up with the proper words to respond.

"What about you?" he asks after the longest thirty seconds of my life. Maybe it was a minute. Maybe it was only ten seconds.

I don't know.

"What about me?" I croak, clearing my throat.

"Do you think about me as much as I think about you?"

Yes, my brain screams. *I never stop thinking about you.*

I should be real with him like he's being with me. I just—I don't know how.

I'm too scared.

He shifts even closer, and I can't move. I'm trapped, but I don't mind. He reaches for me, settling his hand on my waist, his fingers pressing into bare skin, and a shuddery breath leaves me at first contact.

Oh God.

His body heat seeps into me, warming me from the inside out, and I tilt my head back. His gaze drops to my lips, lingering there, and holy shit, is he going to kiss me?

"Yo, Nico—oh." Coop comes to an abrupt stop when he catches us, and Nico removes his hand from my body, turning so he can face his friend.

Me? I scurry away like a scared little mouse and resume cleaning the kitchen. My hands are shaking, my breath rattles my lungs, and I try my best to spy on their conversation, automatically giving up when I can barely hear them speaking above the running water.

Closing my eyes for a moment, I take a deep breath, trying to calm my racing heart. I'm completely rattled, and it's all Nico's fault. And I just know he was about to kiss me. I know he was. And I would've gladly welcomed it. Most likely enjoyed it too.

Maybe it was a good thing that Coop interrupted us. Once we take it to that step, nothing will stop us from pursuing it further. Until the next thing I know, I'm naked in bed with Nico.

And that sounds . . . amazing.

I chance a glimpse over my shoulder, wanting to make sure they're not arguing or anything stupid like that, but they appear friendly. Coop even slaps Nico on the shoulder at one point, both of them looking in my direction, and I hurriedly turn away, embarrassed I got caught.

I wonder what they're saying to each other. What are they talking about?

Me? Us? I hope not.

I finish loading the dishwasher, doing my best to ignore the conversation currently happening between my roommates. Though it's unfair of me to think of them in that way. They're more than just roommates to me already. I consider them my friends.

One of them specifically a friend I have a massive crush on.

This isn't good. Not even close to being good, but there's a small part of me now filled with hope, thanks to Nico's confession.

Beautiful, grumpy Nico, who's frustrated because he can't stop thinking about me. Looks like Sienna was right after all. He's frustrated by his feelings for me.

Feeling is mutual, bud.

By the time Coop leaves us alone in the kitchen, I can feel Nico's eyes on me. I'm wiping down the counters, putting my all into it rather than facing Nico because I don't know what to say to him.

I'm also afraid of what he might say to me.

Eventually I finish wiping down the counters and return to the sink, rinsing out the dishrag I was using when I feel him approach. He stops just behind me, his presence wrapping around me like a hug, though he's not even touching me.

"I'm sorry if I made you uncomfortable earlier," he murmurs.

"It's fine." I turn off the water and brace my hands on the edge of the sink. "I never did answer your question."

He's quiet for a moment before he asks, "What do you mean?"

"You asked me if I thought about you as much as you thought about me."

Nico shifts closer, setting his hands on either side of mine along the sink's edge. "And?"

He's so close, I can feel his chest rise and fall with every breath he takes. And when I glance up at the window, I can see our reflection thanks to the overhead light. He's watching me with that intense expression on his face. The one I think he's wearing because he's upset with me, or irritated.

But now I'm starting to wonder if it's something else.

"Maybe I do think about you as much as you think about me," I whisper, swallowing down all the anxiety that comes with admitting your real feelings. Leaving yourself raw and open to pain.

He doesn't say anything, and the longer the silence drags out, the worse I feel.

"We can't do anything about it, though," I say hurriedly, whirling around to face him. He pulls his hands away and takes a step backward, giving me space, and yes. Yes, that's exactly what I need. Getting involved with Nico is going to bring me nothing but problems, and I don't need that.

I don't want it. I know what I said to Sienna earlier, and yes, I considered what she said, too, but ultimately I think it would be a huge mistake and lead me to nothing but miserable heartache.

I'd much rather deal with indifference after breaking up with a long-term boyfriend instead of getting involved with a larger-than-life, too-handsome-for-his-own-good superstar who'll only leave me with a broken heart.

I can barely stand the thought.

"We can't?"

I slowly shake my head. "It would be a huge mistake. Don't you think?"

Nico says nothing, staring at me, his brows drawn together. Like he's confused because he can't figure me out.

"Yeah." He says the word slowly, dragging it out. "It probably would."

"You're not looking for anything serious."

He squints at me. "And you are?"

I nod, my voice solemn when I admit, "I'm nothing but a serious kind of girl."

And I believe that with my entire heart.

"Maybe you're right." He says those words, but he also sounds full of doubt.

No worries, Nico, I want to tell him. *I'm full of doubt too. More than anything, I'm talking out of my ass and trying to convince myself that I'm not into you like that.*

"I think I am." I thrust my hand out toward him like the awkward weirdo I've suddenly turned into. "Cool if we just remain friends?"

Reluctantly he reaches toward me and clasps my hand in his, giving it a gentle squeeze. I feel the pressure of his fingers settle into an incessant throb between my thighs, and I'm desperate to ignore it. "Okay. Friends."

We shake on it. The biggest lie we've ever told each other.

Wonder how long we'll keep up the pretense.

Chapter Twenty

Everleigh

We're halfway through the quarter, and classwork has ramped up to the point that I'm in a state of constant overwhelm. Between that and work and taking care of my agreed-upon responsibilities at the house, I'm swamped. I try to do homework locked up in my room, but even with my old AirPods stuck in my ears, I can't drown out the sound of my roommates and their various friends playing video games. Because when they play, they're loud.

They don't have a lot of faults—wait, I'm lying, they totally do. We all do. But for the most part, we're living a mostly peaceful existence together, especially if I avoid Nico.

Things have worked in my favor lately, though, and I don't run into him often. Especially the last couple of days since our "agreement." I'm able to sneak through his bedroom and use the bathroom to take a shower, doing my best not to leave my "girlie stuff"—Coop's description, not mine—strewn all over the counter. He hasn't been around much, and I wonder if that has to do with our "just friends" agreement.

Did I insult him? Has he run off and found someone else to mess around with? Is she prettier than me . . . ?

Wait a minute. I need to stop thinking like that. I don't care if she's prettier than me. I don't care if he's hooking up with twenty women who are more attractive than me. At least I'm not the one he's stringing along and pretending to care about. Nico Valente is a dangerous man.

Dangerous when it comes to my precious feelings, which are still a little raw after our last interaction.

Men. They're better left alone if you ask me.

Giving up on listening to the endless string of curses coming from our living room, I pack up my stuff and my laptop in my backpack and leave the house, heading for the campus library. It stays open till midnight Monday through Friday, which is ideal for situations like this. Though I don't want to stay there too late. I have to be at work tomorrow morning at six thirty.

Groan.

Ten minutes later I'm walking through the library, grateful as always that our house is close to campus. I move through the somewhat crowded tables, shocked to see so many students here bent over massive textbooks or tapping away at their laptops. Everyone's got headphones on or earbuds in, and hardly anyone is talking. It's so quiet in here I feel like I'm too loud, thanks to the slapping noise my flip-flops make as they hit the bare floor.

Clutching them with my toes to make them a little quieter, I slip through the maze of row after row of books, heading deeper into the library. Not as many people sit in the back, and that's my favorite place to work. Much more peaceful.

And that's what I'm seeking tonight. A little peace.

I turn left at one point, heading for my favorite quiet nook of tables and chairs, and come to an abrupt stop when I see who's sitting there.

It's Nico, his focus entirely on his laptop, his fingers moving slowly across the keyboard. Oh, and he's wearing glasses like he's freaking Clark Kent or something.

Damn it, he's adorable with the glasses, because of course he is.

Panicking, I'm about to start walking backward and get the heck out of there when he glances up, his eyes widening when he spots me. He whips off his glasses, an embarrassed smile on his face.

"Hey, friend."

That's what he's been calling me the last week or so. He's saying it just to get under my skin, and guess what?

It's working.

"Hey." I offer him an awkward wave because that's my usual mode of operation when I'm near the guy. "I'll leave you alone."

I'm about to turn away and leave him when he says, "You can sit with me if you want."

I shouldn't want. I absolutely should not want to sit with Nico but . . .

I do.

Turning back to face him, I smile and reach for the chair directly in front of me, pulling it out so I can settle in. "Thanks."

"What are you working on?"

"I have a research paper I need to finish."

"Ah." He nods. "I'm working on an essay."

"Sounds like we both have a lot of work to finish." I wrinkle my nose. "And I'm not the best writer."

"I do all right." He shrugs those impossibly broad shoulders, drawing my attention to them. To him. He's hard to look at because he's so attractive. Currently I'm avoiding his face, my focus zeroing in on his chest.

He's wearing a white Dolphins T-shirt with Billy the mascot in the center. The cotton stretches across his shoulders and chest, and his skin is tan from spending so much time outdoors. The man practically oozes with sex appeal, and I've made a huge mistake, agreeing to sit with him.

It's too much. He's too much.

"What's up with the glasses?" I ask, needing to focus on something fairly nerdy about him, because trust when I say there is nothing nerd-like about this man.

"Oh. These." He reaches for them, curling his fingers around them and picking them up. "They're the blue-light ones. My vision gets fuzzy if I stare at a screen for too long."

Ah, another flaw.

"You should probably get your eyes checked," I suggest.

"I already have. They suggested these." He holds up the glasses and then slips them on his face. "I look like a dork."

He is the furthest thing from a dork.

"You do," I say with a nod. He chuckles, about to take them off, but I shake my head. "Keep them on if they help you."

"You won't make fun?"

I slowly shake my head. "Never."

We smile at each other, and oh my God, I wonder what I'm doing. This doesn't feel like two friends working together in the library.

More like it's a man and a woman who are desperately attracted to each other, trying to fight their feelings while they work together in a library.

"Mind if I put these in?" I hold up my AirPods case.

"Not at all." He unzips the front pocket of his backpack and pulls out his own case. "I'll plug in too."

I scroll Spotify for my favorite playlist I like to do schoolwork to and turn it on shuffle before I grab my laptop and set it up. Within minutes I'm typing, trying my best to remain focused on the task before me. I'm last minute with this one since it's due at midnight tonight and the professor already declared there will be no extensions. I'm about halfway done, so it shouldn't be a problem, but . . .

The man sitting across from me is an utter distraction. I can smell him. That spicy cologne I know he uses, because I see it on our bathroom counter, hits my senses every time I breathe in. Then there's the fact that I can just feel his presence. He's like a magnetic force sitting across from me, radiating heat and sexiness. Is that even a thing?

The longer I sit here and try to avoid him, the more unavoidable he becomes. I chance a look in his direction, lifting my gaze to peek at him from above my laptop to catch him already watching me.

His gaze jerks away from mine. He returns his attention to his computer screen, sitting up a little and twisting his neck to the left, then the right.

I drop my gaze back to my screen, the words blurring as I stare at them.

Is this going to work? Or do I need to leave and sit in another section? That would be incredibly rude of me, but I'm feeling desperate. The clock keeps on ticking—I check the corner of my laptop screen and see that it's almost seven thirty—and I've got to get this paper done.

Now.

Determination filling me, I tap through the songs on my playlist until I get to one with a fast beat, telling myself it's go time. No more outside distractions.

I'm going to get this paper done.

Within seconds I'm writing it, 100 percent focused, the music fueling me. Occasionally I have to do some research and look up some facts, but for the most part, I'm putting this paper together with all the energy I can muster. Another thing urging me on is the fact that I have to go to work so early tomorrow. I don't want to stay up too late tonight because I'll pay the price in the morning.

I'm not risking it.

After a while I'm so focused on the research paper I'm putting together, I don't even notice what Nico's doing any longer. I don't even smell him. I'm in the zone, bopping my head every few minutes to the beat of the song I'm listening to, skipping the ones I know the lyrics to. Singing along with a song always ruins my attention span.

The first time Nico's foot nudges against mine, I don't acknowledge it. I'm sure it's an accident, and I don't want to take the time to talk about it.

But then it happens again. I jerk my foot back, frowning. Still not looking at him.

It happens again. This time, his foot slides along mine, his leg curling, like he's trying to . . . what? Trap me?

I lift my gaze to find him watching me, his too-sexy lips curved up in a closed-mouth smile.

Turning off the music, I stare him down, but he doesn't say anything. "Are you trying to distract me?"

"You're super focused."

"I need to finish my paper."

"How much longer until you're done?" He lifts his brows.

I check the word count along with the pages I've already written. "Probably another page and a half."

"Cool." He nods, his glasses slipping a little down the bridge of his nose, and he uses his index finger to push them back into place.

My stomach flutters at the cute gesture. I should not be turned on by him pushing his glasses up his nose, but here we are.

"I'll leave you alone," he says when I remain silent.

I turn the music back on and hope like crazy he keeps his word.

Looks like coming to the library was a giant mistake.

Chapter Twenty-One

Nico

Ever is fucking adorable when she's concentrating. Her fingers were flying over that keyboard just a moment ago, her mouth turned down into the slightest frown as she nodded along with whatever song she was listening to. I'm done with my essay. When she bumped into me earlier, I was close to finishing already, but I wasn't about to lose my opportunity to talk to her. Just the two of us.

Alone.

Yes, I've been avoiding her, but I've also been busy. I have a stack of assignments this week. It's that time of the quarter when everything hits hard and it's make or break. I'm not about to break. I don't have much longer to do this school gig, and I'm going out on top.

I study her as covertly as I can, taking in what she's wearing. The oversize light-gray sweatshirt I assume she got from Sienna, with the light-blue *UCSM* across it. The neckline is stretched out, revealing the turquoise strap of her sports bra, and I focus in on that spot. Wondering how soft her skin might be. I bet no one touches her there. Wonder what she'd do if I kissed it—

Probably kick me in the balls and scream at me to never touch her again. That's what she'd do.

Damn. Just thinking about it makes my balls want to shrivel up and disappear.

Her declaring us as "just friends" didn't help matters. She's all I can think about.

It's worse now. I'm borderline obsessed with the woman. I can hear my mother's voice now. She's told me this time and again.

You always want what you can't have.

Yep, you're so right, Mom. I do. And right now, I want my roommate.

I stretch out my legs, accidentally brushing against Ever's foot, and I retract my legs back into position, but she doesn't even react.

Huh.

This time I do it on purpose, looking for any kind of reaction. Now it's her turn to pull her foot back, like she's the one who knocked into me, but otherwise, no outward reaction.

Feeling like a little kid who kicks the girl he likes because he doesn't know how to tell her his feelings, I do it again, rubbing my foot against hers. Trying to curl my leg around her leg even. The sweats she has on ride up a little bit from my nudge, and I'm touching bare skin. Which is a real fucking disappointment considering I have my Nikes on.

A missed opportunity.

This time she looks up, irritation flaring in her pretty eyes. "Are you trying to distract me?"

I shrug, playing it cool. "You're super focused."

"I need to finish my paper." Yep, there's irritation in her voice.

"How much longer until you're done?" Maybe she'll want to get out of here. Go get a drink.

Yeah. I'm guessing her answer would be no.

"Probably another page and a half," she answers.

"Cool." I nod, pushing my glasses back into place when they start to fall.

Her eyes flare with an unrecognizable emotion, and I wonder what that's all about. Otherwise, she says nothing.

"I'll leave you alone," I finally say, returning my focus to the computer screen.

She remains quiet and starts typing again while I add some finishing touches to my essay before I finally turn it in to my professor via email. I grab my notebook and glance over the list I made Monday morning, checking off the assignment, reading over what's left that still needs to be done.

I have two tests Thursday, which sucks, but I can manage it. As long as I focus on getting one item done at a time, it'll be easy.

Somewhat.

I hear Ever sigh and glance up, watching as she snaps her laptop shut and shoves it into her backpack. I'm frowning, wishing she'd talk to me, but she's still quiet. She gathers her things and puts them all away before she rises to her feet, jerking her backpack over her shoulder.

"I need to go," she announces when she catches me watching her. "See ya."

That's it. No *I'll see you at home* or *Hey, that was fun*.

Just a simple *see ya* before she hoists her backpack strap higher on her shoulder, turns on her heel, and scurries away.

I glance around the table, wondering what the hell that was about.

Then I scramble, shoving everything I brought into my backpack, zipping it closed as I stand and go after her.

It's darker back here in the depths of the library, but I think I spot her in the near distance. I hurry my steps, wondering what the hell could be back here that she's seeking out, when I spot it.

The restrooms.

She pushes her way through the door marked **WOMEN**, and it slams shut with a rattle. I glance around, wondering if anyone is in there. Where we're at is pretty much empty, all the action happening at the front of the library, and I hesitate for a moment, contemplating my next move.

I wait for what feels like forever but is probably no longer than a minute. Maybe two. Enough time passes to make me contemplate if I should go inside. What if something's wrong with Ever? I don't want to invade her privacy but . . .

Fuck it.

I barge my way into the women's bathroom, stopping short when I see Everleigh standing in front of the sink, washing her hands.

"Are you following me?" She shuts off the water and grabs a couple of paper towels, drying her hands as she studies me.

Great. Now I feel like a stalker.

"I was worried about you." Which is partly true. But she looks great. Normal.

I overreacted.

"Really." She tosses the paper towels in the trash. "Well, I'm fine. No need to worry."

"Okay. Good." I hesitate, watching her for a moment. I feel like an idiot. I shouldn't have run into the bathroom, but here I am. "It's just that you . . . took off so fast. You didn't give me a chance to say anything."

Her shoulders sag, and I realize her backpack is propped against the wall nearby. I do the same, letting mine drop by the door.

"What could you say, Nico? Are you mad I didn't give you a chance to say goodbye?" She sounds weary. Poor thing. She's overworked lately.

"No, of course I'm not mad." I approach her carefully, not wanting to scare her or, worse, make her run. "It's just that . . ."

"I left you because I couldn't focus," she blurts, clamping her lips together the moment the words leave her. Her eyes are wide and a little panicked. Like she regrets just admitting that.

"Why couldn't you focus?"

A sigh leaves her, and she waves her hand in my general vicinity. "Look at you. You're a walking, talking distraction."

Maybe I should be insulted, but I'm not. More like I'm relieved.

"I feel the same way about you," I admit, taking small steps toward her. I'm so close, I can almost touch her.

She takes a couple of steps in the opposite direction, still facing me, until her back hits the white-tiled wall. "We're supposed to remain just friends. Remember?"

"Uh-huh." I close the rest of the distance between us, my hands going to her waist, lightly pinning her to the wall. She tilts her head back, her gaze troubled, almost defiant. I shift even closer to her. Until I can feel her body heat absorbing into mine. "Hey, guess what?"

Ever frowns, a little line forming between her eyebrows. "What?"

"You're a walking, talking distraction too." I dip my head, my mouth hovering above hers. She's trembling. I can feel her body shake. Can tell by the way she breathes. I shouldn't push her. I shouldn't put her in this position, but it's like I can't help myself.

"Nico . . ." My name is like a sigh, and when she curls her fingers into the front of my T-shirt, that's what does it for me.

That's what makes me lose control.

I kiss her. Testing her. I don't come on too strong or press too hard. I keep my touch light, a barely there promise.

She responds, returning the kiss, her body straightening, her other hand settling on my chest. Not to push me away . . .

No, she's got handfuls of my T-shirt clutched in her fists, like she needs to hang on for dear life.

Our mouths connect and break apart again and again, her lips parting more and more until I take my chances and slide my tongue against hers. A whimper sounds low in her throat, and then it's on.

We're kissing. I pin her against the wall with my body, pressing my hips against hers. She runs her hands up my chest, curling her arms around my neck, and I slide my hands around her waist, jerking her to me.

She goes willingly, whimpering again, and when I circle my tongue around hers, that whimper turns into a full-fledged moan.

Fuck.

I devour her mouth, holding her to me, kissing her with everything I have. Warm lips and tangling tongues and soft sighs. Her even-softer body seems to melt into mine, and I shift my hands downward, just about to pick her up so she can wrap those long legs around my hips, when I hear someone gasp.

And it's not Ever.

We stop kissing at the same time, our heads swiveling toward the open door of the bathroom. An older woman is standing there, an employee badge hanging from a chain around her neck, and I swallow hard, trying to control my breathing.

"Young man, this is the women's restroom," she says in a shrill voice.

I reluctantly pull away from Ever, sending her a look before I turn my focus—and charm—to the librarian. "Sorry about that. I got . . . lost."

She crosses her arms in front of her ample chest. "Uh-huh."

I amble my way toward her and grab my backpack from where I left it by the door. Glancing over my shoulder, I send Ever a quick look before I flash a smile at the older woman. "Excuse me."

The librarian steps out of my way, and I exit the bathroom, turning almost immediately to the right so I can wait for Ever in between the rows of dusty old books.

I can hear the librarian talking to Ever, and then they're both leaving the bathroom.

Together.

Shit.

They start to walk past, and I make a weird whistling sound, catching Ever's attention. She spots me, her eyes wide before her gaze shifts to the still-walking librarian, and thank God Ever stops, leaning against one of the shelves.

I wait a few seconds, wanting the woman to be long gone and out of earshot before I speak. "That was a close call."

Everleigh's response is to sigh, shaking her head. "We should've never done that."

"Why not?"

"You know why not." She marches toward me and pokes me in the chest. So hard I take a step back, rubbing at the spot where she did some damage. "I asked you to keep things between us as just friends."

"I was keeping it friendly." I put on my most innocent face, because come on.

That kiss was pretty fucking friendly.

"And you got us in trouble."

"You were at fault as much as I was," I remind her.

She glares at me, seemingly at a loss for words. All she can manage to say is, "You're annoying."

Like I haven't heard that one before. "Tell me you didn't feel anything when we kissed."

Ever remains quiet, but she's breathing hard. Like she's battling a massive internal struggle.

"See? You can't say it." I'm feeling smug. And positive that we're going to take this back to the house and make some more magic happen. Hopefully in the privacy of my bedroom.

Only because I have the bigger bed.

"I felt absolutely nothing when we kissed." She stands up straight, flicking her hair behind her shoulder. "There. How does that make you feel?"

Before I can respond, she's gone, shooting down the aisle and most likely heading for the front of the library. Her scent still lingers, though. As do the taste of her lips and those breathy little whimpers she made too.

I rub at my chest again, pressing against the spot where she poked me. A direct hit on my heart. What she said just now?

Makes me feel like shit.

Chapter Twenty-Two

EVERLEIGH

"Exactly how many people are coming to this party, anyway?" I ask Sienna as we compete for space in front of the full-length mirror that is currently leaning against my wall. I keep meaning to hang it and always forget.

"It'll be the biggest bash the team has this season, and they rarely throw parties because they're too busy with football. But you can count on them always having this party every year during their bye week. It's the one time they can cut loose on a Saturday night with no major consequences. Nothing but fun." Sienna tugs at the bodice of her black strapless dress, trying to contain her boobs, which currently look like they're going to pop straight out at any second. "Maybe I shouldn't wear this."

"You look stunning," I tell her, because it's true. "Wear the dress."

She smiles, shimmying her shoulders as she watches herself in the mirror. "Coop will probably flip."

"Don't let him see you." I make it sound simple, but the house isn't that big.

From what I've seen, though, the party will spill out into the backyard. There's a keg stand set up out there ready to roll, and Frank gathered a bunch of folding chairs from somewhere, scattering them all over the yard. We have one of those outdoor firepits that's full of kindling and newspaper and already lit.

After the long week we all just experienced, I'm ready for it. The entire party is going to be lit, according to Frank. He's calmed down with all the love bombing, as Sienna calls it. I think he's found someone else he's interested in, and I'm so grateful for it. Not that he's been chasing after me, but he's been so down the last few weeks because of his shoulder. He even asked me to give him some special shoulder stretches so he could work on strengthening it on his own. I gladly gave him some tips and hope they help.

We shall see.

Frank has turned into a true friend, but he's definitely seemed preoccupied by someone else over the last week. When asked about it, he's played coy, which I found odd. He's not one to hold back his feelings. He'll always tell you what's going on and who's involved. Not this time around, though, which leaves me curious.

Maybe he'll invite this new friend—woman, whatever he wants to call her—over tonight. That should be interesting.

It'll also be interesting to watch Sienna and Gavin interact this evening. She's avoided him for almost a week, which she admits has been difficult for her and she's had to use tremendous willpower to stay away. I'm proud of her. I'm thinking the more she stays out of his life, the more he'll want her in it, but who knows?

I can't figure men out.

I do know the one man who's been haunting my dreams on a nightly basis seems to be staying away from me, and I'm pretty sure he's doing it on purpose. After the disastrous kiss in the library bathroom, he's kept his distance. He doesn't act annoyed with me or hostile in any way, which I would totally deserve because I completely rejected him.

No, it's much worse than that. More like he's polite and almost—indifferent every time we're around each other. He barely speaks to me beyond a greeting or an *excuse me* or *thank you*. That's it. While I know this is all my fault . . .

It kind of sucks. Doesn't matter that I was the one who said we needed to keep it friends only and then ultimately rejected him—I still can't help the way I feel. While he acts like he can turn his feelings off and on like a light switch.

Maybe deep down he's an unfeeling asshole and I dodged a bullet just in time. Then again, maybe it's a lie I'm telling myself. I don't know.

I don't know what to think or how to feel when it comes to this man.

Doesn't help that I had an over-the-top sexual dream where Nico was featured in a starring role last night. We were in my bed, both of us naked. His mouth was *everywhere*. His hands. His fingers. I could feel him pressed against me, hot and hard and insistent, and when I woke up, my hand was literally in my panties.

I get a little sweaty just thinking about it.

"You'll have to help me with that," Sienna says, interrupting my dirty Nico thoughts. "Avoiding my brother. Like, I'll need you to distract Coop if he goes in search of me, which I doubt he will. Though I don't know, he's been a little tense lately."

Ever since he found out that his sister has a thing for Gavin, though I don't remind her of that. There's no point. Everyone knows what's going on with everyone else. We're all kind of twisted up in each other's business.

"I guess the yoga classes aren't working for him if you think he's tense," I say jokingly.

"For real. I need to come do another session with you guys. I enjoyed it, though all I did was try to get Gavin's attention." She rolls her eyes. "Like I'm doing now. When am I going to give this behavior up? I need to find someone new. Focus on another guy, because it feels like I'm wasting my time with this one. Maybe I'll come to one of your yoga sessions when Gavin isn't there."

The problem is Gavin's always there. He's been spending a lot of time at our house lately, and I'm not exactly sure why. It's definitely not because of me. After that tense night over the dinner table—something I never told Sienna about, because what she doesn't know doesn't hurt her—things have shifted with my friendship with the guys. Not in a bad way at all, but I do notice that they're not really hanging out with me.

"You should definitely do yoga with us again soon," I tell Sienna. "Or just come over and hang out with me one night. I've been lonely."

All my roommates and Gav have kept up gaming every night, and it's so boring, I usually end up locked away in my room doing my home-work—always a good thing—or scrolling mindlessly on social media.

"I will." Sienna flashes me a quick smile. "I promise."

I step closer to the mirror, rubbing off some stray mascara from underneath my left eye. "Do I look ridiculous? Please be honest."

I'm wearing a gold stretchy dress that clings to my body probably a little too much. It's short and strappy, and while my boobs aren't spilling out like Sienna's, they're definitely on display. The fabric is so tight, I decided not to wear panties tonight, which feels rather bold.

But as I continue staring at my reflection, the doubt trickles in. I thought the dress was flattering when I tried it on in the store, but now I'm second-guessing my every decision.

Typical.

I blame Sienna for convincing me to buy this dress in the first place. It was on sale, so that was a plus because I'm trying to save as much money as possible. But much like the workout set I bought a couple of weeks ago, when Sienna saw me in this dress at the store, she insisted I had to buy it. She is good for my ego but bad for my bank account.

"You look like a goddess," she gushed as I stood in front of the dressing room mirror, turning this way and that, trying to catch all the angles. "Seriously. They're all going to lose it."

"Who exactly are *they*?"

"The guys. Any guy. Whatever guy you want to attract, you will definitely attract him with this dress. It's foolproof."

Was she right? I'm putting it to the test tonight, so we'll see.

"I already told you it was perfect," she continues, and I can tell she's losing patience with me. "You're stunning."

"Thank you, so are you," I tell her, because she is.

"Why thank you." She waves a hand in front of her as if she's fanning herself. "Wonder if Gavin will notice."

"I thought you were going to focus on someone else," I tease.

Sienna's expression falls a little, and I feel bad for what I said. "You're right. I should focus on someone else, but it's so . . . difficult."

"Try one more time with him. I suppose it can't hurt." I haul her into a hug, squeezing her close. I hate seeing her so down, especially because she's so very rarely sad.

Noise comes from the living room, and I can tell that people are starting to arrive. Nerves eat at my stomach, and I rest my hand against it, reminding myself that whatever happens tonight, I'm going to have fun.

It's going to be fun.

"You look scared out of your mind," Sienna says, her wide eyes meeting mine.

A nervous laugh escapes me, and I drop my hand to my side. "It's the first big party I'll actually be a part of since arriving here." We've gone to the bars and hung out. Sienna dragged me to a frat party once, but I stayed outside for most of it, too intimidated to talk to anyone.

Her expression turns sincere. "You're still liking it here, right? Living with the guys? Your job? Your classes?"

"I love it," I say truthfully. "School's getting a little harder, but I love a challenge."

Sienna rolls her eyes. "You would say that, Little Miss Overachiever."

"Hey, I want to do well in school. And I like my job. The hours are perfect. And the guys are great."

They really are. They're respectful of my space, they appreciate my cooking, and they try their best to keep the house tidy. They know I can't help but pick up after them if they leave their stuff lying around. I don't like a messy house. I dealt with that living with my mom. I saw it whenever I was at Brad's house, which was often. I don't like it when people are sloppy.

"I know I've said it before, but I'm so glad we've become friends." Sienna smiles at me. "It's nice to have someone here who understands what it's like, being around these guys."

I've come to realize over these last few weeks that it's almost a privilege that we get to hang out with so many members of the football team. I get why they keep to themselves and don't let just anyone into their inner circle. There are a lot of fame chasers on campus, both men and women.

But especially the women. I'm guessing we'll have a house full of them tonight, and most of them will be trying to get the guys' attention. I understand why they want it. The guys are all handsome. Charming. They command attention wherever they go, and people are drawn to them.

Like me. Especially one in particular. Who I just rejected. Even after he kissed me. And God, what a kiss. The hottest moment in my life took place in a library bathroom of all places.

Sometimes I wonder if I'm a complete idiot.

"Come on, let's go out there and get drunk." Sienna takes my hand and drags me toward the door, throwing it open. We're blasted by loud music and even louder conversation when a deep male voice yells, "Yeah, let's get it!"

The party has officially begun.

"You're that girl who lives here, right?" This very tall, very thin woman is swaying on her feet, watching me with glassy eyes as she clutches a red Solo cup in her hand. She's obviously drunk, and I'm worried she might pass out and fall forward, taking me with her.

We're outside in the backyard standing near the firepit, which is keeping me warm. I can hear the ocean crash against the shore in the near distance, and the wind coming off the water is cold enough to leave me shivering.

I'm sort of regretting my dress choice. Regretting even more my decision to be outside, but Nico is inside, and just like Sienna is avoiding her brother, I'm avoiding Nico as much as possible.

Not like he's noticing me anyway. He's surrounded by an endless throng of girls, all of them clamoring for his attention. Every single one of them hotter than me. Prettier than me. He has his choice of women tonight. Any night.

I remember the look on his face when he told me he couldn't stop thinking about me. Or right when we first started to kiss in the bathroom, before we got caught by the pissed-off librarian. I'm sure each situation was just a fleeting moment. A symptom of wanting someone he can't have, because we both know what a mistake it would be, messing around when we live together.

It would turn into an actual, giant mess, and we already know I don't like messy things.

"I live here, yep." I nod, glancing around the backyard in search of a familiar face. Even Nico would be a welcome sight so I could escape this very drunk woman.

"You're so lucky," the girl says, lurching forward so hard I step out of her way. I knew she was close to falling. "I'd pay to live here just so I could see Nico every day. Talk about a dream come true."

Seriously? Why does it feel like everything centers around Nico?

"Yeah, you would definitely have to pay rent," I tell her before I turn and walk away, leaving her by the firepit. With determined steps I march back into the house and spot Coop, who is at the kitchen table, a.k.a. our makeshift bar, pouring himself a drink. I stop right beside him.

"Whatever you're having, make it a double for me," I say firmly.

He does a double take at my demand. "Seriously, Ever? You don't drink much."

"I do tonight."

"Better watch it." He sounds fatherly with the warning. "You're such a little thing. The liquor will go right to your head."

"Everyone is a little thing compared to you." I give him a sharp nudge in the side, making him yelp. "Serve me up, bartender."

He does as I request, handing me a Solo cup full of some sort of alcoholic concoction that has me feeling brave. I take a massive swig, nearly choking on it when it goes down, but fortunately I swallow it all without spitting it back up like a wimpy little baby.

"Delicious," I rasp, my eyes watering.

He chuckles. "You're going to be wasted in like thirty minutes."

"Good. That's the goal."

Coop's brows shoot up. "You work tomorrow?"

I shake my head and take another drink. "It's my day off."

"You're lucky, because you're gonna need to sleep off the hangover."

"Okay, Dad." I tap my cup against his, and we both drink at the same time. "Where's your sister?"

"I haven't seen her all night. Figured she's wearing some sexy dress that'll make me want to cover her up." I gape at him, making him laugh. "Apparently I'm correct."

"You're dead on." I shrug one shoulder. "She's just trying to have a little fun."

"I know. And she deserves to, but every one of these guys in here doesn't deserve her," he says vehemently, gesturing at the crowd of mostly guys in the house. "God, this is nothing but a sausage party."

I'm laughing because he's so right. Nothing but dudes as far as the eye can see. "There are plenty of women outside. I was talking with one of them, and she's already pretty drunk. She practically fell on me."

"No thanks. I like my women somewhat sober. I don't take advantage of drunk girls." He shakes his head. "Be careful tonight, okay, Ever? I don't want you to end up with some jackass who tries to hook up with you."

"Maybe I want to hook up with someone." I stand up straighter, saluting him with my cup. "That sounds kind of fun."

"If you say so." The doubt in his voice is clear, and I'm about to call him Dad again when I feel someone tugging on my arm. I turn to see it's Sienna, who's currently wearing an oversize denim jacket that's actually really cute. And completely hides her scandalous dress. "What's up, homie?"

She wraps me up in a hug, laughing. "Someone is feeling herself."

"At least someone is feeling me, even if it's only you." I pull away from her to finish off my drink, smacking my lips together. "Another round, bartender!"

I practically shove my cup into Coop's chest.

"There you are," he says to Sienna as he takes my cup and sets it on the table. "I haven't seen you all night."

"There's a reason for that." She tucks the front of her jacket together, hiding the dress. "Are you corrupting my friend with copious amounts of alcohol?"

"She's the one who asked for a double." He gets to preparing me another, and I hop up and down with excitement, my head already spinning. "And that's my roommate you're referring to."

"Whatever, she likes me most." Sienna swings her arm around my shoulders and presses her cheek to mine. "Right, snookums?"

"You know it, babycakes." I kiss her cheek, which of course has a few of the guys starting to chant, "Kiss her! Kiss her!"

God, men are such pervs.

"Do not kiss her," Coop says with a grimace as he hands me my drink.

"I would never." I take a sip. Damn, I think that's even stronger than the first one. "I'm not here to put on a show for the guys."

"Good, because they're all assholes." He glares at the group of chanters, silencing them just like that. Impressive. "There. They'll leave you alone. Now go about your business."

Sienna and I share a look before we hurriedly leave Coop behind at the table and wander around the house together, only stopping to talk to someone she knows, which is often. I continue sipping my drink, going a little slower this time around. I can feel the liquor flowing through my veins, warm and languid and making my bones feel like they could turn to mush at any moment. I'm feeling good.

Beyond good.

It's definitely the alcohol talking, but I'm feeling pretty freaking great.

Until I spot a beautiful blonde with a nasty expression on her face glaring at me as she enters the house.

My house.

It's Portia.

Chapter Twenty-Three

Nico

The party is off to a great start. There are so many people filling our house and backyard, the majority of them I don't even know. Coop is acting as bartender at the moment, and Dollar is manning the keg with a couple of other teammates outside.

Me? I'm wandering around both the house and the backyard like the consummate host that I am. Smiling and greeting everyone. Offering them a drink. Directing the scantily clad and cold-looking women over to the firepit so they can warm themselves up.

Doing my best to avoid my roommate every time I spot her, which is far too often for my taste.

Speaking of taste, she appears pretty fuckin' tasty in that gold dress she's wearing. It's tight and clings to her curves, showing them off to perfection. There's this constant smile curling her lips that makes her positively radiant, and I can see it in the way the other guys are watching her, interest glowing in their eyes. They notice her.

And I hate it.

Fuck, I can't even look at her. I'm not supposed to think about her like that since we kissed in the library and she ran away from me. Hell, by kissing her I already broke our promise after we shook on it, so I guess that's on me. But I wasn't the only one participating in that kiss.

She was into it too. She was into me. Until the crotchety old librarian had to walk in and bust up our little secret party of two.

Deep down, I know I can't hook up with her or fuck her or whatever the hell I was thinking. Talk about a colossal mistake.

But I can't stop watching her. The way that dress looks on her.

All I can think about is taking it off. Her sprawled across my bed, me lying between her legs. Slowly lifting it, exposing her bit by bit. Kissing and licking every inch of her skin on display . . .

My thoughts are fueled by the alcohol I'm consuming—and I'm drinking a lot. Which is something I don't normally do during football season. None of us guys on the team really do.

But this is the one weekend when we don't have to worry about hangovers for at least a couple of days. Our coaches will slap us into shape come Monday, but tonight?

I'm drinking until I'm fucked up, and I'm going to have a good time doing it.

Our teammate Jonesie eventually enters the backyard through the side gate, bringing with him at least six beautiful women, all of them with friendly smiles on their faces and looking hot.

"Told you I'd bring some ladies," he greets me, making me laugh.

I point them in the direction of the keg, where they all go eagerly, and the last woman who walks by me trails her fingers along my stomach as she passes. A tempting smile curves her red lips, and I send her a look, one that says *I'm definitely interested*, because fuck it.

I am.

Anything to help me get the pretty brunette in the gold dress off my mind for at least the night.

"You're such a dog."

I turn to see Gavin standing there with a Solo cup in his hand and a big ol' grin on his face. All I can do is shrug at him in return.

"I can't help it if the ladies love me."

"So modest." He takes a drink, scanning the backyard for a moment. "I'm over this."

"Over what?"

"Partying. Drunk people puking in the yard. Kegs. A girl giving a guy a blow job in the bathroom. All of that is going to happen tonight. It might even be happening right now at this very moment, and I'm tired of it. Aren't you?"

I study him, surprised by his outburst. At the weariness in his tone. He definitely sounds over it, and I'm surprised. "I had no idea you felt that way."

"I've been feeling it for a while. Don't you think you're just too old for this scene?"

"I'm twenty-two," I remind him. "Same age as you."

And no, I'm not over it. Or tired of it. This is college, and it's our last year. We're supposed to party and get shit faced and have fun. Real life is waiting for us on the other side, and I plan on living it up as much as I can before I have to face reality.

"I'm tired, man. Sometimes I feel older than twenty-two. Like I've already been through it." He shakes his head, and I go to him, gripping him by the shoulders.

"The best is yet to come," I remind him, giving him a shake. "Don't give up on us now."

"Trust me, I'm not giving up on us. Don't worry about that. I'm just—tired of the party scene. Meaningless conversations. Meaningless hookups. I want something real." He steps away from me, and my hands drop from his shoulders. "You really feel okay with how this season is going?"

"Hell yeah," I say without hesitation.

"I'm freaking out," Gav admits. "Feels like everything is riding on us winning. If we lose one game, it'll make the rest of the season that much harder. We lose two? We're completely fucked."

I say nothing because he's right. Everything is riding on us winning, and losing even one freaking game puts so much at risk. But I don't have the kind of pressure that Gav deals with as the quarterback. What he deals with is on a whole other level.

"We're not going to lose," I tell him, confidence bleeding into my every word. I believe that with all I've got.

"Easy for you to say," he grunts.

"It is. Look." I rest my hands on my hips, contemplating him. "I believe in you. I believe in all of us. We're doing everything we can to make this season—our last season—epic. But some of it is out of our hands. We just have to try our best and work with what we've got. Not get too caught up in our heads over it."

He studies me for a while, his expression serious. "When did you become so fucking logical?"

"Not sure." I shrug. "The words just came to me."

Gav laughs. "It was perfect—you don't know how badly I needed to hear that."

"Good." I smile a little. "So did I."

He peers at me, like he can see right through me. "You doing okay, though? Really?"

I remain quiet again, unsure if I should be completely honest. He's dealing with his own problems, and he doesn't need to worry about mine.

"Come on. Tell me the truth."

I blow out a harsh breath and shake my head, both hating and liking that he's got me figured out.

"I've been a little—fucked in the head lately. It's not affecting my game play or anything," I admit, my voice low. I quickly add, "That's why I have zero problems with this party tonight. I need the distraction." I don't want him freaking out that I'll turn into shit on the field.

"From?" He lifts his brows.

"Everything."

He remains silent, waiting me out.

"Fine. From her."

"Which her?" Gavin draws his brows together.

Is he acting like this on purpose? I thought it was obvious to everyone that I have a thing for Everleigh.

That she most likely has a thing for me too.

"Her." I wave a hand toward the vicinity where I know for a fact Everleigh is standing. Laughing. Hanging on Sienna and having the time of her life, that skirt riding up higher and higher on her thighs. If I stick around long enough, I might see her panties. Or better yet, maybe she's not wearing any at all. "The girl in the gold dress."

He angles his head to the right, looking for Everleigh. "Oh, right. You mean your roommate."

I nod, and Gavin—one of my very best friends, a person I confide all my secrets to—starts laughing his ass off. He doesn't stop, either, when he sees me starting to fume.

Such a dick.

"You are so fucked," he says between bouts of laughter, practically clutching himself while I stand there glaring at him. "Seriously. You're a mess."

"Thanks." I throw my hands up in the air, letting my frustration rip. "What am I supposed to do? Fuck her like I want to?"

She already basically turned me down. Twice.

"Not that she's interested," I tack on before Gavin can say anything. "She already told me she wants to be friends only. But ignoring her isn't helping me much."

"Wait, she said to your face she isn't interested in you?"

"Yeah," I rasp, feeling like an idiot.

"Ballsy," he murmurs.

"We had a talk a few days ago." I scrub the back of my neck, gripping it for a second before I let go. I decide not to mention the kiss in the library. "We decided we'd be better off as just friends."

"When did this happen? I've been hanging out at your house all week and never noticed this little interaction."

"We're not about to chat about shit like that in front of you assholes," I mutter.

"I can't believe it. She rejected you. *You.* That's gotta sting." Gav is grinning. "She's cute."

"Tell me all about it."

"I like the dress." He pauses. "It's short."

I hear the amusement in his voice, and even though I know he's only giving me shit, I'm tempted to threaten him just to get him to shut up.

"It's too short," I grumble, which has him laughing all over again. "Seriously, bro?"

"You got a crush, Valente? Is that your problem?" Now he's actually clutching his sides, having a grand ol' time at my expense. "I never thought I'd see the day."

"You're being an asshole," I mutter.

"Please. You've been an asshole for the last three years. A cold, callous asshole when it comes to women especially. It's nice to see someone get under your skin."

"You enjoy watching me suffer?"

"Absolutely. I never thought I'd see the day." He finally gets himself under control, wearing a straight face when he asks, "What's so different about this one? Is it the yoga? How she cooks dinner for you guys? What a deal that is. I meant what I said when I called her wifey material."

"That pissed me off," I admit.

He's grinning again. "I remember. It's why I brought it up."

I'm glaring. "Now you're just trying to piss me off."

"A little bit." He pauses. "What is it about her that you're attracted to?"

"I don't even know." That's a lie. I like everything about her, but it's hard to come up with a list for Gavin. "Maybe it's because I'm not supposed to have her?"

"Forbidden fruit." Gav nods like he understands.

"Right. Sure. She's sweet. She tolerates my ass. She's nice to Dollar."

"No one is nice to Dollar," Gav says.

It's true. He's such an easy mark. Always gets worked up when someone gives him grief, which everyone does.

"Exactly. She's running yoga classes in our backyard." I make a face. "All these jackasses from the team stretching and shit. Doing the lone-dog-tree position or whatever you call it. Unbelievable."

"I've been enjoying the classes," Gavin says, his expression thoughtful. "They really help with stress. Like, they clear my mind."

I hate to admit that I didn't mind the classes either. But is it only because I like to watch Ever the entire time in her cute workout outfits? Probably.

"Is that why you're coming over all the time?" I ask him.

"Nah. I need the distraction. If I sit around at home too much, I start thinking about everything and freak myself out. Playing video games with you guys is a lot more relaxing. Oh, that and Everleigh's nightly dinners. It feels like she's taking care of us, you know?"

"You don't even live here," I remind him.

"Yet I'm reaping some of the benefits. Look, when it's just us, we're lazy. We DoorDash everything or we're eating pizza all the time. The house is a mess. It starts to smell. We drink too much beer or we play too many video games. But with Everleigh around, I feel like I need to be on my best behavior. I don't want to be a slob around her. Girls don't like that shit."

"You think she makes us better people?" I never thought of it like that before.

"Definitely," he says with a nod. "Even you."

"Ha, thanks." I give him a shove, and he pretends to topple over a little bit. "Maybe it's working on you too."

"I'd like to think it is." He smiles.

We both turn to see Cooper approaching, his sister and—oh shit—Everleigh accompanying him.

"Gavin." Sienna walks right up to him and wraps him up in a hug. "I haven't seen you in forever."

"Figured you were avoiding me." He returns the hug, his arms springing away from her in seconds. Jesus. Talk about someone who needs to admit to himself that he might have some minor feelings for someone else. "Looking good, Sienna."

"Why thank you." Her cheeks are bright pink, and maybe it's the alcohol, but I'm guessing it's the compliment coming from the guy she's had a thing for since her freshman year. "You're looking good yourself."

Gavin is wearing a black crewneck sweatshirt and jeans. Nothing special. But I'm guessing it works for Sienna.

"What are you ladies up to, hanging out with Coop?" Gav asks.

"We dragged him away from his bartending duties," Everleigh says. "And got someone else to take over."

"Who?" I ask Everleigh.

She barely looks in my direction. It's like she can't. "I don't know his name."

"It was Jonesie," Coop says. "He wanted to do it. Supposedly he has skills."

"He made me a special concoction, and it's delicious." Sienna lifts her cup in a cheers gesture before she takes a drink.

Everleigh giggles, sipping from her own cup, and I stare at her like some sort of perv, unable to speak. I can feel Sienna watching me, her lips curving into an amused smile, and when I finally chance a look her way, her smug expression has my smile fading.

Caught. Yet again. I need to stop making an ass of myself.

"I was talking to our coaches about your yoga class," Gavin says to Everleigh, his voice casual.

Her eyes go wide. "Why would you do that?"

"I was telling them how much it helps all of us and that you're a certified yoga instructor and all that. And then I suggested you should come to our practices sometime and lead everyone through a quick session. Like a warm-up before we go out on the field," Gavin explains.

"Oh, I don't know . . ."

"They said they were interested. And they'd even pay you," Gav tacks on.

Everleigh's eyes light up with interest. She's always looking for a way to make money. "Really? They'd pay me?"

"They said they might if it seems to work out for us. You want to come in Monday before practice starts and talk to the coaching staff? They'd love to hear what you have to say."

"I definitely would." She nods eagerly.

"How exciting! If you need an assistant, I'm your girl." Sienna glances over at Gavin, her gaze full of longing. "I'd love to help you."

Everleigh and I share a look, something passing between us. Like we both know who Sienna is stuck on and that particular person is still somehow clueless about it.

Freaking Gavin. Sometimes he's a dumbass when it comes to women.

Just like I am.

"I don't know if they'll let me have an assistant, but I'll definitely keep your offer under consideration," Everleigh says, nibbling on her lower lip. "I could only come to practice Monday and Wednesday. I have school on Tuesday and Thursday, and I end up working most Friday afternoons."

"I don't think that's a problem." Gavin's gaze locks with mine. "What do you think, Nico?"

"Me?" I shrug. "Not a bad idea."

"You'll all need yoga mats," Everleigh suggests, her brows drawing together. "Maybe I should write up some sort of proposal for your coaches on what I could provide."

"That would be a great idea." Gavin grins at both women, and they get a little too bright eyed at the sight of it. He may not know much about love or relationships, but he's pretty good at putting on the charm.

Me, though?

I'm better.

Chapter Twenty-Four

Everleigh

I eventually walk away from Gavin and Nico, my head spinning from Gavin's offer to meet about giving yoga lessons to the team.

And then there's the fact that when that much testosterone is aimed directly at me, I get a little flustered. It becomes difficult to think clearly. I'm having a difficult enough time already trying to keep my thoughts from straying to other . . . things.

Like Nico.

He looks extra appealing tonight wearing a pair of jeans and a Dolphins hoodie. That's it. The outfit is truly nothing special, but the fact that it's him wearing it?

Beyond gorgeous.

Meaning I have a problem.

That secret look we shared when Sienna was going on about being my assistant while staring at Gavin was unexpected. My stomach flipped the longer Nico stared into my eyes, and I finally had to look away first.

I told myself he didn't matter, but I was lying. I still have a massive crush on Nico, made worse by our kissing session in the library. I think he's still into me as well, which is just . . . mind blowing. Even if we were to act on our impulses, this would go absolutely nowhere.

That's what I need to keep reminding myself.

I escaped to the backyard just to avoid a run-in with Portia, and I sort of forgot that she was even here when the guys started talking to me. But I spot her again now, smiling and flirting with, of all people, Frank, who seems totally into her. Is she the one he's been preoccupied with lately? This week he's left the house late at night twice but always returns before the sun rises.

Watching them standing by the sliding glass door and the way Portia keeps touching his chest while he watches her with giant moon eyes, I sense she is definitely the one he's been sneaking out and seeing. Which makes me worry that . . .

She's up to no good.

"What the hell is she doing here?"

I stiffen at the sound of Nico's familiar voice coming from directly behind me. I can feel the warmth of his body seeping into mine, and for a minute there, it's like I can't move. I'm enjoying his warmth way too much.

"I forgot to warn you," I admit, not looking at him.

He steps even closer, if that's possible, his chest brushing my back, his mouth at my ear. "Forgot to warn me what? That she's at the party?"

I nod, trembling at his closeness. At the sound of his deep chuckle, his warm breath touching my neck. "I saw her arrive earlier. That's why I came outside."

"I don't blame you. I would've run from her too." He pauses, and I wonder what he's thinking. "Are you cold?"

He must see me—or feel me—shivering. "A little."

It's a lie. I'm warm from the alcohol and him. The only reason I'm trembling is from him standing so deliciously close to me.

"You should come stand by the fire."

"I'll be fine." I offer him a weak smile.

"Want to wear my hoodie?" I turn at the same time he makes the offer, my mouth dropping open when he starts to take it off. He lifts the hem, taking his shirt with it, exposing the perfection that is his muscled abdomen, and I immediately bat at his hands, trying to stop him. My fingers accidentally brush his abs, and oh my God, they're rock hard.

My face is on absolute fire.

"I don't want to take it from you, but thank you. I'm fine," I reassure him. He keeps his sweatshirt on, frowning at me. "Really."

His gaze falls to my chest, blatantly checking me out, and I swear to God I can feel my nipples growing tighter. "You look pretty cold to me."

"Stop," I chastise, my voice soft. "I'm going inside."

I'm about to turn on my heel and walk away from him, totally embarrassed by what he said, but he grabs my hand, preventing me from leaving. I angle my head in his direction to find a contrite expression on his handsome face.

"Sorry." He swallows hard. "I just . . . it was obvious."

My cheeks are still warm, and I'm sure I am red in the face. "It's okay."

"Come on." He tugs me closer, letting go of my hand only to slide his arm around my shoulders. "Let's go inside."

I briskly walk ahead of him, his arm falling away from me, but I don't look back. I can feel him looming behind me, hear him greet people as we walk past them, and all I can do is smile because most of them are complete strangers to me.

What's it like to have so many people know who you are? To adore you for what you do out on the field? He's like a celebrity on this campus. What did Sienna call them?

The kings of the campus.

That's the perfect description.

We're approaching the back sliding door when I realize Frank and Portia are still standing there, and she's so very obviously wrapped around him, her hands everywhere. I wish I could tell him that she's just using him. But I can't. I don't want to hurt his feelings.

I try to think positive. Maybe she's not using Frank at all. Maybe she actually likes him. He's nice. He's good looking. He's a football player, which seems to be her type. And he'll do anything for the woman he falls for . . .

"Oh, hey, Nico," Portia says, her voice way too casual, her fingers curling around the waistband of Frank's jeans. "Still with her, I see."

The disdain dripping from her tone makes me tense up.

The way Nico oh-so-casually slings his arm around my shoulders yet again doesn't help.

"What are you doing with Dollar?" he asks Portia, his voice edged with hostility.

"What does it look like?" She focuses all her attention on Frank, tipping her head back like she's waiting for a kiss while Frank just appears confused.

The pout that forms on Portia's face when Frank doesn't do what she wants almost makes me laugh. But the heavy weight of Nico's arm is a reminder that I need to act like I'm . . . what?

His *girlfriend*?

That thought almost has me laughing as well.

"Uh, Nico . . . ," Frank starts, and I'm sure he's remembering that his friend, teammate, and roommate used to be with Portia. "It's not what you think."

"It's exactly what you think." Portia steps in front of Frank and grabs his arms, wrapping them around her, settling her hands over his. "We're together."

"We are?" Portia jabs her elbow into Frank's ribs, and he coughs. "I mean, we are."

I can feel Nico tense beside me, and I wonder if that bothers him, or if he misses Portia.

I mean, look at her. She's gorgeous. And she knows it. The helpless look on Frank's face is downright comical. I'm sure he's stunned that this beautiful woman wants to be with him when the poor guy is always chasing some girl.

"It's cool, Dollar. You can have her." His arm tightens around my shoulder, and Frank notices, his gaze zeroing in on Nico's fingers skimming my upper arm.

Uh-oh.

"What, so you two are together?" Frank sounds incredulous.

"Frank, it's not—" I start, but Nico cuts me off.

"We're giving it a shot. Seeing where this might take us. Right, Ever?" He gives me a little shake, gazing down at me, and I glance up at him, noticing the faint pleading in his eyes.

Go along with this. Please.

"R-right. That's wh-what we're d-doing." I'm stuttering like an idiot, and the last thing I want is to see Frank's reaction.

I'm sure he's hurt. Angry. He has every right to feel that way too.

Portia laughs. "Sounds like the two of you are sooooo confident about your relationship. Good luck with that."

The last sentence is directed at me, and I'm suddenly fuming.

"We're very confident," I tell her, my voice firm, my gaze still on Nico, who's now glaring at Portia. "It just happened so quickly and . . . unexpectedly."

"Right." Nico glances down at me again, and I rise on tiptoe, resting my hand on the solid wall that is his chest right before I do something I've imagined doing countless times since the bathroom incident.

I press my lips to his.

A surprised huff of breath escapes him the moment our mouths connect, and I remain there, trying to kiss his immobile lips.

But it lasts only for a second. Next thing I know, his hand is cupping the back of my head, and he's returning the kiss. Over and over, his lips eventually parting mine.

His tongue slipping inside for a quick, teasing lick.

I end the kiss the moment our tongues touch, taking a stumbling step backward, but he doesn't let me go. He's got me firmly pinned in place against him, and all I can do is stare up at his gorgeous face. Note the concern I see in his gaze, the faint confusion. His brows are drawn together, and the jovial smile that's always on his face is gone.

I swallow hard.

So does he.

"Seriously, Nico?" Portia screeches, pushing Frank's arms away from her as she stomps toward us. "You're such an asshole!"

Feels like the entire backyard goes quiet at her screaming, and it startles both of us into action. Somehow my hand ends up in his yet again, and he's dragging me into the house, Portia hot on our heels.

"You're such a fucking piece of shit, Nico! Leaving me like you did, and for what? This girl? She doesn't even look good in that stupid gold dress!" Portia is shouting at us as she follows us through the house, causing a scene, but Nico doesn't say a word.

Neither do I. I just let him lead me toward the short hallway, a gasp escaping me when he yanks me into his bedroom and slams the door in front of Portia, cutting her off from entering the room with us.

He turns the lock just as she starts pounding on the door, making it rattle. "Let me in, you chickenshit! We need to talk!"

"Go away, Portia," he calls to her. "There's nothing left for us to discuss. We ended it months ago."

"I wasn't ready! You never gave me a chance! You don't give anyone a chance." More pounding on the door until I hear Cooper's steady, deep voice sounding from the other side.

"Hey, Portia. Calm the fuck down, or I'm going to have to kick you out."

"Just try it, asshole! I have every right to be here."

"Jesus." Nico glances over at me, shaking his head. "She's unhinged."

"She's really mad," I agree, though it feels more like an understatement, describing her that way.

Nico is tapping away at his phone, and I wonder who he's texting.

"Come on, babe. Let's go get you something to drink." Now I hear Frank talking to her, trying to calm her down, and all I can think is *This poor dude.*

"Do not call me babe!" she shrieks in response, followed by more banging on the door.

Nico shakes his head. "He doesn't know what he's getting into."

Most likely she's going to trick him into thinking that she cares and hurt him in the end. But if I were to warn him about Portia? He wouldn't listen. He's probably mad at me and Nico, thinking we started some sort of secret relationship right under his nose, which wasn't what happened.

How can I tell him that? And what am I going to do right now, stuck in Nico's bedroom while his ex is trying to bang down the door?

Talk about ruining my Saturday night.

Chapter Twenty-Five

NICO

I'm constantly texting Coop, practically begging him to get rid of Portia and kick her out of our house for good. He's trying, but he also feels like a jackass telling her to leave. Frank is defending her to Coop, and he feels caught in the middle. I get it.

But she's relentless and won't leave us alone. She's still banging on my bedroom door every few minutes, screeching my name. Doesn't matter that Coop is trying to entice her with alcohol. She won't even listen to Dollar as he tries to sweet-talk her into leaving with him.

She's lost it. More like she lost it at seeing Everleigh kiss me, which, not gonna lie, was surprising.

And pretty fucking good once I took over.

It was a bold move on Everleigh's part, and while I was enjoying it, I felt kind of bad when we kissed in front of Portia and Dollar. I'm sure he's hurt, believing we were hooking up behind his back.

That makes me feel like shit. I love giving Frank a lot of crap, and yeah, he bugs me sometimes, but he's a good dude. A good friend.

Now he probably thinks I'm a terrible friend. At the very least, a big ol' liar. That sucks. I don't want whatever's happening between us to mess with the team dynamics. Right now, everything's going good for all of us. I can't risk an argument with Dollar throwing the team off-balance.

Sliding out of the chat with Coop, I send Dollar a quick text.

Me: We need to talk.

I wait for his response, which comes sooner than I thought.

Dollar$: There's nothing to talk about. You two make a great couple. Hope you're happy with her.

He says nothing else.

"Shit," I mutter, shoving my phone into my jeans pocket.

"What's wrong?"

I turn to face Everleigh. She looks stressed the fuck out, and I feel terrible for dragging her into this. Even if she was a willing participant with that kiss.

My mind drifts to that too-quick moment. How soft her lips were. How sweet she tasted. Just like I remembered. I would've kept it going on longer, but she ended it first.

It's still my fault that we're locked away in my bedroom.

"Dollar is mad at me," I tell her, deciding to be honest.

"He's probably mad at me too," she says with a sigh, collapsing on the edge of my bed. "He looked so hurt when he thought we were together."

"Now everyone probably thinks we're together," I say, curious to see her reaction.

"I'm sure they find that hard to believe," she retorts, wrapping her arms around her middle like she's cold.

Frustrated, I tear off my hoodie and hand it over to her. "Put this on," I demand.

She takes it from me and slips it on without protest, rising to her feet to let the hoodie drop to practically her knees. It's huge on her, covering her entire dress, and honestly? I'm relieved.

Seeing her in that dress has me thinking all sorts of thoughts, none of them productive. All of them dirty. Touching her earlier, kissing her—that didn't help.

What the hell are we doing, anyway? The constant back and forth is confusing.

"Why would you say that?" I ask when I realize I haven't responded to her. "Is it so hard to believe that you'd want to be with me?"

She barks out a laugh, covering her mouth immediately, but that doesn't stifle the sound. "Are you for real right now? More like they're wondering what *you* are doing with *me*."

"No one would wonder that," I say.

"She would." Everleigh waves a hand toward the door.

"Portia doesn't count. She's just jealous."

"You know she's using Frank to get back at you." Everleigh sounds sad.

"Yeah. She probably is." I run my fingers through my hair, pushing it away from my face. "I wanted to explain to him what's going on, but he's not in the mood to talk to me right now."

I'm positive he's angry with me, but shit. It was automatic, pretending that Everleigh is with me. We tried to sell that to Portia already, and we need to stay consistent.

I glance toward the door, realizing it's become fairly quiet out there, and I go to it, pressing my ear against the wood.

"I think she's gone," I whisper to Everleigh.

"I'm not gone!" Portia screams, making me leap away from the door, anger filling me all over again.

"This woman is making my life a living hell." I walk past Everleigh and throw back the thick comforter on my bed, kicking off my shoes before I climb beneath the sheets and jerk them back over me, covering my lower half.

"What are you doing?" Everleigh asks, her blue eyes extra wide.

"You going to hang out at my door all night, Portia? Huh? Do you want to hear us having sex? Is that what you're waiting for?" I'm yelling. Goading her. "I'll make her moan extra loud just for you!"

I don't give a fuck about her feelings anymore. She's pushed me right over the edge.

"Nico," Everleigh whisper-hisses at me, but I ignore her.

"Fuck you, Nico!" Portia screams as she begins pounding on the door yet again.

My phone buzzes with a text.

Coop: For the love of God, stop egging her on.

Me: She won't leave me alone so I'm giving her exactly what she wants.

Coop: No, you're pissed and you're being a complete douche. Knock it off. Stay quiet and she'll leave you alone.

Damn it. I know he's right, but I'm too fired up to take his advice. I toss my phone onto the nightstand, folding my arms beneath my head as I lie there against the pillows that are propped against my headboard. I decide to make myself comfortable because it looks like I'm not going anywhere else this evening.

Stuck in my bedroom with Ever isn't such a hardship, is it? I guess it is when I've got my ex yelling at us from outside a locked door.

And Portia is still yelling. Calling me every creative name she can think of. I can hear Frank trying to calm her down, but she won't listen to him. She's pounding on the door. Think she might've even kicked it at one point.

"If you dent my door, you're paying for it!" I yell at her just to be an asshole.

My phone buzzes, but I ignore it. Probably another text from Coop telling me to stop.

Here's my problem. I've never liked being told what to do. Since I was a kid, I've constantly rebelled against authority. Made my parents nuts, but someone trying to boss me around and tell me how I should act or feel?

It never sits right with me.

Yeah, the coaching staff can get on our asses and demand we do something, but it's always for the betterment of the team. That I don't mind. That's what being a coach is all about.

That's what being on a team is all about too. We're in it together, just like I told Gavin earlier. Sometimes I'm a selfish bastard, but very rarely am I selfish when it comes to football. Catching the ball and running it into the end zone is enough of a glory moment for me to get my accolades in.

But this woman I went out with—damn, I can't even call it that; more like we fucked around for a couple of weeks, tops—is now determined to make my life a living hell, and I don't get why. It's not like we had a solid connection. Not yet. And while I hated how bossy she was all the damn time—I don't like being told what to do—I know I'm the one who ruined everything between us, not that I regret it. I didn't treat her the best, though, which looking back on it, was pretty awful on my part.

I'm not a great guy, especially when it comes to women. I screw up all the time. I'm careless. Thoughtless. I've had a few women even tell me I'm heartless.

Maybe they're right. I don't know. I'm thinking after tonight, I need to reassess my behavior and start treating women with a little more respect. Because this situation is god awful.

"You must've really upset her." I glance up to find Everleigh standing at the foot of the bed, adorable in my hoodie as she twists her hands together. Her teeth are sunk into her lower lip, and she seems hella stressed out.

"I did." I decide to be honest. "When we were . . . seeing each other, I treated her like garbage."

"Yikes." Her brows shoot up. I think I surprised her with my honesty. "Now I guess she's getting you back?"

"Apparently. I think seeing us together triggered her." I drop my arms and cross them in front of me. "I suppose I deserve this."

"Well, maybe. Though no one deserves to be harassed." She offers me a sympathetic smile. "I guess we're stuck in here for a while, huh."

"Guess so." I shrug.

"What should we do to occupy our time?" She looks around my room, and I wonder what she thinks. I'm not a slob like Cooper, thank God. That guy's room is always a mess. I don't know how he's able to find anything ever.

"Got any suggestions?" I ask, my mind overflowing with all sorts of ideas. None of them involving us wearing clothes.

Every one of them dirty.

Everleigh slowly shakes her head. "Scroll on our phones and wait it out, I suppose."

"Is that what you want to do?"

"I don't know what I want to do." She throws her arms up in the air, the hoodie rising, flashing her slender thighs at me. "I was having a good night until *she* ruined everything. I don't even think I have a buzz anymore."

"Same." I lean over and check the bottom drawer of my nightstand. I pull out a bottle of mezcal I hid in there from the last time we had a party over the summer and I didn't want anyone drinking it. "We can continue the party with this if you want."

Her eyes light up at first sight of the bottle. "Seriously?"

She sounds amused, and I smile, the tension easing inside me a little. "Seriously. Come here." I pat the other side of the bed, indicating I want her to sit next to me.

Maybe even slip under the covers with me.

Whatever she's comfortable doing. I'm not about to push myself on her, especially after we promised each other we were going to keep this friendly.

"You sure that's a good idea?" One delicate brow arches, and her lips curve into a faint smile. "You can't try anything funny."

"Define *funny*."

A tiny laugh escapes her, and she shakes her head. "You know what I mean."

"Come on." I pat the empty spot beside me again. "Let's settle in, share some mezcal, and relax. Hopefully by the time we polish off this bottle, Portia will finally get the hint and leave us alone. What do you say?"

Chapter Twenty-Six

EVERLEIGH

What Nico is suggesting is dangerous. I know it is. I should say no and leave—though technically I can't because I'm not about to walk out of this room knowing Portia is lingering on the other side of the door.

She might, I don't know, attack me or something.

My gaze goes to Nico, who's waiting for me, an expectant smile on his face. His fingers are wrapped tightly around the bottle of mezcal, which is sitting in his lap. Practically nestled against his junk.

I think about that. His junk. What he might look like naked. I've not seen a lot of naked men in real life. In fact, I've only seen one, and that was my ex, because Brad is the only guy I've had sex with. While it was decent at first and I believed we were madly in love, eventually the excitement seemed to fade, and by the end of our relationship, we were just going through the motions. He never seemed to care if I had an orgasm or not. He rarely went down on me, so I decided to be a petty bitch and never give him a blow job.

Yeah. We were in such a healthy relationship, huh?

My gaze roams over Nico, taking every bit of him in. The faded gray T-shirt he's wearing says *Property of Santa Mira Dolphins* on the front, the school mascot in the dead center. It's a little tight on him, accentuating the sheer size of his chest and shoulders and upper arms, and I think of Brad. How slender he was. We probably weighed the same, or maybe he was just a little more. I don't know. Not like we were weighing each other and sharing our numbers.

I wonder what it's like, being with a man who's so . . .

Large.

The smile on Nico's face slowly fades, and he sits up straighter, setting the bottle on his nightstand before his gaze returns to mine. "If you want to leave, I get it."

Does he, though? He's not in my head, so he has no idea what I'm thinking, but I'd guess he's making assumptions.

"I want a drink of that if you're willing to share it." I incline my head toward the bottle sitting on his nightstand.

"You know I'm down. I already made the offer." His smile is back, dazzling in its brightness, and I wonder how anyone can resist it. No wonder Portia is pounding on his door. She probably misses this: his easygoing yet somehow effortlessly sexy demeanor.

The man is magnetic and he knows it. I made a fool of myself already by kissing him in front of the entire party. I mean, he definitely kissed me back, but was that only because I attached my lips to his? Or because he was merely playing along since he already told Portia that we were together? Was he trying to make the kiss appear convincing?

Well, he definitely did that. At least to me.

Realizing that he's waiting for me, I approach the bed, unsure how to go about this. The closer I get to him, the more I can smell him, and his scent is heavenly. Like spicy, sexy, clean man skin.

Okay, I need to get a grip. I am losing it over here while he's just being a nice guy. Though it *is* his fault we have to suffer through this moment together, being locked up in his room. He'd probably rather be anywhere else but here.

I can hear the party raging on both in our house and out in the backyard. There's lots of laughter, and loud music is playing, the bass a throbbing beat that rattles the walls. I can only imagine all the incredibly drunk people stumbling around, having the time of their lives. Couples are hooking up. Some are probably leaving to go hook up.

Hmm. There will be no hooking up between us tonight. We're just roommates stuck together. I need to remember that. Treat him like a friend, like we promised each other only a few nights ago. This is no big deal.

Not a big deal at all.

Taking a deep breath, I sit on the edge of the bed, leaning against the stack of pillows and stretching my legs out. His hoodie covers me almost to my knees, but when I sit, the hem rides up, exposing my legs. His gaze flickers there for a moment, lingering on my thighs before he looks away to grab the bottle of alcohol.

I tug the covers up into my lap, watching as he uncaps the bottle and takes a swig from it. His lips are still wet once he swallows before offering the bottle to me, and I take it from him with a murmured "thank you," our fingers grazing.

That little finger graze sends a cascade of tingles all over my body.

I lift the bottle to my lips and take a tentative drink, wincing once I swallow the alcohol down. "Oh my God."

He chuckles. "You can't drink it like that. You just have to chug it."

"I don't know—"

"Watch me." He swipes the bottle from my hand and takes another big swig. "Do it like that."

I take the bottle from him and try again, reminding myself I need to just go for it. Tipping my head back, I take a couple of long swallows, choking it down before I thrust the bottle back at him, gasping.

"That a girl," he praises, sounding pleased.

I sit up a little straighter at his words, watching as he takes another, even longer pull from the bottle. I stare in fascination at the way the strong column of his throat moves when he swallows. How he licks his lips when he's finished, like he wants to catch every last drop. I'm so caught up in watching him, I don't even realize he's offering the bottle to me until he's saying my name.

"Everleigh. It's your turn."

I take the bottle from him without comment and drink. It's becoming easier now, and I savor the warm sensation of the alcohol flowing through my veins. "It's kind of awful."

"Yet you keep drinking it." He sounds amused.

"My goal tonight was to get trashed," I admit.

Chuckling, he drinks from the bottle, his gaze stuck on mine. "Same." He hesitates. "You trying to forget something?"

I blink at him, caught off guard by his question. "What do you mean?"

He shrugs. "People drink sometimes to forget what's going on in their lives. Or they're trying to forget—someone."

"I'm not trying to forget anyone," I say, my voice soft.

Nico offers me the bottle, and I take it yet again, drinking from it like he just did. We're starting to run out, so I guess we should pace ourselves. "Lucky you."

His comment leaves me confused. "What do you mean by that?"

His expression actually turns bashful, and he slowly shakes his head, averting his gaze. "Never mind."

"Never mind?" I turn and set the bottle on the nightstand on my side—I'm impressed that he has one on either side of the bed—and face him once again. "You can't just say never mind after you drop a bomb like that."

He chuckles. "It wasn't a bomb."

"Sort of felt like one."

"It definitely wasn't one." He waves a hand. "It was nothing at all. Hand me the booze."

"Not until you tell me what you were referring to. Or more like *who* you were referring to."

"It was no one."

I study him for a moment. The way he won't make eye contact is so telling, though I shouldn't keep pushing him. I probably don't want to know who he's referring to, and besides, it's none of my business. By pushing him, I'm probably just asking to get my feelings hurt. He's probably crushing on some new gorgeous girl after I rejected him, and I'm just the annoying roommate he's stuck with and now getting drunk with.

Because that is definitely happening, at least for me. The getting-drunk part. Yep. YEP. Yeppers.

Wow, that didn't take long.

"Nico . . ." I draw his name out, emphasis on the *o*.

"Ever . . ." He clamps his lips shut. "Do you like being called Ever or do you prefer Everleigh?"

"Ever is fine." I shrug. I noticed that he shortened it earlier, and I liked it. He's the only one of my roommates who insists on calling me by my full name most of the time. Even Coop calls me Ever sometimes. "Everleigh is a lot."

"It's a pretty name."

My insides light up at the compliment, and I tell myself to knock it off. "It's definitely different. That was my mother's goal."

"You get along with your mom?"

I wince. "It's kind of a touchy subject."

"Oh." He nods. "Sorry."

"Don't think you're off the hook, though." When he frowns, I explain myself. "You never confessed who you're trying to forget."

Why do I keep pushing again? Because deep down, I hope he's talking about . . .

Me.

"My economics professor." He says it with such a straight face, I almost believe him.

Almost.

"You're a liar." I grab the pillow from behind me and try to toss it at his head, but it's heavy, and he blocks me with his hand, snatching it from my grasp. "You're also really fast."

"I do this out on the football field every single day. Don't test me." He's grinning. "I will win every time."

"So cocky."

"You don't know the half of it." His voice is a sexy drawl, and from the way my body goes on high alert, I'm here for it.

I grab the other pillow behind me and sit up, clutching it close to my chest. He watches me with a wary gaze, completely onto me. "You never know. I might catch you when you're not paying attention."

"Just try it," he taunts like the arrogant football player he is. "Like I said, I will beat you every time."

"You're drunk. Your reflexes might be slower."

"Not that slow. And I'm not that drunk."

I smile at him, realizing that I am indeed that drunk. "I might be."

The side of his mouth kicks up in a faint smile. "I can tell."

I'm frowning. "How can you tell?"

"Your body is doing this . . . swaying thing." He chuckles, and he must see the flash of panic on my face. "Don't get freaked out. I think it's cute."

He thinks it's cute? Oh, come on.

"You don't see me like that." I tilt my chin up with a sniff, steeling myself for his agreement. "I'm just your roommate, remember? We made a deal."

"Oh, I remember." Nico's gaze never wavers from mine as he brings the bottle to his lips and takes a long swallow, nearly finishing it off. "You think I don't notice you?"

"Of course you don't," I retort, waggling my fingers at him. "Gimme the bottle."

Without hesitation he hands it over, and I'm the one who polishes off the mezcal, setting the empty bottle back on the nightstand while smacking my lips and making a satisfied *ahhh* sound.

"There goes our party," he murmurs, which for whatever reason makes me laugh.

"I think our party ended when Portia started screaming at us," I tell him.

"True." His expression turns somber. "Sorry about that. I didn't know she'd lose it like she did."

"It's okay." I shrug. "And it's not your fault."

"It kind of is." He studies me for a moment, his lips parting and then closing. Like he was about to say something but changed his mind.

I wish I knew what he was going to say.

"You're pretty cool, Ever," he eventually murmurs, his gaze dropping to my mouth. "Going along with my bullshit story for Portia."

"Not sure if she believes it." I roll my eyes, trying to lighten the moment, but the air suddenly feels heavy around us. Humming with invisible energy, as if something major is about to happen.

"Don't forget that you kissed me. And I think it was pretty convincing." His gaze is still on my lips.

Mine is on his.

"You kissed me back," I whisper, swallowing hard. I can feel my body swaying, just like he pointed out to me, and I try to rein myself in so I don't fall into his lap. "That probably helped."

He chuckles. "It definitely helped."

We're quiet for a moment, and I close my eyes, breathing deep. When I open them again, I find he's still watching me, his brows drawn together and a concerned look on his face. "You okay?"

"Head spinning a little." Not really, but what can I tell him? That he overwhelms me in the best way, and I'm trying to remind myself that this is nothing? Just two roommates getting a little drunk on a Saturday night. Nothing more.

Nothing less.

"Too much alcohol?"

"Not really." Oops, that was a too-honest answer.

His gaze turns knowing. Does he realize he's the one who's making my head spin? His delicious scent, his stupidly handsome face, me engulfed in his hoodie, sitting on his bed, alone in his room, a little buzzed from sharing a bottle with him?

"I have a suggestion."

"What is it?" I ask warily.

"I think we should make out."

Chapter Twenty-Seven

EVERLEIGH

Wait a second.

Did I hear him correctly? Did Nico Valente just say he wants to make out?

With me?

It's like I'm on a ten-second delay, his words slowly sinking into my brain and taking a moment for me to absorb. "You're kidding."

His face switches into an expressionless mask. "If you don't want to, it's cool. Just a suggestion."

His voice is way too casual, which has me suspicious.

"It's not that I don't want to . . ." I clamp my lips shut, wondering where I'm going with this. On the one hand, I would love to make out with Nico. That one kiss in front of Portia wasn't enough. It was like a tempting little snack before the actual feast.

While we feasted on each other a few nights ago, that wasn't enough either. It's like the more we kiss, the more I want it.

Does he feel the same way?

Casually kissing my roommate with tongues involved is not something I thought I would do. How am I going to feel after tonight's proposed make-out session? Will I move on with my life, or will I crave more?

Knowing me, I'm guessing it'll be the latter.

"I get it. You've already told me you don't want to do this. That I'm not your type."

Why does he sound so . . . defeated?

He makes no sense.

I peer up at him, swaying backward until I basically collapse against his headboard, nearly knocking my head on it. He lunges for me a little too late—see, I knew his reflexes would become slower from the alcohol—and his hand comes around to cup the back of my head, lifting me away from the headboard.

"You okay?" He's holding me like I'm some sort of Disney princess laid out on his bed. Hovering above me like my very own Prince Charming. "Did you hurt yourself?"

"No," I whisper, my gaze resting yet again on his perfectly shaped lips.

They're nice lips. The bottom one is fuller than the top, and when he smiles—like he's doing at me right now—all my brain cells seem to scatter like leaves in the wind. Leaving me dumbstruck.

Breathless.

"You're definitely not my type," I admit.

The smile fades. "Right. You've already mentioned that."

"If you're having an insecure moment right now, please let me reassure you that I only say you're not my type because you're just—you." I lift my hand, flicking my fingers at the perfection that is his face. "And I'm me."

"What do you mean by that?" He sounds even more confused.

"You could have anyone here tonight. Every woman at this party would fall at your feet," I tell him, savoring the way he's still cradling me in his arms.

"Except for the one that I want."

We stare at each other, and I swear I'm not even breathing. Not when his gaze drops to my lips. Not when his head starts to descend . . .

And definitely not when his lips touch mine.

A spark ignites between us at first contact, and I feel his exhale all the way down to my soul. It brings me back to life, has me sitting up, swiveling in his lap until his back is against the headboard and I'm straddling him. My hands are in his hair, my fingers twisted in the dark, silky strands, my mouth still attached to his.

We're kissing. Our mouths connecting. Parting. Reconnecting. With every pass, my lips open more and more, until our tongues brush against each other. Tentatively seeking. Circling. Tangling.

Tingles sweep over my skin when he slips his hands beneath his hoodie I'm still wearing. They slide upward, running over the stretchy fabric of my dress until they're touching the bare skin of my back, skimming along my spine. Making me shiver.

Making me moan.

The sound startles me. Brad didn't make me moan, especially not at the end of our relationship. Did we kiss much? If we did, it would always lead to mostly boring sex that never lasted long.

Now that I'm out of one, I realize being in a relationship is hard work. Why would I want another one again?

That's right. I don't.

All thoughts of relationships evaporate the longer Nico and I kiss. It's like we can't get enough of each other. We're lost in each other's taste, the kiss going deeper. Lasting longer. I scoot closer to him, drawn to all that heat and muscle, and when I nudge against what is unmistakably his erection, I freeze, breaking away from his still-seeking lips.

"Maybe we shouldn't take this any further," I whisper, my breaths coming as fast as my heartbeat.

"Further like how?" His voice is a deep, rough rumble that has my stomach doing backflips.

"Nothing but kissing."

He presses his forehead to mine, the sound of his ragged exhale making my insides tremble. "You're serious."

I nod, my fingers raking through his hair. God, it's soft and so thick. The murmur of approval he gives when I do it again has my heart fluttering. "You're the one who said you just wanted to make out."

"I'm an idiot." He kisses my cheek. Soft, sweet little kisses he trails across the side of my face until his mouth is at my ear. "How drunk are you?"

My answer is immediate. "Not too drunk for this."

"You sure?" He pulls away slightly to stare into my eyes.

I nod. "I want this."

I've never wanted anything more in my life.

His smile is slow. Devastatingly sexy. "Oh yeah?"

"Mm-hmm." I suck in a breath when he presses his face into my neck again, his warm lips tickling against my skin.

"How about I kiss you . . ." He shifts up, nibbling on my earlobe. "Everywhere."

I feel like I'm in freefall at his words, and I grip him closer. He turns his head, our lips now close enough that we could be kissing, but I need answers first. "Like where?"

He's smiling again. Probably because I want details. "Where do you want me to kiss you? Your neck?"

Before I can respond, Nico dips his head, pressing his hot mouth to the side of my neck. He kisses and licks me there, making me gasp. "You like that?"

I can't answer because my voice has disappeared, but yes.

I love it.

His fingers tug on the front of my hoodie—his hoodie—pulling it down so he can drop a kiss on my collarbone. "We need to get rid of this."

Without a word I lift my arms, and he tugs the sweatshirt off, exposing me. My skin is covered in goose bumps, and the skirt of my dress is hiked up almost to my hips.

Reminding me that I have no panties on.

He kisses a fiery path across my bare shoulder. Then the other one. He gently nudges the strap of my dress down, and it falls to my upper arm, exposing more of my chest. I close my eyes, savoring the feel of his mouth on my skin, trying to remind myself that this isn't the move. I'm only going to end up wanting more, and that will only lead us to trouble.

But it's like all logical thought has been erased from my brain upon the first touch of his lips. I just want more.

This is looking to be the best make-out session I've ever had.

His hand drops to my rib cage, resting just under my right breast, and I suck in a breath, my core aching with anticipation. He slowly sweeps his thumb across my breast. My nipple.

I melt into him, pressing myself against his erection, and he rears his head back. I can feel him staring at me, and I slowly open my eyes to find his dark gaze locked with mine.

"You're not wearing panties."

"I know," I whisper.

The smile that appears on his wickedly handsome face is filthy, and he shifts his hand so it's fully covering my breast. "You're a bad girl, Ever."

I'm laughing. Is it the alcohol? The tone of his voice? The way his fingers gently massage my breast while I'm basically grinding on his dick? "No one has ever called me a bad girl in my life."

"You're the one who didn't wear panties." He presses his face against my neck, seeming to breathe me in.

"I didn't want weird lines under my dress," I admit, my hands sinking into the hair at the back of his head.

It's like I can't get enough of it. Enough of him.

Chuckling, he slides his hand down, gently cupping my rib cage before dropping to my waist. My hip. His mouth finds mine once again, and I kiss him back with everything I have, tugging on his hair. Desperate to get closer. I want him to consume me.

I want to consume him.

His hand falls to my thigh, resting there as our tongues twist, his fingers drawing lightly back and forth. Teasing me. Driving me out of my mind with anticipation.

"Your skin is so soft," he whispers against my lips, and everything inside me clenches tight. My head is spinning, though I'm not that drunk. It's from Nico's touch. His mouth. His teasing fingers and soul-stealing kisses.

All thoughts of this being a mistake have fled my brain. I can only focus on the way his fingers play with the hem of my dress, perilously close to where I want them the most. And when those fingers slip beneath my dress and trace the spot where my pelvis connects with my thigh, a shuddery sigh escapes me—it's not a place where I'm touched much beyond by my own hand.

"I can smell you," he murmurs once he's ended our kiss, his gaze dropping to the spot where he's touching me. "We probably shouldn't do this."

If he stops touching me, I'll scream like Portia did. My entire being is focused on the one place on my body where his fingers are. I cannot imagine him stopping, or what I might do if he does.

"Do you want me to stop, Ever?"

Swallowing hard, I slowly shake my head. "Please."

It's the only word that I can get out.

"Please what?" His fingers trace along the top of my thigh, getting closer. "Please stop? Please don't ever quit doing what you're doing?"

"The last one," I manage to say, a whimper leaving me when his fingers brush the front of me, tangling in my pubic hair. I used to keep it waxed, but Brad didn't really care, so what was the point?

I wonder if Sienna knows of a good wax technician.

His fingers slip lower, dipping inside, touching me lightly. I wind my arms around his neck and hold on, afraid I might melt into a puddle if I don't have something to grip while he plays with me.

And oh, how he plays with me.

He swirls a slow circle around my clit with his index finger before dipping lower, sliding back and forth, searching every part of me while his mouth finds mine. He kisses me fiercely, his touch remaining gentle yet insistent between my thighs, and when he slips a finger inside me, I cry out against his lips. Wanting more.

Needing more.

"You like that?" His voice is pure sin, and I can't respond. All I can do is hum my approval, and he adds another finger. "Fuck, you're tight."

No one has ever said those words to me, but every time Nico so much as makes a sound, I swear I get wetter. His fingers are probably drenched, and maybe in another lifetime I'd care.

But not now.

His mouth never leaves mine as he continues to fuck me with his fingers. I move with him, lifting my hips, needing him deeper. Moaning when he presses his thumb against my clit and rubs it. Everything inside me focuses on that one spot where his hand is so busy, his thrusting fingers filling me. Teasing me. I rub against him shamelessly, panting against his lips when the sensations become too overwhelming and I can't concentrate on anything else.

Just this.

Just him.

"You're close," he murmurs, and I love that he can tell. That he's paying attention. Listening and watching for my cues.

My nod is frantic, and I try to spread my legs wider, essentially riding his hand.

"Shhh." His fingers go still, though he leaves them inside me. I wait there, hanging on the edge of orgasm, my entire body trembling. Aching for release. "Don't move."

I do as he says, waiting. Breathless. Anxious. He removes his fingers from my body, both hands going to my hips, and the next thing I know, I'm falling backward onto the mattress, my head at the bottom of it, and Nico's head . . .

Right between my legs.

His mouth hovers over my pussy, his breath wafting across my sensitive skin, just before he dips down and licks me from my clit to my ass.

"Ohmygod." The words come out as one, and I clamp my hands on top of his head, keeping him there as he sucks my clit in between his lips. He slips his fingers back inside me, fucking me at a steady pace, and I rock against him. Barely able to take it.

I close my eyes, lost in the sensation of his searching tongue. It feels so fucking good. Too good. Unbelievably good.

And then I'm coming, the intensity of my orgasm leaving me unable to think. Breathe. Function. I just clutch him to me, my entire body going still before I fall completely apart.

I'm crying out as I lift my hips, my toes freaking curled into my feet like I'll never be able to straighten them again as wave after wave sweeps over me. I tilt my head back, completely overwhelmed by the tremors that rack my body. He never stops licking me, fucking me with his fingers, and then all at once, it's too much, and I'm pushing him away. Begging him to stop.

He pulls to the side, wiping his face off on the inside of my thigh, and again, I imagine the old me would've been mortified he did that. Like it's a bad thing I'm wet.

But I think he liked it. He wasn't hesitant about going down on me at all and my God . . .

The man is really good at it.

"You all right up there?" he asks after a couple of seconds of my shaky breathing.

I blow out a slow breath, trying to control my racing heart. Pressing my lips together when I feel him kiss the inside of my thigh.

If he does that again, I might request a repeat performance.

"I'm—I'm fine," I finally manage to say.

"You sure?" He's smiling. I can hear it in his voice, and I finally dare to open my eyes to find that, yes, Nico is definitely smiling while still lying between my legs.

This is the most surreal moment of my life, I swear to God.

"I can't believe you just did that," I whisper.

"What? Made you come with my mouth? I think you needed it, Ever." Oops, there he goes again, kissing the inside of my thigh, his hot lips like a brand.

"What if I told you I might need it again?" Hope rises in my chest, and I mentally bat it down, reminding myself I shouldn't be greedy. He already gave me one orgasm for the night. I doubt I could come one more time anyway. "Wait, never mind."

"Never mind? What do you mean?" He sounds genuinely confused.

"I'm more of a one-and-done type of girl when it comes to—that," I say somewhat primly.

He actually laughs, and when our gazes meet, I see the determination there. His eyes are actually twinkling, and I recognize that look. It appears every time he talks about football. "Are you implying that you can't have multiple orgasms in one night?"

"I never have," I confess.

"Ever?" He's grinning.

"Ever," I stress.

"You can't challenge me like that."

"What do you mean?"

"I mean, I'm now determined to make you come again." His mouth shifts up higher. "Maybe even two more times tonight, if you're lucky."

His hands shift to the inside of my thighs, spreading them wider, and everything inside me clenches up tight in anticipation. Oh my goodness . . .

I think I've died and gone to heaven.

Chapter Twenty-Eight

Nico

I startle awake, cracking my eyes open only to slam them shut against the obscenely bright light shining through my uncovered bedroom window.

Goddamn, it's sunny out there. Guess I forgot to close the blinds last night.

Keeping my eyes closed, I reach for my phone on the nightstand, slapping my hand around until I finally find it. Once I've got my phone, I roll over and stretch my arm out to see if there's anyone still in bed with me.

But the other side is empty, the sheets cool to the touch.

Disappointment floods me. She's gone.

Once my back is to the window, I open my eyes again and see that it's after one o'clock in the afternoon. Closer to two.

Damn. I slept in.

Yawning, I check my notifications and see there isn't anything exciting, so I shut my phone off, rolling over onto my stomach.

Only to discover I've got a serious case of morning wood going on, and lying like this is contorting my dick into an uncomfortable position.

I roll back over and sit up, running my hands through my messy hair. Remembering how much Everleigh touched it last night. She kept tugging on it, especially when I ate her delicious little pussy.

Three times.

She's so fucking responsive. Easy to make come, and when I finally let her touch me, she gave me the best hand job of my life.

No joke.

Of course, I was so ramped up from constantly going down on her, it's no surprise I came with an intensity I don't remember experiencing before. After the second orgasm, I finally stripped her completely of that gold dress, and fuck, her body is insane. Sweet little tits that are a perfect handful, with rosy nipples that were so hard, they were practically begging for my mouth.

So I gave them what they wanted.

Just thinking about what we did has my dick getting harder, and I slip my hand beneath the covers, wrapping my fingers around my shaft. Lazily stroking it while I think about her.

Everleigh.

Ever.

I wish she hadn't sneaked out of my bed in the middle of the night. I miss her. Her pretty face and her flushed skin. The sounds she makes when she comes. When I'm kissing her. The way she melts against me. I swear I can still feel her. Smell her on my skin.

I can't stop thinking about her.

Grabbing my phone once again, I bring her contact up, calling her via FaceTime without even thinking about it. There's no room for doubt or worry. I'm just working on pure impulse right now.

I wait for her to answer, frowning when it keeps ringing, and I'm about to give up when she finally answers. Her expression is harried, and she's clearly somewhere out in public from what it looks like. I hear voices. Music. There are shelves filled with knickknack-type crap, and I assume she's out shopping.

"Where are you?" I ask in greeting.

She glances around, her ponytail swinging like it always does. Next time we fuck around, she needs to wear her hair just like that so I can tug on it. Hold her in place. Maybe when I'm pushing my dick into her mouth for the first time. "I'm out."

"Out where? I miss you." I'm grinning.

She is most decidedly not. In fact, that's a pretty deep frown on her face. "Nico—"

"My dick misses you too." I start to dip my phone lower to show her my hand moving beneath my comforter as I stroke myself, when I hear someone shriek.

"OH MY GOD, NICO VALENTE! Are you making a sex call to your roommate?"

Jesus. I know that voice. It's Sienna.

"Nico, stop," Ever whispers, turning away from Sienna and bringing the phone closer to her. "Um, can I call you later?"

"Only if you promise to suck this—"

The call ends before I can finish my sentence, the screen going blank.

"Shit." I toss the phone onto my bed and give up on showing myself a little self-care.

There's a knock on my bedroom door, and before I can say anything, it's swinging open, revealing Coop standing there with his hands on his hips.

"You slept the entire day away. Do you realize how late it is, young man?" Though he's trying to appear stern, he keeps breaking out into a smile and eventually gives up.

"Yeah, yeah, I don't need the lecture." I punch the pillows beneath me and fluff them up before I prop myself against them, bunching the comforter around my lap. "How did the party go?"

"There were people passed out on the lawn this morning, and I had to kick them all out. That's how it went."

"So pretty well."

"I think you had a better time." I don't say anything, and Coop barely waits me out because it's obvious he's got something he wants to tell me. "Saw a certain someone sneak out of your room early this morning."

"How early?"

"About three."

Damn, she didn't stay at all after I passed out.

"And who did you see?"

"You know who." He leans against the doorway, crossing his arms in front of his chest. "You sure you wanna go there?"

"Too late." I'm grinning. "I went there. And it was pretty fucking great."

Coop's expression remains serious. "You better not break her heart."

My smile fades. "I won't."

The now-skeptical look on my friend's face tells me he doesn't believe a word I'm saying.

"Seriously. I won't," I stress.

"Nico. Be real with yourself right now. You break every woman's heart. You had a hysterical ex at this house in the middle of our party last night trying to bang your door down, she was so pissed at you. Especially because you were locked away in there with Everleigh and you said you were going to make her moan, just for Portia's sake." Coop shakes his head again. "That was kind of fucked up, you know."

"What Portia did was majorly fucked up. I'd even call it harassment."

"That's a stretch."

"Not really."

A deep sigh leaves him. "You've egged her on before, Nico. You know this."

Right. He's right. But . . .

"Did you hear her, Coop? She was screaming at me. *Threatening* me."

"You're a big boy, Nico. You can handle her. After all, you're the reason she lost her damn mind in the first place."

"So this is my fault." He's ruining my mood with all this.

"No, but you didn't help matters." He shakes his head. "You've said so yourself that you can't commit. You tried with Portia, and look where that got you."

In hell is what I want to say, but I keep my mouth shut.

And maybe I do want to commit. It's hard for me to admit out loud, but I want to pursue something more with Ever. Does she want the same?

I'm not sure.

"I like Everleigh. I like how she's changed the vibe in this house. We don't party as much. We don't eat out as much. She's got us doing yoga and getting all Zen and shit. I like it. I like her a lot." He clamps his lips shut when he notices the look I'm giving him. "Oh, get over yourself, I don't like her like that. She's a friend. My roommate. And a really nice, sweet girl."

Unease slips down my spine at the lecture I know is coming my way.

"If you're not serious about her, end it now. I'm asking you to think about someone else for once in your life versus just yourself."

"Are you saying I'm selfish?" I'm actually offended by his remark. "She's a grown-ass woman who can make her own decisions."

"Right, and was most likely a little drunk and horny, and all you had to do was flash that smile at her, and boom. Her panties flew off."

"She wasn't wearing any in the first place."

He actually pales. "There's a detail I didn't need to hear."

"Sorry about that." I shrug. I am not sorry at all for saying that to him.

"She's like a sister to me," Coop adds.

"And she's currently with your sister." I don't bother telling him what happened on the FaceTime call.

"I know. Sienna came over, and they took off together about an hour ago."

"Where did they go?"

"I don't know. And even if I did, I wouldn't tell you. You're a grown-ass man. You can ask her yourself."

And with that, Cooper exits my bedroom, shutting the door behind him.

Frustrated, I grab my phone and send Ever a quick text.

Where are you?

She doesn't reply, and after five minutes of waiting, I take a shower. Jerk off because I still have a raging hard-on. Once I'm finished, I step out of the shower and grab a towel, wrapping it around my waist and checking my phone immediately like some needy asshole to see she still hasn't responded.

Fuck, I think I'm being ignored. And I'm not used to that.

Not at all.

I dry off. Shave extra carefully to make sure the face is nice and smooth. Though women never seem to mind when there's a little bit of stubble on the cheeks. Some of them even claim they like the friction in certain places . . .

I slap on some aftershave like I'm an old man and enter my bedroom to get dressed, leaving the towel on the bathroom floor. I'm standing bare-assed naked in front of my dresser when my bedroom door swings open, and I'm about to yell at Coop to get the fuck out, but this time it's Ever standing there.

A gasp escapes her when she spots me, and she covers her eyes with her hand, reaching for the door handle with the other. "Oh my God. I'm *so* sorry."

I dash toward her, grabbing her about the waist and pinning her against the door, using her body to slam it shut. "Not like you haven't seen it before."

"Not like this." She drops her hand from her eyes, but they're still squeezed shut.

"Ever." I give her a gentle shake, my arms tightening around her body. I've missed her. How is this possible? "Open your eyes."

She does as I command, her gaze staying on my face and not straying at all. "I went out with Sienna. We grabbed lunch and did a little shopping."

"Buy me anything?" I grin at her, but she doesn't smile back.

"No." She shakes her head. "Nico . . ."

"Ever . . ." I mimic her serious tone, trying to ignore how soft she is in my arms. I can smell her, fruity and sweet, and there are a few stray tendrils of dark hair framing her pretty face.

A sigh leaves her, and she rests her hands on my chest, her fingers pressing lightly into my skin. "I don't know if this is going to work."

Unease prickles over me, making every hair on my body rise. "What are you talking about?"

"You. And me. What happened last night." Her eyes are extra wide, and I wait for her to say something else. Mentally preparing myself for the blow. "It was probably a mistake."

"A mistake?" My voice is weak, and I'm frowning so hard my face hurts.

What the hell is she talking about?

"We're roommates. We're . . . friends. And like I told you a few days ago, we should probably keep it at that. Friends."

It's too late, I want to tell her. *We've taken it too far. I've kissed you. All over your body. I know the taste of your pussy. I know what you look like when you come. I've come all over your hand and was hoping to come in your mouth next. Today.*

Tonight.

Now.

I'm up for anything.

Anything but what she's saying.

"Friends," I repeat, hating that word with my entire being.

She nods, her ponytail gently swinging. "Continuing along this path we started last night only complicates things. And I was just in a relationship that was terrible. I'm not ready to jump back into another one. Not that what we're doing is a relationship but—you know what I mean."

Ever is really going to compare me to her ex, the douche? Fucking Brad?

Give me a break.

"You're really pulling the friend card back out?" I ask, my voice tired.

Hell, I am tired. Exhausted by the back and forth. Just when I think we're making progress, bam.

It's ruined.

I drop my hands from her body and take a step away from her, but she remains leaning against the door.

Her gaze narrows. I probably offended her. "I'm not pulling out any sort of card. This is how I feel."

"And I guess I can't argue with how you feel, right? You want to be friends, and all I can think about is kissing you. You're just my friend, and all I want to do is get you naked."

Ever goes quiet. So do I.

"I think we might want different things," she whispers.

I should tell her how I feel. Right now. In this very moment, I need to admit that I care about her. That I want something more with her. But damn, putting yourself on the line like that?

It's scary.

Chapter Twenty-Nine

Everleigh

I'm trying to remain strong and stand by my convictions. My opinions, feelings, whatever you want to call them. Going out to lunch with Sienna and being able to talk about everything that happened last night between me and Nico was just what I needed. I'd been full of nonstop doubt ever since I sneaked out of his room, my head swirling with confusion after I left Nico sleeping alone in his bed. I went to my own bedroom, locked the door, and then just lay there thinking.

Thinking.

It was the most earth-shattering sexual experience of my life, but it also left me a mess—and not in a positive way. Good sex is one thing, and we didn't even do the actual deed yet. I didn't think I was this type of woman, but maybe I fall a little in love with a man who knows how to rock my world.

Nico rocked my entire universe with ease. Like it was no big deal for him to give me an intense orgasm with his mouth and fingers while I was left lying there in the middle of his bed, a gasping, overwhelmed bundle of bewilderment. A fumbling fool who tried to give him an adequate hand job. Who probably should've done more for him, but after three orgasms, I was sleepy.

Exhausted, really. And a little drunk.

I passed out only to jolt awake about thirty minutes later, my heart racing after the dream I just had. More like nightmare.

We were in a giant house where I lived with my current roommates. I went looking for Nico, but I couldn't find his bedroom anywhere. I opened door after door, and eventually I found him in a bathroom.

Fucking Portia while she sat on the edge of the counter, a triumphant smile on her face, aimed right at me.

Feeling sick to my stomach, I sneaked out of his bed and went to my own, totally distraught. I barely slept. When Sienna sent me a text asking if I wanted to go to lunch, I immediately said yes. And the moment after we made our order and the server walked away, I spilled my guts.

Told her everything that happened between me and Nico the night before, though I saved a few details for myself. Like I refused to tell her his dick size, and trust that she tried her best to pry the information out of me. I repeatedly said it was sufficient and left it at that.

She had a moment of supreme jealousy because *stupid Gavin will never make a move* on her, direct quote. I let her have her moment of getting all her frustration out, but then she asked me a difficult question.

What do I want from Nico now?

I couldn't give her an answer.

And this was what brought me to this point of being in his room and wrapped up in his arms while he's naked and smells so freaking good since he just got out of the shower. His dark hair is wet and slicked back from his gorgeous face, and his cheeks are as smooth as a baby's butt because I assume he just shaved, and he's so tempting.

Beautiful.

Flirtatious.

A little demanding—in a hot way. Not in an *I'm the man, do as I say* way.

Yet I'm turning him down. I'm telling him what happened last night was a mistake and it's best we remain friends. That's it.

What in the world is wrong with me?

But seriously, how can I remain his friend when I know how good it is between us? How it has the potential to be even better if we just give it a chance?

"Wait a sec. Did you just compare me to your shitty ex?" He sounds a little pissed.

"You're nothing like Brad," I immediately say.

"No kidding," he mutters.

I've told my roommates enough about Brad that they all hate him. He is the complete opposite of every single one of the guys I live with.

Especially Nico.

"But you're not great in a relationship. You've admitted that to me before," I remind him.

"We can't just fuck around and see where it takes us?" he asks hopefully.

Heaven forbid we put a label on what we're doing.

"You'll get bored with me." My voice is flat, my annoyance on full display. I'm not interested in "fucking around" to see where it takes us.

He studies my face, his eyelids falling to half-mast, giving him this sleepy, sexy look that has my heart beating a little faster than usual. "What if *you* get bored with *me*?"

"I doubt that will happen." I actually snort, which is sort of embarrassing.

His lips curve into a closed-mouth smile that only adds to his appeal. "I won't get bored with you, Ever. Not after last night."

I should not take that as a compliment. I don't even know what he means exactly. "What are you talking about?" I ask warily.

He dips his head, his mouth at my ear, his hands pressing against the door on either side of my head, caging me in with his big body. "You were a dirty girl."

That sort of remark should not make me want to melt, but here I go, my bones feeling like they could turn to mush at any second. "Not really."

"You are." His lips skim the edge of my earlobe, making me shiver. "I practically had you bent over backward last night when I was going down on you. Remember?"

Oh God. He's right. At one point I felt like a gymnast, my body contorted in all sorts of unusual positions.

"And don't forget that I had you begging for it," he continues in that smooth, seductive tone.

"I was?" Hmm. I don't remember begging. Did I?

Probably.

"Uh-huh." He licks me behind my ear, his mouth drifting down the length of my neck. I can feel him getting hard, and I spread my legs a little to accommodate for it. "Kept saying please over and over when I asked if you wanted me to tongue-fuck you."

I lock my knees so they don't buckle. "I did not."

He chuckles, the sound making me throb between my thighs. "Yeah, you did."

I slide my hands up his bare chest, savoring his smooth, hard skin. He's warm and solid and so freaking ripped. I take him in, the midafternoon sun spilling into his room from the uncovered window, highlighting all his best parts, which are . . . every single part of him.

There's a patch of dark hair between his developed pecs. He's got six-pack abs that I still think about licking, and I wish he wasn't so tightly pressed against me so I could check him out from the waist down.

No, the annoying voice in my head screams. *You don't want to check out his dick or his thick thighs or his lickable abs. You want to friend zone this dude. He will break your heart.*

Shatter it into a bazillion pieces if you're not careful.

"Come to bed with me." Oh, his words, combined with the deep timbre of his voice, are the epitome of seduction.

He makes it sound so easy.

Come to bed with me.

"Maybe we—"

The words die in my throat when he hauls me into his arms with ease, carrying me over to the bed while I cling to him, impressed by his strength. My arms are wrapped around his neck, and my legs are clamped around his waist tightly, but I know he won't drop me.

Deep down, I know he never would.

Nico deposits me on the bed, and I bounce on the mattress, ready to say something else, ask him what he's doing, though I know. I know exactly what he's trying to do, and I'm a willing participant in all of it.

But then he's on me. All six feet plus, two hundred pounds of muscle of him covering me completely. He grips either side of my head with his big hands, holding me in place as his mouth finds mine and he devours me.

Kissing me like his life depends on it.

I return the kiss with all the pent-up emotion that's been growing within me since I left this very bed in the middle of the night. I kiss him with such ferocity that when I try to roll him over and end up on top, he lets me do it. I'm sitting on him still fully clothed while he's completely naked, his erection poking me in the ass.

I brace my hands on his chest, staring at him unabashedly. Vaguely angry with my choices because this is exactly what I told myself I wouldn't do.

Yet here I am doing it. Enjoying it.

"You've got too much clothing on," he murmurs, his hands going for the front of my denim shorts, undoing the button there. I let him, savoring the sensation of his hands touching the same spots that he did last night, his fingers skimming along the waistband of my panties. "Wearing panties today? How unfortunate."

He's a talker, a commentator even, and I'm not used to that. Brad was the furthest thing from that, and I love the commentary.

I think it actually makes me wetter.

Nico's fingers dive beneath the front of my panties, but my shorts are too tight for him to go much farther, and the disappointment that hits me at this realization is . . .

It's a lot.

"Are you serious about keeping it as just friends between us?" His fingers brush the sensitive skin just above my panties, making my stomach muscles constrict. He knows exactly what he's doing, and I love it. "Because I'll stop if you are."

He's also not playing fair. Looking like that naked. Those dark-brown eyes watching me carefully as he slowly withdraws his hand from the front of my open shorts, resting it lightly on my thigh. The velvety tone of his deep voice, the warmth of his body seeping into mine. Even with me fully clothed and sitting on top of him, it's like a perfect fit.

We are a perfect fit.

Swallowing hard, I think of all the many reasons why we shouldn't continue this. They are numerous. Endless. I'm most likely going to end up the injured party here when it's all said and done between us. I keep going around and around on this point, yet I always find myself here.

With Nico. Wearing that persuasive smile and oozing confidence. Confidence that's not fake. It comes naturally to him, like breathing.

If I could gain even an ounce of confidence from this man, I'd probably conquer the world.

"You haven't answered me, Ever." He stares into my eyes, and I lose myself in them for a moment. "It's obvious to me that we're good together."

"Good together, as in sexually?" The question tumbles from my lips without thought.

He nods, his hand sliding down to curl around my knee. "I made you come three times last night."

Like I could forget that important point. Though I'm not used to talking about how many times a man can make me come, so this conversation isn't normal for me. At all.

"Well, you are quite . . . talented." I'm blushing. I can feel the heat fill my cheeks.

His smile grows. "You're not so bad yourself."

"I gave you a quickie hand job. That's it." I'm shaking my head, about to slide right off him, but he tightens his hold on me, keeping me in place.

"Why are you always downplaying what you do?"

I frown. "What do you mean?"

"I'm trying to give you a compliment and remind you how hot you were last night." He drags his index finger across my knee. I feel that touch to the very depths of my soul. I'm literally shaking. "And you act like what you did was nothing."

"It was noth—"

"It was something. You're something." His gaze lifts to mine, his eyes full of sincerity. "You're beautiful. You're smart. You have this . . . way about you that everyone likes. Coop called it a vibe."

Pleasure blooms in my chest. "A vibe?"

"He said he likes the vibe you've brought to the house since you moved in. I do too." His hand is on my thigh again, his fingers playing with the hem of my denim shorts. "I can't stop thinking about last night."

"Yeah?" I croak, swallowing hard. I forget all about what I said. How we should just be friends. That pursuing this further will only end up in disaster. I'm mesmerized by the words he's saying. The look on his face. The way he's touching me.

"I know what you said, and I want to respect your wishes, but my thoughts about you, Everleigh? They're way too friendly." His gaze locks with mine, and I can't look away. I'm finding it difficult to breathe. "I keep thinking about what it'll feel like, being inside you."

I don't know how to respond to him. I'm in a haze, one easily constructed by this man's way with words and how he's touching me . . .

Realization strikes and my heart drops. Is this a line? Is this what he tells all the women he's been with?

Is this what he said to Portia?

Without warning I'm climbing off him, nearly tripping over my own feet when I make it off the bed. I'm practically to the door before he actually has a chance to say anything.

"Where are you going?" He sounds confused. Vaguely irritated. I'm always running from him, secretly hoping he'll chase after me.

Except in this moment.

"I—like I said, Nico. I don't think this is going to work." I say the words to the door, unable to face him.

I exit his bedroom before he can say anything else, desperate to escape his convincing ways. He's good at this.

Too good.

Chapter Thirty

NICO

I arrive at practice Monday afternoon ready to get out some aggression on the field, wishing I was a lineman so I could smash into someone extra hard. It would feel pretty fucking great to punch something right about now.

Anyone.

I'm not one who uses violence to get out my anger, but damn.

Rejection sucks. Especially from a gorgeous woman who tastes delicious yet panics every time I try to tell her how I feel about her. I'm starting to wonder if I'm complete shit at this, because anytime I start talking, she starts walking.

I suppose I can't blame her for running away from me. I do have a reputation, and she's heard all about it. I'm positive Sienna filled her head with all sorts of stories about me and my shitty behavior with women.

And here I thought Sienna was a friend.

Unfortunately, my reputation and behavior, all of it is true. Sienna is also Everleigh's friend, and I'm sure she told her the truth: *Nico Valente is a risk. Look at his situation with Portia.*

I can hear Sienna saying it now. Laughing about it. I'd almost guarantee Ever didn't laugh about it at all. She lived that moment with me when Portia tried to break down my bedroom door. It was bad. Made me look bad too.

Maybe I *am* bad.

Fuck.

The moment I come storming into the locker room like a massive black cloud about to rain down upon everyone in my path, Gav is giving me shit. "Whoa there, buddy. You look ready to kick some major ass."

"Don't tempt me," I practically snarl, sending him a death glare.

Gavin actually has the nerve to laugh. "Damn, bro. Did Portia finally sink her claws into you again? Back in the day she always put your ass in a bad mood."

That he would dare to bring up Portia has me wanting to tear him apart. And he's one of my best friends, so this isn't normal for me.

"Keep this up and I will definitely kick your ass," I mutter as I go to my locker and open it, shoving my backpack inside.

The room goes silent, and I can just imagine everyone sharing a look. I ignore all of them and strip off most of my clothes, changing into my gear and practice uniform with jerky movements, not saying a word to anyone. Not even to Coop, whose locker is right next to mine. I can feel his eyes on me, but I refuse to look at him.

I can't lose it on him. I live with the guy. I respect him. I respect Gav, too, but I hate it when he gives me shit. I've turned into the epitome of *He can dish it out but can't take it.*

Yep, that's me.

My teammates eventually start changing into their practice gear, even Gavin, and by the time I've got my emotions under control and I'm shutting my locker, the team is mostly dressed and ready to go.

Turning on my heel, I come face to face with Dollar, nearly smacking into him. I shove at his shoulder, putting a little more force behind it than usual. "Watch where you're going."

I realize a second too late that I pushed his injured arm and immediately feel like a complete dick.

"*You* watch it. What the hell is your problem?" Dollar takes a step back, glaring at me as he gently massages his shoulder. "You're an asshole."

I'm fuming. He didn't even give me a chance to apologize.

"And you're a stupid fuck who believes anything a woman says to you," I toss back at him, referring to Portia.

His gaze narrows. I've pissed off Frank Dollar more than once. More like multiple times. But I don't think I've ever seen him look this furious.

"You better watch what you say about Portia," he mutters, taking a step closer to me.

I don't back off. Hell no. Dollar is giving me exactly what I've craved since I woke up this morning.

I thrust my face in his, reminding him that I'm taller and bigger than he is and I'm not injured. Meaning I could totally kick his ass if I wanted to.

Not that I want to.

"Are you with her?" I hope he doesn't think I care, or worse—that I still might have feelings for Portia.

Hell no.

Dollar lifts his chin, his golden gaze meeting mine. "That's none of your damn business."

I'm guessing that means they're not. She's playing her usual games and leading him on, which she tried on me. But I'm a game player, too, and I was always the one who had her running to me.

God, I regret some of my past behavior, considering it's helped me lose my chance with Everleigh.

"Listen, take it from a friend. She's going to end up making you look like a complete asshole," I warn him. Rationality comes into play again, and I take a few steps back, away from Dollar. "If you don't watch it, she'll have you doing and saying things you never believed you're capable of."

"Like screaming at her while locked inside your bedroom during a party on a Saturday night?" Dollar's brows shoot up.

A couple of the guys start chuckling, and I scan the room, glaring at all of them. They immediately shut up.

"Exactly," I tell him. "Just—watch out."

"Hey, let's get the fuck out of here and head out to the field," Gav calls. They all fall into line, and he leads the team out of the locker room, leaving me and Dollar alone with Coop lingering nearby. Ready to break us up if needed.

"Portia provoked me," I start, but Frank interrupts me.

"Nah, dude. You started that mess Saturday night, and now I'm the one who's gotta clean it up. I think she's still hung up on you." Dollar sounds absolutely miserable, making that confession.

I'm confused. "Then why are you trying to get with her? She's just playing your ass—"

"It's so easy for you," he says, interrupting me again. "You can have any woman just by snapping your fingers, while I'm over here trying to do everything possible to get a girl to just pay attention to my ass at least once. I'd treat them like gold if they gave me the chance, and you discard them like trash every single time. You don't know how good you've got it."

I open my mouth, ready to defend myself, to give him tips on how to not be such a little bitch boy all the time, but he keeps talking.

"I liked Everleigh. A lot. But I never had a chance because of you." It's Dollar's turn to shove at me, and I go stumbling backward, unprepared for the force of his strength. "You're such a lucky fucker, and the worst part of it all is you're not even aware of it. That's just your life. It's like nothing ever touches you, and I have to say—I hate you for it."

Dollar stomps out of the locker room before I can respond, the door slamming so hard I flinch. My gaze goes to Coop, who's got his foot on a bench in front of him, tying his shoe.

"He's not wrong" is all Coop says to me.

Jesus, I cannot win with anyone lately. "What the fuck, Coop? Can't you be on my side for once?"

"I'm always on your side. I defend you to everyone, especially Dollar. That poor guy, he just wants a shot. He'll take whatever scraps he can get."

"Like Portia," I mutter.

"Like Portia," Coop confirms. "He did like Ever. He told me so the first night she moved in."

"And what did you tell him in response?"

"I told him it was a bad idea, just like I told you. Just like I keep telling you." The pointed look Coop sends me lets me know he's onto my bullshit.

"Well, you'd be happy to know she rejected my ass once and for all and hasn't talked to me since. I haven't seen her since she ran out of my bedroom yesterday afternoon." I rest one hand on my hip, running the other through my hair, pushing it out of my eyes, but it just flops back into my line of vision. Goddamnit, I need a haircut.

Hell, I need a lot of things, but it's like I don't have time for any of it.

More like I don't want to make the time. For anyone or anything.

The one person I thought I was willing to make time for told me no, and damn, that still stings.

"I'm sorry," Coop finally says once he's finished tying his shoe. "But it was probably for the best."

"You sound just like her," I practically snarl. "What's so wrong with my ass anyway? Am I that horrible of a person?"

"Bro, I don't have the time to list everything that's wrong with you, though I can confirm one thing—you're not horrible. You just do horrible things sometimes."

Oh, great. No big. I'm just a careless, callous jerkoff who doesn't give a shit about anyone but myself.

No wonder Ever ran away from me.

"Look, we have to head out to practice. Just . . ." His voice trails off, and he approaches me, grabbing my shoulder and giving it a not-so-gentle shake. "Think about how you talk to people. How you treat them. The world doesn't revolve just around you, Valente. People have feelings, even if you don't."

Coop's words linger with me as I trail after him out to the field. It's obvious he doesn't want to walk with me, and that's fine. I want to stew in my own head for a few seconds anyway. Before we start practice and get shit rolling.

But I come to a complete stop when I see who's standing with the coaching staff on the sidelines clad in a pair of navy leggings and a matching sports bra.

It's Everleigh, looking fine as fuck.

Goddamn, those matching outfits are going to be the death of me.

There's a breeze blowing across the field, whipping her dark ponytail around, and the temptation is back, just like that. I'm dying to grab that silky ponytail and drag her off the field, reminding every single guy on the team that she's mine. This one belongs to me.

Even though she doesn't. Not really. I can't claim her.

Ever rejected my ass, and according to one of my best friends, I deserved it.

The entire team is in a row facing the coaches, and I join them, standing on the far edge of the group, wishing I were anywhere but here. I can't even find refuge in practice, my one last safe space on this goddamn campus. I've got Dollar pissed at me, Coop disappointed in me, Gav eager to give me shit, and Everleigh avoiding me like I'm a contagious disease.

It fucking sucks.

I stare at Everleigh, trying to get her to look my way, but it's like I don't even exist. I can feel some of my teammates watching me, most likely not-so-secretly enjoying my obvious failure, and I send everyone who's looking in my direction a dirty look. Even Gav.

Fuck all of them. Fuck the cute girl who's currently talking about helping us stretch by holding a yoga session for us to kick off practice. I am not in the mood for this, and I interrupt her midspeech.

"What if we don't want to do it?"

All heads swivel in my direction, including Ever's, whose eyes are full of disappointment.

"You don't have a choice," Coach answers for her, his voice firm and his focus only on me. "This is a part of practice. You know how it goes, Valente."

I do. This is my fourth year. My last year on this team.

"I don't want to participate." I cross my arms, figuratively digging in my heels.

Being a complete idiot. But hey, I don't half ass anything. I'm going all in.

"Like I said, you don't have a choice." Coach pauses for a moment, his steely gaze boring into mine. "Unless you want to leave practice."

Leaving practice is worse than getting kicked out. Leaving means you don't want to stick around for your team. Getting kicked out means you're acting like a shithead and the coaches don't want to deal with you anymore.

I'm definitely trying to get kicked out.

"I'll just chill on the sidelines and watch everyone," I drawl, my gaze scanning across my teammates, who are all wearing sour expressions of varying degrees. "Whatcha think, guys?"

"Fuck that, Valente. Stop being difficult," Gav calls good naturedly. "I thought you liked Everleigh's yoga classes."

"Not anymore," I say, my voice loud and clear.

Dollar mutters under his breath.

Coop groans.

I am digging my own grave, and I don't give a shit.

"Valente, you're being a distraction." Coach glares. "You either agree to run through this yoga session—twenty minutes tops, so it'll go by quick—or I'm kicking you out of practice."

I slowly shake my head. "I'm not doing it."

"Get the fuck out of here, then."

It's the Monday after a bye week. We need to have our heads in the game and get ready for this weekend's match with one of our biggest rivals. I am dying to play this game. They need me to play this game.

But if I keep fucking off like this, they'll have no choice but to boot me out of this Saturday's game.

My gaze shifts to Everleigh, who's watching me, her expression sad. If I could flip them all off, even her, I would.

But I don't. Instead, I leave, heading back to the locker room.

Regretting my life choices every step of the way.

I'm in my truck headed home when my phone starts ringing. It's my mom.

"Why are you calling me right now? You know I'm supposed to be at practice" is how I answer her.

"Then why are you answering my call if you're supposedly in practice?" She sounds worried.

I blow out a harsh breath. "Sorry, Mom. It's been a—rough day."

"You're all right, though? You're not hurt and in the back of an ambulance?"

"No, I'm fine." Moms. They worry a lot, and it's unnecessary most of the time.

"Thank God." Damn, she's dramatic. "I suddenly had a weird feeling about you and thought I'd call."

"What do you mean, a weird feeling?"

"I don't know. I could sense something was . . . off." She pauses for only a second. "What's wrong? Why aren't you at practice?"

I'm close to my mom, but I haven't talked to her as much this quarter. She's always understanding about how much football keeps me busy, and I appreciate her support, but lately I've been trying to do my own thing. Not depend on my mama as much.

But she called at the right time. Right now, I need her.

Taking a deep breath, I tell her the whole story, leaving out a few more private details, but I'm pretty honest with her overall. Once I'm done complaining, she softly exhales. "Can I be honest with you?"

"Please."

"My father used to always say this when I'd complain about having a bad day and how everyone treated me terribly—if you think everyone is being an asshole, that usually means you're the asshole."

I go quiet. I've heard her say this before and always blew it off. I'm not an asshole. I'm the good-time guy. The fun guy. I'm laughing and smiling and flirting and drinking and catching pretty much every single ball that's thrown at me out on the field. You'll never see me being a dickhead.

Lately, all I've been is a dickhead.

Or an asshole.

Take your pick.

"Are you calling me the asshole?" I ask.

She bursts out laughing, and I can't help but smile. My mom's laughter always cheers me up. "Yes, Nico. I'm calling you the asshole. You never fight with your roommates or Gavin."

"Yeah, you're right."

"Is it because Everleigh moved in with you? Is she causing tension among you all?"

"It's me," I admit. "I'm the one causing the tension."

Over Everleigh, which is dumb. They all like her. They think she's great. She is great. I like her too.

But it's more than that, what I feel for Everleigh. She's not just a friend. I want to explore more with her.

Pretty sure I fucked up my chances.

"What did you do to her to have her running so scared?"

I showed her my true colors, and she didn't like what she saw.

But I can't tell my mom that. She'll defend me to the bitter end, even when she's calling me an asshole at the same time.

"My reputation with the ladies isn't the best." I wince, glad I'm not face to face with her while saying this.

"Oh, Nico." She sighs. "Sometimes I worry that's all my fault."

"What? No way, Mom. You're great."

"You didn't see a healthy relationship growing up. Your dad left us, and I channeled all of my energy into you."

"And I appreciate that." I pull onto our street, turning into the driveway almost immediately. "You're not the reason I won't commit."

"My relationship with your father influenced you, though. Even if you can't see that. He ran away from his commitments and never looked back."

Shit. She's right. I refuse to be like that guy. He ditched us and left my mother alone to pick up the pieces. Am I avoiding relationships so I won't do the same?

"If you're really being the asshole in this situation, Nico, you need to make things right," Mom says. "With everyone."

"I will," I say, my voice fierce. "I promise."

Chapter Thirty-One

EVERLEIGH

I wait for my roommates to finish practice before we all walk home together. Normally Nico is their ride home, but since he got kicked out of practice today because of me . . .

Here we are.

"Are you coming to practice tomorrow?" Frank asks me. "That session you led was great. Everyone said so. Right, Coop?"

Coop grunts in response.

"I can't because I have class. And anyway, today was just a test run. Your coach said he'd let me know if they want me to come back again." I'm guessing when their star offensive player basically asks to get booted from practice, they're going to reconsider if they want to use me or not.

"Fucking Nico. He better not have ruined it for you with how he got kicked out," Frank mutters, shocking me. I don't hear him curse much. "He's been a complete jackass lately."

"It's no big deal." I put on a brave face, trying to smile through the humiliation.

Well, I'm not feeling so humiliated anymore, but I sure was when Nico was standing there in front of his entire team, rejecting me. I sound dramatic, but that's what it felt like. He refused to do my class.

Just flat-out refused.

Who does that?

Is he mad at me for rejecting him? I ran out on him Sunday afternoon, and we've barely spoken since. I'm too embarrassed, and now I'm realizing he's too angry.

See? This would've never worked. We're already in a bad place. We should've never done what we did Saturday night.

Though deep down, I don't totally regret it. That was the best night of my entire life. The three orgasms he gave me are more than proof of it.

"Don't let what Nico did bother you." This comes from Coop, who hasn't said an actual word since we started walking home. "He doesn't call the shots for our team."

"He's one of our captains," Frank reminds us.

"So am I," Coop says.

"Right. And Gav too. But if Nico ruined this opportunity for Ever . . ."

"He hasn't," Coop interjects. "I talked to Coach right after practice. They're definitely interested in Everleigh participating in a couple of practices every week."

"Really?" I remind myself to remain calm and not get my hopes up. This would be such a great way to make more money and have fun while doing it. As long as the guys cooperate.

Meaning Nico.

"Yep." Coop nods. "Expect a call from one of the coaches tonight."

"Wow. Thank you, Coop."

"That's great," Frank says, and I can tell he's truly pleased for me. "Now everyone is going to see how helpful yoga is."

"Aw, thanks, Frank. You're my biggest fan," I tell him with a laugh as we turn onto the walkway that leads to our front porch.

I debate my decision the rest of the walk home, going over various scenarios in my head. Should I agree to do this? Or am I wanting to do it just to spite Nico? Am I secretly vengeful?

No and no. I need as much money as I can get. I asked for more hours at the café, but they can't give them to me right now. If helping out the team actually happens, it means I won't have to lead yoga sessions at home. I can do it all at practice and get paid for it.

Sounds like the perfect setup.

Hopefully Nico won't have a problem with this. With me. Watching him walk away from practice earlier filled me with bitter disappointment—and a hint of guilt. Is he trying to avoid me so badly that he'll get himself kicked out of practice? He's putting himself at risk, pulling that stunt. What if they don't let him play Saturday?

Ugh, that's the problem. He's so good out on that field, they'll let him play no matter what. He has to do something truly awful to get benched. And he's not that dumb.

We enter the house, and the first thing I notice is that the living room is clean. Not a leftover glass or discarded beer can in sight, which is a typical problem and one I take care of in the morning before I go to work.

Not this morning, though. I was still frustrated and not in the mood to be helpful.

The video games are in a neat stack on top of the console that sits just below the TV, and there's even a lit candle sitting in the middle of the coffee table.

Weird.

Coop closes the door, looking around the room. "Did you clean up before you came to practice?" he asks me.

"I haven't been home all day." I shake my head. "This isn't my doing."

Music is playing. I can hear it coming from the little speaker in the kitchen, and I head toward the room, coming to a stop when I see another lit candle sitting on the counter and the dining table is perfectly set for six, a large bouquet of fresh flowers in a vase sitting right in the center.

Huh.

"What the hell is going on?" Frank asks, sounding as baffled as I feel.

The sliding glass door opens, and Nico emerges from it, carrying an empty plate in one hand and a pair of tongs in another. He stops short when he sees us, a contrite smile on his face. "Oh, hey. You're finally home."

"We took longer because we didn't have our normal ride," Coop reminds him, though he doesn't sound pissed about it.

"Yeah." Nico's expression turns apologetic. "That's on me. Sorry about that."

"It's cool." Coop nods. Nothing fazes this guy, while Frank and I say nothing. I need more than a *sorry about that*, because what Nico did at the start of practice?

Felt personal. And rude.

"Whatcha up to?" Coop asks him.

"I'm making dinner."

"What are you making?" Frank asks warily. Like he doesn't trust him. *I feel the same way, Frank.*

"Barbecuing some steaks. Got some garlic bread already in the oven. Everything will be ready soon." Nico's gaze shifts to mine, slightly pleading. "You make the best salads, Ever, and I was hoping you'd help me out? I already bought the ingredients."

I lift my chin, ready to tell him he can stuff that salad up his butt, when Coop speaks up first. "He's right, Ever. Your salads really are the best."

"They're delicious," Frank chimes in.

How can I tell him no when my favorite roommates are praising my salad-making skills?

I give in.

"Fine." I head for the fridge, hip-checking Nico when I walk past him, and he practically leaps out of my way. "I'll make one. Who else is coming to dinner?"

"Me!"

We all turn our heads to see Sienna standing in the kitchen entry-way clutching a giant bottle of wine in her hand. "I brought the spirits, just like you requested, Nico."

"Thanks, Sienna." He's smiling at her, looking relieved, and I would love to tell him the things she called him just last night while we were on FaceTime for almost two hours. She listened to me go on and on about him, which means she's a saint and I owe her one.

Next time she needs to have a bitch fest about Gavin, I'm all ears.

"That's five," Coop notes. "Who else is coming over?"

"Gav," Nico answers, his gaze shifting to Coop. "Come outside and check out these steaks with me."

"I'm going to wash up," Frank says, his expression impassive. I'm sure he's still upset with Nico because of the Portia stuff. And the me stuff.

It's been a little messy around here the last few days.

Only when Nico and Coop head to the backyard and the sliding glass door is closed do I speak. "When did he invite you over?" I open the refrigerator door and start pulling out the ingredients I need to make my beloved salad.

"He called me about an hour ago and filled me in on his assholish ways." When I send Sienna a confused look over my shoulder, she explains further. "He told me how he got kicked out of practice."

"He did?" I'm surprised he'd admit it.

Sienna nods. "He feels bad about it too."

I whirl on her, clutching a head of lettuce. "Don't you dare fall for his smooth-talking ways."

Sienna bursts out laughing. "Is that what we're calling it now? Look, I'm not the one who has major beef with him. I can be nice when I need to be. And when he told me he was making a steak dinner as an apology for being such a jackass? I absolutely took him up on the invitation."

I roll my eyes as I set all the salad ingredients on the counter. "Looks like I'm too late. You already fell for Mr. Smooth Talker."

"No way." Sienna shakes her head, watching me as I start to rinse off the lettuce in the sink. "I'm on your side, sister. These men need to get their heads out of their asses and figure out what they're doing."

My gaze goes to the sliding glass door. I can see Nico at the barbecue with Coop standing by his side. He's tending to the steaks on the grill, and it seems like Coop is giving him an earful. For a man who doesn't speak much, his mouth is moving nonstop.

"I think your brother is chewing out Nico," I tell Sienna.

"Good. About time someone was real with him." She settles onto one of the stools that sit by the counter. "How are you holding up?"

"In regards to him?" I wave the knife I'm using in Nico's general direction. "Not so great."

"He feels bad over what happened." Sienna watches me as I begin to chop the salad, unleashing all my pent-up aggression.

"You already mentioned that," I tell her, still chopping away. It feels good to cut the lettuce into tiny pieces, and when I scoop it up with my hands and drop it into the bowl, I catch the amused look on my friend's face. "What are you laughing at?"

"You want me to be real with you right now?" I lift my gaze to hers, tempted to say no, but I remain quiet. "I think both of you are scared."

"Nico Valente scared? No way." I shake my head and grab a cucumber, ready to slice and dice that sucker.

"I'm serious. You make him nervous. And I know he makes you nervous."

Sighing with exasperation, I set the knife down and focus all my attention on her. "He's not scared. He had no problem doing what he did Saturday night. He was ready for a repeat performance Sunday, and I'm the one who ran. Remember? I'm the nervous Nellie in this situation. Not him."

"I think he wants to make it up to you." Sienna walks over to the sink and turns on the water, washing her hands. "Why don't I finish that salad up for you, and you can go change? Maybe even take a quick shower."

"I promised the guys I would make it—"

"And you did. Mostly," Sienna interrupts, shutting off the water. "Go. You need to clear your head."

I reluctantly leave the kitchen and head for my bedroom, stopping in the doorway when I see what's waiting for me inside.

There's a small bouquet sitting on my desk and an envelope with my name on it propped against the vase. The flowers match the ones that were on the dining table, and I know without looking at the card inside that they're from Nico.

My heart tumbles over itself, and I give myself a stern mental lecture that this means nothing. I snatch up the envelope and open it, pulling out the plain white card inside with shaky fingers. The handwriting is bold, taking up almost the entirety of the card, and I read it.

I'm sorry I ruined your first practice with the team. Please let me make it up to you.

He didn't sign his name or add a sweet endearment, either, but this is almost—not quite but almost—enough.

At the very least, I think as I tuck the card back into the envelope before I hide it away in my desk, *he's on the right track.*

Now it's up to me to make some progress with him.

Chapter Thirty-Two

NICO

By the time I'm bringing the steaks into the house to let them sit for a few minutes, I find Sienna in the kitchen making the salad. A glass of wine is sitting next to her, and the music is cranked up.

None of the soft jazz that Ever likes to listen to when she cooks. Nope, Sienna is blasting the Nicki Minaj song "Want Some More." She's singing every word as she sprinkles cut-up tomatoes on top of the already full salad bowl, snapping her lips shut when she sees me standing there with a plate of still-sizzling steaks.

"That was quick," she says, her gaze going to Coop, who just came inside after me. "And those steaks smell delicious."

"Where's Ever?" My appetite threatens to vanish. If she left because of what I did earlier . . . what I've been doing . . .

The disappointment crashes into me like a giant wave. I've fucked everything up.

"Oh, I sent her away to take a shower. She seemed—frazzled."

My relief is instantaneous, but the knowing look on Sienna's face tells me she's aware of everything I've done. Even more than what I told her on the phone earlier.

I'm not surprised. Ever has become close to Sienna since she moved in, and I think it's great.

"You really messed everything up, you know," Sienna says as she turns off the music.

"I'm gonna go call Gav. See where the hell he is." Coop holds up his phone as he rushes out of the kitchen, leaving me alone with Sienna.

Who seems ready to give me a lecture.

"I know I messed everything up with Everleigh." I go to the oven and peek inside to see the garlic bread is browned nicely. I go ahead and turn the oven off as well as the timer. "You don't need to remind me."

"Well, she messed up with you too."

I turn to look at her, surprised she'd bash her friend. "What exactly do you know?"

"I know that you tried to make a move and she panicked and bailed on you Sunday afternoon." She shrugs. "You two are both scared. I told her that, and she completely disagreed."

"Right, because she's not scared at all to stand up for her feelings."

"No, she said you're the one who's not scared. She ran away from you, which makes her feel like a chickenshit."

Leave it to Sienna to tell it like it is.

"I'm trying to do better." I walk the platter of steaks over to the dining table and set it down. "You know I'm not good at this relationship thing."

Sienna laughs and takes a big sip from her wineglass. "No kidding. But I think you're on the right track with this dinner."

I pause, trying not to get my hopes up. "You really think so?"
Sienna nods.

"I left her flowers in her room."

"Aw." Sienna rests her hand on her chest. "That's sweet."

"What else should I do? I need input. And I'm clueless."

"Just—if you're into her, let her know. Show her that you like her. Even better? Tell her. Say out loud that you want to pursue something with her." She pauses. "You do want to pursue something, right?"

"I do." The words leave me without hesitation, and I realize I'm speaking the truth.

I do want to pursue this. I want something meaningful with Everleigh. I like her. A lot. I care about her.

A lot.

"Let her know. And be serious. Don't be all Mr. Player. The big man on campus who can get any girl he wants with a wink and a smile." Sienna rolls her eyes.

"I don't have to wink. I usually just smile and they come running." I'm grinning.

She plucks a cherry tomato from the salad and tosses it right at my head, but I catch it just in time. "You know what I mean."

Before I can say anything, Coop and Gav enter the kitchen, Gavin's nose in the air. Damn, that guy got here fast. "What smells so fucking good?"

"That would be dinner," I tell him, my gaze shifting to Sienna once more. "Could you pull the garlic bread out of the oven, please?"

"At your service." Sienna salutes me, heading over to the oven.

Sienna and I work as a team to get everything on the table while Gav and Coop gather drinks for all of us. Frank eventually wanders in and makes small talk with me—progress. I am dying to ask him what's really going on with Portia, but no way am I saying her name. There's no need to bring her up right now. It'll probably only end up pissing Dollar off all over again.

By the time Ever enters the kitchen, we're all seated at the table, passing around the bowl of salad. The only empty chair left is the one to my right, and she sits down, smiling tentatively at me when I hand her the salad bowl.

Everyone remains quiet once we've got food on our plates, no hesitation as we all start to eat. Gav, Coop, and Frank are just shoveling it in like they haven't been fed in days while the girls start in with their salad.

I'm the only one with no appetite. I'm too nervous.

Clearing my throat, I decide I need to say something and get it out of the way.

"I'm glad you all came tonight," I start, causing them all to pause, their heads swiveling in my direction. "I haven't been . . . easy to deal with lately, and I want to apologize to all of you."

Frank sets his fork on the edge of his plate, giving me his full attention. "Go on."

"I was a dick this weekend at the party. And I was a major dick today at practice. I know I need an attitude adjustment. I'm working on myself." I nod once. "Go ahead and keep eating. Don't let your meal get cold. I just needed to say that. Thank you for being my friends, and I'm sorry."

Gavin, who is sitting to my left, slaps me on the shoulder. "You don't have to apologize, bro. Everyone has a bad day here and there."

"Thanks, man." I smile at him, grateful for his comment.

Gavin nods, his attention switching to Dollar. "Tell us what's up with you and the blonde. Portia."

I inwardly groan. That was the last thing he should've brought up.

Frank's cheeks actually turn ruddy. "Nothing much."

"You don't need to hold back, Dollar Bills." Gavin is teasing him. "She's hot."

The annoyance on Sienna's face is obvious. "Don't forget she used to date Nico."

"Oh, I remember. She was wild." Gav chuckles. "I'm guessing she still is."

"Probably not the best topic to focus on right now," I tell Gav, who completely ignores my warning.

"So tell us—are you with her or what?" he asks Frank.

Dollar glances in my direction, looking like he might shit his pants at any moment. "We are—casually seeing each other."

"Keep it that way," Gavin says with an approving nod. "No need to get serious with anyone right now."

I want to stomp on my friend's foot to get him to shut up, but I restrain myself.

"That's terrible advice," Sienna blurts.

Gavin tilts his head. They're sitting directly across from each other, and I know Sienna planned it that way. He didn't notice, though.

Or does Gav notice and not give a shit? Does he enjoy having Sienna follow him around like a fangirl? Does it feel good to him knowing that she'll always have his back no matter what?

If he's not interested in her, he needs to stop toying with her emotions. Full stop.

"I don't see you in a steady relationship," Gavin challenges her. "And hey, I figured you'd agree with me. You always agree with me."

Oh God.

Dollar actually groans out loud. Ever and I share a look, seemingly always in sync when it comes to these situations.

"For once in my life, I'm definitely not agreeing with you." Sienna grabs her steak knife and points it in Gav's direction. "You're an oblivious asshole."

The chuckle dies on Gavin's lips, his gaze going to me. "I thought Nico was the asshole tonight."

"You're all assholes." Sienna points at every guy at the table with the knife, pausing on Coop. "Even you."

"Me?" Coop rests his hand on his chest. "What the hell did I do?"

"You exist. You have dicks and a shitty attitude. You treat women like garbage, or worse, you ignore them completely, like they're meaningless." Sienna drops the knife, and it lands with a clatter onto her plate. She leaps to her feet, taking her wineglass with her. "Nico, I appreciate your apology. If you could just get your head out of your butt and realize there's a pretty great woman sitting beside you who might change your life for the better—that would be perfect."

I blink at her, my gaze finding Ever's once more, but she looks away quickly, her cheeks pink.

"And if you could stop being so overprotective all the time, maybe I could find a little independence," Sienna says to Coop, taking a big gulp from her glass, her attention shifting to Frank. "I'm not mad at you, Dollar, but you gotta know that Portia is toxic as fuck and she will ruin you. Run while you can."

All Dollar can do is blink at her.

"Then there's you." Sienna waves her glass in Gav's general direction. "You're blind. Or an egomaniac. Most likely a combination of both. You know how I feel, yet you still lead me on. As my dear old dad would say, Gavin, it's time for you to shit or get off the pot."

She raises her glass in a cheers gesture, polishes the rest of the contents off in one long swallow, and slams it down on the table before she turns on her heel and exits the kitchen.

The front door slams shut seconds later.

"Should I go after her?" Ever asks, pushing back her chair.

"No." Coop shakes his head. "Someone else should."

The table goes silent, which has been a common theme tonight. I thought my dinner was going to bring us together and we'd have a good time.

Things really veered offtrack from my original intentions.

"I'll go," Frank starts, but Coop shuts him up with just a look.

"You think *I* should go after her?" Gavin actually has the nerve to ask. "I wanted to finish my steak."

"You know what, if you want to finish your steak, go for it. I'm thinking Sienna finally realizes that you don't care about her anyway." Ever patiently cuts her own steak, keeping her gaze on her plate.

"I do care about her. She's a good friend to me. It's just—"

"What?" She turns to him, her expression scarily calm. "You don't see her like that? Have you ever told her beyond that one drunken night when she was a freshman and basically threw herself at you?"

The shock on Gavin's face is almost comical. Even I know about that night. And from Coop's complete nonreaction, I'm guessing he knows about it too. "She told you about that night?"

"She's told me a lot of things."

"I knew about it too," I add.

"Same." Coop nods, which is shocking because he acted clueless about those two only a couple of weeks ago.

"She even told me." Dollar shrugs.

"Jesus," Gav mutters, jumping to his feet. "I'll go talk to her."

He's gone in a flash, and we all look at each other from across the table.

"Look, I'm still starving." Coop plucks another piece of garlic bread from the basket and shoves half of it in his mouth. "They'll figure their shit out. Just like you guys will."

Chapter Thirty-Three

Everleigh

I knock on Nico's partially open bedroom door before I walk inside, knowing that he's in there.

Knowing that we still need to talk.

"Come in," he calls, and I enter his room, lingering by the door.

He's sitting on the edge of his bed wearing a pair of black sweats. Nothing else.

I swallow hard, trying my best not to look at his glorious, naked chest, but it's difficult when there's that much bare skin on display.

"Hey." I offer him an awkward wave. "I wanted to thank you for the flowers. And the apology."

"You're welcome." Both his voice and his expression are solemn. "Dinner turned into a shit show, huh?"

"The food was really good." I smile at him. "The best steak I've ever had."

"I'm glad you enjoyed it." He leans back, pressing his hands into the mattress behind him, putting his torso on complete display for my greedy eyes. I'm enjoying this feast too. "Sorry everything went sideways."

"That wasn't your fault. And I'm thinking all of that needed to be said. Have you heard from Gavin?"

"No. I texted him, but he hasn't replied."

"I tried texting Sienna, but she's quiet too." I lean against the door-jamb. "I hope they're okay."

"I'm sure they are. If I were to guess, I'd say they were probably fucking each other's brains out at this very moment."

The moment the words are said, they hang heavy in the air, making me think all kinds of things, every one of them involving the two of us. Naked.

I wonder if he's thinking the same thing too.

"If that's what she wants, then more power to her."

His gaze locks with mine, dark and oh-so serious. "And what do you want, Ever?"

"In regards to what?" I ask shakily, ignoring the nerves suddenly rattling around in my stomach, making it twist.

"Me. And you. Did I fuck it all up? Have I blown all of my chances?" His brows lift in question.

The words get stuck in my throat, and I swallow down the lump that formed there. "No. You haven't blown all your chances."

He smiles.

"Yet," I tack on.

The smile fades, and then he's shaking his head. "You know just how to bust my balls."

"Someone has to."

"My mom would like you." I go still at his casual comment. Men with flirtatious *I'm a player*–type reputations like Nico's don't usually want the women in their life to meet. "I talked to her today. She was the one who put my head on straight."

"How?"

He sits up, the muscles in his stomach rippling. God, he is a beautiful male specimen. "She has a theory she learned from my grandpa. Want to hear it?"

"I would love to."

"Come here and sit by me, and I'll tell you." He pats the mattress, his gaze shooting to mine. "I won't try anything. I swear."

I push away from the door and sit next to Nico on the foot of the bed, keeping a respectable but not-too-far distance from him. "Tell me."

"It goes like this—if you're having a bad day, if you think everyone in your life is a jerk. Treating you like crap. If you keep thinking that over and over, with every encounter you're having, sometimes you need to take a step back and wonder—am I the asshole?"

"Okay." I nod, absorbing his words, a little laugh escaping me. "I think I get it."

Nico reaches out to take my hand in his. "I'm the asshole. I was an asshole over the weekend, and I was a giant one today at practice. I'm sorry, Ever."

He squeezes my hand, and I feel that touch all the way to my soul.

"Thank you for apologizing. I can't lie—you *were* a total asshole at practice today." He ducks his head, a faint smile on his face. "But you weren't an asshole on Sunday. Or Saturday either."

"Yeah?" His smile is faint. "So you don't regret what happened between us?"

"No. I wanted it." He turns to fully look at me, my hand still in his. "I wanted you."

"And then I came on too strong Sunday."

"You were coming on *really* strong. And while it was flattering, it was also shocking. That kind of—scared me."

"That's why I lashed out at practice." He interlaces his fingers with mine. "I'm not used to rejection."

"Aw, poor Nico." I'm teasing him. "A girl rejected him."

"You did. You ran straight out of my room." He settles our linked hands in his lap, and I can feel the heat of his body through the thick cotton of his sweats. "I've missed you."

I melt at the sincerity in his voice.

"It's been barely twenty-four hours," I remind him.

"Doesn't matter. It didn't feel right, not being able to just talk to you." He tugs me a little closer. "Did you miss me?"

Old me would've said no. Old me would've played this off and tried to change the subject.

But if he's willing to change, then I should be too.

"Yes," I admit. "The minute I ran out on you, I regretted it."

His gaze lingers on my face, dropping to my lips. "I need to do this right."

"Do what right?"

"You." He laughs when I poke at his side with my free hand. "I mean you and me. Us."

A little thrill shoots through me at his using the word *us*. "How are you going to do this right?"

"I need to treat you like a woman I'm interested in versus my room-mate whose bedroom is conveniently located across the hall from mine." He's grinning, and the sight of it steals my breath.

My thoughts.

"I mean, that *is* pretty convenient." I lean into him, pressing my cheek against the solid rock that is his shoulder. I remain there, savoring the simple joy of feeling connected to him, and he releases his grip on my hand, shifting his arm so it slides around my shoulders.

"Want to go on a date tomorrow night?"

"A date?"

He grabs hold of my hand again, sliding his fingers between mine. The seemingly innocent touch sets off a fresh wave of tingles sweeping over my skin, my breath catching when he slides his thumb back and forth along the side of my hand. "Yeah. I'll take you to dinner. Maybe catch a movie?"

"That sounds—normal."

Nico chuckles. "Normal?"

I'm nodding, even with my head still pressed to his shoulder. "Like something a regular couple would do."

"What do you say?"

"I'd love to go to dinner and a movie with you." I pull away from his arm so I can smile up at him, and he leans down, brushing my mouth with his in the gentlest of kisses.

"Thanks for giving me another chance," he murmurs, pressing his forehead against mine. "I'm going to do my best not to fuck it up."

I can't help myself—I start to laugh. "That instills a lot of confidence in me."

He chuckles too. "I'm going to prove to you that I can do this. I'll be the best boyfriend you've ever met."

I pull away slightly, wanting to make sure I heard him right. "Are you serious? You're saying the word *boyfriend* now?"

His expression solemn, he nods. "Guess I didn't make my intentions clear enough. I'm in this to win your heart, Everleigh Olmstead."

I blink at him, my breaths coming faster. And when he leans in and delivers a heart-stopping kiss to my lips, I almost admit . . .

He's already won it.

Chapter Thirty-Four

Nico

November

Saturday. Game day at home. The stadium is packed. Not an empty seat in sight. The sky is a bright blue, the sun blazing over us, soothed by the gentle breeze carrying over from the nearby ocean.

It's the perfect setting to win a game.

This time of year most of the colleges we play against are dealing with colder weather. Cloudy skies accompanied by wind and rain. Sometimes even snow. But here in Santa Mira?

The weather is great year round. Yeah, we'll have the occasional rainstorm, and we'll sometimes get major fog, but for the most part? It's like we're living on endless vacation around here. Similar to the weather I grew up with too. And speaking of growing up . . .

My mom is here at the game today. She's a nurse, so sometimes it's hard for her to get time off to come to my games, but she's in the stands today, sitting with . . .

My girlfriend.

We've been playing it cool, Ever and I. We go out a lot. Just the two of us. When we're feeling ambitious, those dates turn into study sessions, which we both need. School is getting more intense, and we have to stay on top of it. When we're not cramming for an exam or writing papers, we go to the movies. We mostly stay home, holed up in one of our bedrooms and watching a movie or series on a laptop.

That usually leads to us kissing. Making out in the most intense way possible, though we never take it beyond that. I'm a new man. A changed man. I'm trying to take this slow and savor her. Make her feel cherished and wanted and needed. Show her appreciation and not just use her for hot sex.

That's the most difficult part. Resisting her. I'm being 100 percent truthful right now: this woman is dying for it.

Dying for me.

But I can say that because I'm dying for her too. Goddamn, has it been difficult, only just kissing her. Maybe feeling her up a little bit while we kiss on her bed. Or my bed. Or at the movie theater. Or in my truck. In the back of the library during one of our late-night study sessions.

The one place where we never get too touchy feely? When she's leading the football team through yoga sessions. I'm usually in the back row, my gaze never straying from her as she stretches and moves. The guys treat her with respect—thanks to me giving them a little reminder speech that she's mine and they better back the fuck off—and I've turned into quite the dutiful yoga student.

We kiss everywhere we can without causing a scene because lately anywhere I go I seem to cause a scene, thanks to the football team doing so well. In the past, I loved this sort of attention. Fucking reveled in it.

Now all I can think about is *When can I get some alone time with my girl?*

I rub at my chest, right at my heart. Sounds good calling Ever that, even in my own mind.

"What are you daydreaming about?"

Gav appears at my side, full of his usual swagger. I love my friend and am always loyal to him, but he done messed up big time when it comes to Sienna, who also happens to be sitting with Ever and my mom up in the stands.

I'm still not sure what happened that night during the steak dinner a couple of weeks ago when Gavin went searching for Sienna after she told him off, but it couldn't have been good. Because those two aren't talking to each other. Sienna's not coming around our house if Gav is there. And when she's hanging out with us and Gav shows up?

Sienna leaves.

Ever claims she doesn't know much about it, either, but I think she's just protecting her friend, which I get. I don't push. Someday she'll tell me. Or Sienna will.

Or Gavin.

"Just thinking today is a good day to kick some ass." I grin at him, and he smiles in return.

We're at the front of the tunnel from where we run out onto the field, the game announcers rattling on from their booth about today's game and how important it is to the Dolphins. We're currently undefeated this season, and the odds for today's game are in our favor.

But you still never know what might happen. We could lose.

Doubt we will, though. Thinking there's a chance is a mentality I don't want to touch today. I'm confident we're going to win.

"I figured you were fantasizing about your new girlfriend." Gavin laughs when I shoot him a dirty look. "Stop being so sensitive."

"Stop talking about Ever," I tell him, but he knows I'm giving him shit. Just like he's doing to me.

Ever since Everleigh and I became somewhat official, my teammates love nothing more than to give me endless shit about it. All good natured, of course.

I'm whipped, I'm soooo in looooooove, I'm a simp, I'm a pussy, I'm all of the above. I laugh along with them and tell them all to go to hell, but I never, ever deny it.

Because it's true. Not that I've ever actually experienced it before, but I think I'm a little in love with Everleigh.

Okay, fine, I'm not a little in love. I *am* in love.

With Everleigh.

I just haven't told her yet.

"Guess what," Gav says, pulling me out of my Ever-filled thoughts.

"What?"

"Dollar's starting today."

"No shit?" I glance over my shoulder at the rest of our team filling the tunnel, ready to run out. "That's great."

"I know, right? It was a last-minute decision, and I think it was the right one." Gav nods.

"I'm happy for him. I told him he'd get to play during the regular season," I say, scratching the side of my neck. I'm beginning to feel anxious, which means I get a little jumpy. I wish we'd just get this party started and get on the field.

My gaze catches on Dollar, noting the faint smile on his face, which I haven't seen in a while. The dude has been down in the dumps the last few weeks, which is another reason why Ever and I keep ourselves locked up in one of our bedrooms. We don't want to rub it in his face that we're seeing each other, especially since he's still single. Portia ghosted him after the party at our house, and while he keeps saying he's glad she's gone and that he dodged a bullet, I know deep down he's upset. His pride is hurt.

He deserves a good woman. Someone who'll appreciate him for who he is because he's a stand-up guy.

"And now, ladies and gentlemen, let's give a big, rowdy welcome to our Santa Mira Dolphins football team!" the announcer screams.

Gavin gives his usual signal—a single nod—and we run out onto the field, our roars sounding like a bunch of gladiators filling the coliseum, ready to take on wild animals with our bare hands.

That's what it always feels like to me.

Everyone in the stands is screaming and yelling and cheering. I hear some shouts of my last name along with Gavin's. There are lots of faces painted with the school colors and jersey numbers on cheeks. Women and men alike are wearing our jerseys, and alumni too. One of my biggest fans is an eighty-year-old woman who dyes her hair jet black and paints my number on her cheeks every home game. I make sure to take photos with her when I can because that woman is cool as fuck. She calls herself my adopted grandma.

We get into formation and start stretching on the fifty-yard line. Every chance I get, I'm scanning the crowd, looking for that familiar face that makes me smile the most.

Ah, there she is, seated in the friends-and-family section, which is also on the fifty-yard line. My mom is on one side of her and Sienna is on the other, and while the other women are chatting away, my girl is watching me, her eyes glowing with pride when our gazes meet.

Ever.

I give her a quick little salute, and she does the same, her smile big. She's wearing an oversize Dolphins hoodie that I recently gave her, and her hair is pulled into my favorite style—a high ponytail.

Pretty sure I'm gonna grab hold of it tonight. Might not let it go for a while either.

If somebody had told me a month ago that Ever would be my girlfriend and sitting with my mom while watching me play, I would've called bullshit.

"Your mama is sitting with Ever," Coop says minutes later as we move over to the sidelines in preparation for the game to start.

"I know," I say with a nod.

"You're not worried about that?" Coop's brows shoot up.

"Nah. They seem to get along okay."

Coop watches me with a narrowed gaze, slowly shaking his head. "You've changed."

"I know."

"For the better."

"Hey, thanks."

"I mean it. She's good for you." Coop inclines his head in Ever's direction. "I never thought I'd see the day Nico Valente becomes domesticated."

"Here I am, fully domesticated." I spread my arms, grinning. "Just wait. It'll happen to you someday."

"No fucking way. No woman can tame me."

I start to laugh. "Coop, you're not even that bad."

Not like I was. Or Gav, who is still terrible. Flirting with everyone. Hooking up with everyone.

At least I assume he's doing that.

"I'm unlovable. That's what Sienna told me."

"Damn, bro. That's—harsh."

"Eh, it's whatever. She said I don't talk enough."

She's not wrong. He's pretty quiet.

"And I'm intimidating."

He's a big, bulky guy.

"The tattoos don't help." He holds out his arms, which are covered with them.

"Women don't mind tattoos."

"Yeah, well, Sienna likes to get in my head with her comments, and they work." He shrugs. "Maybe I'll be a bachelor forever. I'll be Uncle Coop to all of the little rug rats you and Ever have."

I immediately start to sweat, and Coop, that asshat, begins to laugh.

"Ha. Finally said something that freaked you out." He points at me, chuckling.

"You had me envisioning babies, and we are so not ready for that," I admit.

"Smart. You've got lots of years ahead of you. And if you're lucky, you'll go pro."

I don't like to think about it too much. I want it too badly, and I don't want to be devastated if it doesn't happen. "You might go pro too."

"Maybe." He shrugs. That's Coop. Always playing everything off.

Gav approaches us, slapping us both in the backs. "Ready to get this game started?"

"Hell yeah," Coop and I both yell.

"Let's go."

Chapter Thirty-Five

EVERLEIGH

My throat is sore from all the yelling and screaming I've been doing throughout this game.

It's been a total nail-biter. Feels like our team's opponents are getting tougher and tougher as we get through the season, and as someone who's never really been into football before, I don't know how they can stand it. The players. My player.

Nico.

But he's currently out on that field playing like an absolute champ. I'm so proud of him. We're leading by a touchdown, and there's less than two minutes left in the fourth quarter. We currently have the ball and are looking to score, but as Sienna explained, our boys are also managing the clock and trying to waste as much time as possible so we don't give the other team enough time to do anything.

I've learned a lot about this game this season, mostly thanks to Sienna, who's lived and breathed football with the rest of her family her entire life.

The game isn't the only thing leaving me on edge. Sitting with Nico's mom also makes me nervous, but she's proved to be a lot of fun. She's easy to talk to and laughs a lot, making me feel comfortable, as if she knows what a nerve-racking experience this is. I see where Nico gets his personality from. And his smile.

Though his is better in my opinion, but I'm biased.

"Ah, look at him." Claudia Valente sighs, her dark eyes flashing with pride. "He's so fast!"

Nico is currently scrambling on the field, dodging every defensive block coming his way. Gav just threw the ball, and Nico holds up his hands without even looking too closely. Just a quick glance over his shoulder and somehow that ball finds his open palms.

The moment he catches it, he's clutching the ball close to his chest, running his ass off and gaining plenty of yardage before a team member for the defense lunges toward him, grabbing Nico around the calves and bringing him to the ground, where he rolls over onto his back.

Claudia gasps, her hand flying to her mouth. Her reaction makes my stomach twist with nerves, and both Sienna and I go quiet along with the rest of the stadium when we realize that Nico isn't moving.

My heart drops into the vicinity of my toes when the other guy rises but Nico doesn't.

"Oh my God," I whisper, pressing both my hands to my mouth, sharing a look with Sienna. She appears just as worried as I am.

"Get up, honey. Please get up," Claudia encourages in a raspy whisper, her attention never straying from where he lies on the field, still not really moving. A few teammates go to him, including Gav. We're all waiting, my legs getting weak, when a couple of the coaches run out onto the field to tend to Nico.

Sienna clutches my arm, her voice determined. "He'll be fine. I'm sure he's okay."

"Right. He's fine," I say weakly. Everything about me is weak. My heart. My head. My legs feel like they could give out at any second. Nico is hurt.

Hurt.

I wish I could run out onto the field, but they'd just kick me out of the game if I even tried that, so of course I don't. I remain where I'm at, my focus fixed on the field. I curl my other arm through Claudia's, and we all stand there, hoping against hope that Nico will be okay. The panic racing through my veins makes me breathe faster. Harder. The same words rattle through my brain, getting me through it.

He's just fine. He's just fine.

Is he, though? Really? Tears threaten, and I squeeze my eyes shut, fighting them off. I need to be strong. Nico is okay.

He has to be.

Eventually he sits up, and the entire stadium erupts in earsplitting cheers. We're screaming, too, the relief flooding my senses at seeing him being helped to his feet making me clutch Sienna and Claudia even harder.

"He's going to be all right," Claudia says with a steely determination that reminds me of Nico. "Look at him. He's walking off the field."

Assisted, but I don't say that. I send a look to Sienna, who still appears vaguely worried, but she smiles at me, nodding her encouragement.

"I'm sure he's fine. Might've got knocked around a little bit, but don't worry," she says.

Her words aren't a comfort. And it doesn't help when they lead him to the medical tent on the sidelines, where he remains for the rest of the fourth quarter.

I worry, distracted, as the clock ticks away. I'm not even paying attention to what's happening when the crowd suddenly roars, and I jerk my attention to the field, leaping to my feet when I see that a Dolphin has the ball in his hands when he most certainly shouldn't.

"Interception!" screams one of the announcers.

Sienna and I are hopping up and down, my gaze going to the back of the guy's jersey. It says *DOLLAR*.

"Oh my God, it's Frank!" I'm screaming. Sienna is too.

He runs the ball all the way into the end zone, scoring a touchdown, and we freaking lose it. Half the stadium is cheering so loudly it's almost deafening, and I swear once Frank runs over to the sidelines, the entire team surrounds him, congratulating him. Supporting him.

Ah man, I have tears in my eyes.

"Are you crying?" Sienna screeches. "'Cause I am!" She points at her face.

We're laughing and blubbering, clutching each other, and I realize in that moment that the team is going to win. With the time still left on the clock and how many points we have compared to the other team, there's no way they can catch up to us.

We've won.

Everyone is screaming their happiness, and while I'm clapping, my gaze never strays from the makeshift medical tent. Nico still hasn't emerged, and I hope he's not seriously hurt.

But what if he is? God, seeing him lying there unmoving on the field was terrifying. It made me realize something.

I love him. I'm in love with Nico. I think I've known this for a while, but I always brushed it off because no way could it happen that quickly, but it's true.

I'm in love with him.

I want to tell him, but will that freak him out? He's not big on serious relationships, yet he somehow has ended up in one with me. Sort of.

Ugh, now I feel unsure and frazzled, and I hate that. I need to see him. Talk to him. Just staring into his eyes is a reassurance.

Pandemonium reigns once the game is over, and we slowly make our way out onto the field along with Claudia, who is practically vibrating with excitement or nerves, I can't tell. Maybe it's a combination of both. She's swiveling her head left and right, her hair swinging with the movement, and at one point, she stops on the forty-yard line and tilts her head back, watching the people slowly empty the stands.

"This stadium is huge." Her wide eyes meet mine. "It still amazes me that this many people come here to cheer on my son and his team."

"They're really good, Mrs. Valente," Sienna reminds her, sending me an amused look.

"Sienna, I don't know how many times I've told you this over the years, but please, call me Claudia."

"Right. Okay, Claudia." Sienna nods and smiles, her gaze then zeroing in on someone to the right and just behind Nico's mom. Her smile fades, and panic flashes in her eyes. "I need to go find my brother."

Before we can say anything, Sienna is gone. Seconds later I realize why.

"Hey, Nico's mom" is how Gavin greets Claudia with a big smile on his handsome face, pulling her into a crushing hug.

This is the new way of things. Anytime Gavin is in the vicinity, Sienna makes herself scarce. She still won't tell me exactly everything that happened the night she left our house in a huff and Gavin eventually went after her, but I know it wasn't great.

He must've said or done something that sent her so far over the edge that she doesn't even want to talk about it, and she pretty much tells me everything.

"Oh, Gav, it's been too long. It's so nice to see you." Claudia hugs him in return before she pulls away, smiling up at him. "You played so well this afternoon!"

"Thank you. So did Nico." His expression turns serious. "By the way, he's all right. He's just being checked out thoroughly by the medical staff before being released."

"Was it a concussion?" Claudia asks, her voice full of concern. "He's had a few in the past. They always worry me. I've told him before it's not good to get knocked in the head all the time."

"I'm not sure yet, but he seems like he's in good shape." Gav glances over in my direction. "You'll be able to see him soon."

"Thanks, Gav." I offer him a smile. He's aware of how close I am to Sienna, but I consider Gavin a friend as well. He may be dead to her, and I can still be his friend . . . but I will always be on Sienna's side.

This type of situation is confusing. I actually really like Gavin, but I also know he's been a complete shit to Sienna. Is his behavior on purpose, or is he really that oblivious?

I don't know.

"Can you take us to him, please?" Claudia asks Gav. "I'd like to see my son with my own eyes."

"Of course."

We head over to the sidelines, where Nico is already out of the tent. He's chatting with the offensive coach, his expression grave, his gaze lifting to search around him every few seconds. The moment he spots me, a smile appears and he says something to his coach before he breaks away from him, heading straight for me.

I don't even think. I run toward him, our gazes locking, my heart in free fall. Only when I feel his strong arms clamp around me and hold me close does it settle back into place.

"I was so worried." My voice is muffled against his chest. He's still in his full uniform, and when I pull away so I can look at his too-gorgeous face, I see something in his eyes I've never noticed before. An unfamiliar emotion that has my stomach fluttering with nerves.

"I'm okay." He brushes the hair away from my forehead, his fingers going to his number written in paint on my cheek. "Don't worry."

"Are you sure?" I run my hands over his chest and stomach, but I can't actually feel him, thanks to all the equipment he's still wearing.

"I'm positive." His focus drops to my chest, lingering there. "You're wearing my jersey."

"I always wear your jersey," I remind him, frowning. He knows this.

"You were wearing the hoodie earlier."

I'm surprised that he noticed, but then again, not. He notices everything about me.

Just like I notice everything about him.

"With the jersey on underneath." I smile, rising on tiptoe. "You're being silly."

"Hey, I can't help it that I like seeing you in my jersey. And for some reason, it looks especially good on you right now." He dips his head, his mouth finding mine for a too-brief second before he ends it, turning his attention to his mother. "Ma, you look ready to cry."

"Oh, my Nico." Claudia's face crumples, and he wraps her up in a comforting hug, kissing the top of her head.

"I'm fine," he reassures her, his gaze finding mine once more. "They think it might be a slight concussion."

My heart trips over itself at his revelation. "What does that mean?"

"I'll need to take it easy for the rest of the weekend. They'll monitor me, but I'll probably be back to normal come Monday afternoon." He smiles. "I'm fine. Really."

"What happened out there?" Claudia asks.

"Not quite sure. That dude took me down, and it felt like my head rattled around in my helmet. I think I hit the ground just right, and I even blacked out for a few seconds."

My God, this game is dangerous. Seeing him laid out on the field unmoving scared the crap out of me, and now he's acting like it was no big deal.

"Oh my goodness, Nico. You blacked out?" His mother's level of distress is at about a ten, which is where mine is after his explanations.

"I'm fine. It's okay." He gives her a one-armed hug before he lets her go and comes back to . . .

Me.

My heart soars when he pulls me into his arms again, his mouth at my ear when he whispers, "Want to go to dinner with me and my mom?"

I pull away slightly to stare into his dark eyes. "I don't want to impose. I'm sure your mom wants you all to herself."

"It was her idea. She wants to get to know you better. You were all too preoccupied by the game."

"Right, and then you got hurt." I shove at him a little, unable to help myself, and I immediately regret it. "Are you okay?"

He puffs out his chest. "I'm fine. I promise."

"You scared me."

"If you're going to be with me, Ever, prepare yourself. I'm going to scare you on a regular basis, especially if I keep playing football." His hopeful gaze touches something deep in me, and I realize that I have all the faith in this man.

He's going pro. I just know he is.

"Are you sure it's okay if I go to dinner with you two?" I seriously don't want to interfere. They don't see each other as much as they used to—Claudia told me this before the game started. He's so busy with school and football, and she's been busy with work. They're very close, and she misses him terribly.

Direct quote.

"I want you there. She wants you there. You're the two most important women in my life. What you two think about each other matters to me." The sincerity in his eyes makes me swallow hard, and I'm mentally battling the emotions swirling within me.

"Okay. I'll go," I agree, blinking away the tears at his words.

I mean something to this man. And he means something to me.

I swear I'm the luckiest girl in the world.

Chapter Thirty-Six

Nico

After having dinner with my mom at a small Mexican restaurant that's not overrun with Santa Mira students, Ever and I head to the house while Mom drives back home. I let both women fuss over me during dinner, reveling in their attention and not protesting. I stressed them the hell out when I got injured, and while I didn't do it on purpose, I do feel responsible for almost giving them heart attacks.

Mom is used to it. I've broken bones, torn muscles, and wrecked my body in a variety of ways over the years playing football. But as she so kindly reminded us near the end of dinner, this was the first time I've ever blacked out on the field.

Not gonna lie. That shit was scary. I don't remember much beyond getting tackled. I don't even recall hitting the ground. It's wild how our mind protects us from trauma.

It's only when we're at the house, locked away in my bedroom, that Ever lets her emotions flow freely—by way of tears.

"You scared me so bad," she admits while I've got her pressed against the door, holding her close to me. "You weren't moving, Nico, and it was just—terrible."

"I'm okay," I whisper, brushing the tears away from her cheeks, smiling at her. Needing her to be strong. "I'm fine."

"You have a slight concussion." She tilts her chin up, determination filling her features. "That's dangerous."

"I'm here at home. Resting. Just like the doctors told me I should do." Though I'd rather do something else tonight.

Namely Ever.

We've been playing this *nope, can't have actual intercourse yet* act long enough. Frankly, I'm dying to fuck her, slight concussion be damned.

I know how to take it easy. I won't overexert myself.

"You actually wanted to go to Charley's," she chastises me. I tried to convince her we should stop by after we left the restaurant and my mom, but she wouldn't hear of it.

That's okay because now I'm locked away in my bedroom with her. And there's nowhere else I'd rather be.

"Well, we should get you into bed." She gives me a gentle shove, and I back away from her, letting her make her escape. She heads for my bed, tugging down the covers and patting the mattress. "Come on."

"What am I, three?" I make my way toward her, hurriedly kicking off my shoes before I start shedding my clothes.

She glances over at me, doing a double take when she sees what I'm wearing, which is practically nothing. "What are you doing?"

"Getting dressed for bed." I'm grinning, nearly toppling over as I try to take off my jeans. They're gone seconds later, and I rise to my full height, clad in only a pair of red boxer briefs.

Her gaze zeros in on the front of my boxers before guiltily jerking back up to my face. "You're practically naked."

"This is how I normally sleep."

"We've been falling asleep in your bed for the last few weeks. Together. And you're never this—" She waves a hand at me. "Naked."

"Because falling asleep with you in sweats and a T-shirt isn't how I normally go to bed." I wave a hand at myself. "This is."

Everleigh remains rooted in place, eerily quiet.

"You should give it a try," I encourage softly.

Her brows shoot up. "Are you trying to get me into your bed?"

I decide to be honest. "Yes." I grin.

She rolls her eyes, toeing off her shoes. And to my eternal gratefulness, she slowly undresses, until she's standing by the side of my bed in just my jersey and panties, white socks still on her feet. "How's this?"

"Better," I answer. "The jersey is a nice touch, especially without pants."

"You have a big ego."

"Among other big things." I grin.

She laughs.

"Hey, at least we're getting closer," I say once my laughter dies.

"Closer to what?"

"Getting you naked." I go to my side of the bed and climb under the covers. "Come on. Join me."

She rests her hands on her hips, slightly irritated. "We can't mess around tonight, Nico. You have a concussion."

"*Slight* concussion," I correct. "And you know what's the best cure for a concussion?"

She's frowning. "I don't think there's any type of cure for one."

Well, she's right, but I'm not going to tell her that. "If you get a concussion, you have to stay awake for hours."

"Really?" Her skeptical expression and tone have me thinking she's onto me.

I nod. I remember that's what they used to tell us when I was younger, but the medical team didn't mention anything like that earlier when they checked me out. I'm just trying to convince her that what we're about to do—what I plan on doing to her, with her—has got medical clearance. "Definitely."

"Uh-huh. Shouldn't we stay up by watching something on Netflix or whatever?" She slowly joins me, sliding her body beneath the covers before tugging them up to her chin.

"Netflix and chill?"

"No chill."

"You're no fun." I'm pouting, and I never pout. I always get what I want.

This woman? She makes me work for it. And I can't lie . . .

I love a challenge.

"Don't look at me like that." She laughs when I stick my lower lip out farther. "Is that what you did to your mom when you were little?"

The last person I want to talk about in this moment is my mother. "Quit playing hard to get."

Before she can say anything, I've got my hands on her tiny waist and I'm pulling her close to me, curling one leg around both of hers so she's trapped. I start tickling her sides, and she won't stop giggling, smacking at my chest at one point and begging me to stop.

She won't be begging me to stop soon enough, so I give her what she wants, but I don't let go of her.

It's like I can't.

Ever snuggles up close, her cheek pressed against my chest, right where my heart beats. I reach my hand up and thread my fingers in her hair, combing it out slowly. She likes it when I do that, scooting closer to me until her body is halfway on top of mine.

"You scared me out on the field," she admits, so soft I almost don't hear her.

"Yeah, you said that earlier. And I'm sorry." I kiss her forehead, breathe deep her sweet scent. "I didn't mean to."

"I know. I'm not looking for an apology. I just—I want to tell you how I felt, after seeing you unconscious on the field."

I go quiet, still stroking her hair. Waiting for her response.

"It shook me, in the worst possible way. At first the tackle seemed completely normal. I've watched a few games and seen you get hit numerous times."

"It comes with the game," I tell her, and she nods, her cheek sliding across my chest.

"But seeing you like that, surrounded by your coaches when you weren't moving—I was terrified. It made me realize how devastated I would be if I lost you." She hesitates, her fingers skimming across my stomach, and my dick twitches to life. "I know we've moved really fast, but . . . I care about you, Nico."

My heart swells to twice its normal size at her confession. "I care about you too."

"And I don't want to lose you." She lifts her head, her imploring gaze meeting mine. "I probably shouldn't say this because I don't want to freak you out, but . . ."

Her voice drifts, and she presses her lips together, looking scared shitless.

"Say it," I urge, touching her face. Drifting my fingers across her cheek. "Unless you need me to say it first."

Her lips part, but still no words come from her. She knows me so well already, but I think I still surprised her.

"I'll say it first, then." I cup her face with my hands, smoothing my thumbs across her cheeks, catching those last few tears. "I'm in love with you, Everleigh."

More tears well in her blue eyes, and she closes them for a moment, shaking her head once. "You beat me to it."

"I'm just trying to help you out." I lean in and kiss her soft lips, lingering there. Breathing her in. "I love you."

"I'm in love with you too." Her words come out in a raw whisper that touches my fucking soul. Corny but true. "It's way too soon, right?"

"No. Not at all. My mom always told me, when you know, you know." I kiss her again, because how can I resist her after this major confession between us? "And I know about you, Ever. I love you."

"I love you, Nico. So much." She kisses me this time, and I touch my tongue to hers, retreating when she responds. "Everyone is going to think we're crazy."

"I don't give a fuck what anyone thinks about us," I say truthfully, my voice fierce. "What we have together—it's special."

She rolls her eyes, laughing when I flash her a stern look. "Special?"

"Very special," I emphasize, because damn it, I need her to see just how much she means to me. "I've never said those words to a woman before besides my mother and my older sister. Oh, and my grandma."

Ever blinks repeatedly, like she's trying to comprehend what I just said. "Really?"

I nod, letting go of her face and bracing my hands on either side of her head. "You've come to be my everything. Ever." I grin, wondering if she gets tired of the play on words.

I can't help myself. She really is my everything.

"You're all I think about," I tell her when she still hasn't responded. "I can't wait to see you when we're apart. And I never want moments like this to end. When I'm with you in my bed, even when you drive me out of my mind with lust."

She frowns. "I drive you out of your mind?"

Leaning in, I kiss her. It's a long, tongue-filled kiss, and when I finally end it, she's gasping for air. "I'm tired of being a gentleman and taking it slow. I need to be real with you—I'm dying to fuck you."

"But your concussion—"

"Nope." I shake my head, cutting her off. "I'm fine. Really. Just—I want to show you how much I love you, Ever. I'm all pent up and full of fucking emotion, and I'm worried I might explode if I can't get inside you right now."

Her smile is slow. Confident. I think she's realizing the power she has over me and is loving it. "Okay."

Relief flooding me, I kiss her again, trying to communicate with my lips and tongue how much she means to me.

How much I love her.

How I'm never, ever going to let her go.

Chapter Thirty-Seven

EVERLEIGH

I wind my arms around Nico's neck as we continue to kiss, my fingers sliding into the thick, soft hair at his nape. It feels as if I'm floating on a cloud, overwhelmed by Nico's confession of love. Overwhelmed by my own confession.

When I arrived in Santa Mira, my life was a mess, and it only seemed to get worse. I felt as if I lost everything and was starting over from scratch. The only people I could rely on were my new roommates, and we were basically strangers.

Now they feel like my family, every single one of them. Even Gavin. Especially Sienna.

And then there's Nico.

I didn't know I could feel like this. That it could be this good with someone. I'd become so accustomed to the subpar relationship I had with my ex, I thought that was as good as it gets.

I was so wrong.

We might've had our rocky moments, and Nico might've been a jerk more than a few times, but ultimately, none of that matters. All I can focus on is this beautiful man I love.

And who loves me in return.

He shifts above me, sliding his arm down until his fingers are grasping the hem of my team jersey. "I love seeing my number on you, baby, but we need to get rid of this."

His sexy murmur and the way he just called me baby makes heat flood between my thighs. Eagerly I help him get rid of the shirt, pleased to see the appreciation in his dark eyes when he realizes I don't have a bra on.

"You weren't wearing a bra?" He cups my right breast, toying with my hardened nipple with his thumb.

"I hate them," I admit. "If I could go braless for the rest of my life, I'd be happy."

"I wouldn't protest," he murmurs right before he dips his head and draws my nipple into his mouth, sucking it deep.

Closing my eyes, I sink my hands into his hair yet again, holding him close as he devotes all his attention first to one nipple, then the other. The weight of him on top of me is both arousing and a comfort, and when I curl my legs around his, he settles more firmly against my body, his erection pressing into me.

God, he's already so hard. All for me.

Nico eventually abandons my chest, sliding down my body and raining kisses along my stomach. On one hip bone and then the other. He tugs at the front of my panties, his fingers delving deeper, pushing into my wetness, and I moan, arching my hips.

"You're so wet," he murmurs against my stomach, lifting his head at the same time I glance down, our gazes meeting. His is dark and hot, his fingers slipping deeper, his thumb teasing my clit, setting me on fire. "All for me, baby?"

I nod, licking my lips. His gaze flares with awareness, and then he's disposing me of my panties, tugging them down my legs and tossing them aside before he pushes my thighs open and devours me.

I lift my hips, seeking his mouth, and his hands slide beneath my ass, holding me in place as he licks and sucks everywhere. He leaves no spot untouched, and I'm panting, my body straining, desperate for release. It's almost embarrassing how quickly it happens. I fall apart in an instant, coming all over his face, grinding against his mouth. It's liberating how I don't have to suppress my cries because we're all alone in the house for once.

No one can hear me.

It's as if my crying out only encourages him more, and he doesn't let up. He wraps his lips around my clit, tonguing it in a pulsating rhythm that eases another orgasm out of me within minutes. Until I'm a shaky, overwhelmed mess.

"You taste so fucking good, Ever," he murmurs against my thigh when he's finished. When I'm still trembling and trying to calm my chaotic heart. "I can't get enough of you."

It literally feels like that every time we're together. As if we can't get enough of each other. I love it.

I love him.

Nico eventually gets rid of his boxer briefs, slipping back into bed with me completely naked, wrapping me back up in his arms. I press against him, rolling over so I'm on top of him, his cock in perfect alignment to slip inside my body, and when I feel just the tip of him poking at me, I go still.

"Do you have condoms?" I ask.

Nodding, he's already reaching for his nightstand, tugging at the drawer so hard, it falls completely out of its slot, tumbling to the floor.

I burst out laughing, scooting over along with him as we both reach toward the ground. He finds the box of condoms first. A fresh pack, never been opened.

I don't even want to know how long it's been since he's had sex with someone, but I get the feeling it's been since before he met me. I've not seen him try to hook up with a single woman, and he's had his chances more than once.

None of those women matter anymore anyway. Not even mean Portia. This man is mine.

All mine.

I watch as he tears open the condom wrapper and slips it on his erection, my entire body shivering in expectation. I've waited for this moment for what feels like forever, and anticipation fills me, making me reach for him.

I end up with my back on the mattress and Nico hovering above me, his cock insistent between my legs, my entire body melting in preparation for him.

"Can't go back after this," he murmurs, his voice rough with restraint. "Once I'm inside you, Ever, you're mine."

"I'm yours," I whisper, already knowing deep down that it's true. I'm all his.

And he's all mine.

He slowly slides inside my body, inch after exquisite inch, and I only exhale when he's filling me completely. He pauses, holding himself still, letting me adjust to him, and I close my eyes, savoring the moment. He's huge, and I've never felt so full before.

"Am I hurting you?" The strain in his voice is obvious.

I crack my eyes open, shaking my head. "It's perfect. You're perfect." I wiggle my hips, causing him to go even deeper, making him groan.

He starts to move, pulling almost all the way out before plunging back in, establishing a slow, steady rhythm that already has me seeing stars. Ducking his head, his mouth finds mine, kissing me deep, his tongue doing a thorough search of my mouth, and I lift my legs, wrapping them around his waist. Clinging to him like I never want to let him go.

This is what real connection feels like, I think as Nico rocks into me. I'm so attuned to this man, surrounded completely by him. Locked with him, our bodies melded together.

He's all I could ever want.

I can feel my third orgasm of the night forming. My stomach clenches with every thrust, the tip of his erection nudging a spot inside me that creates a delicious friction I can't get enough of. I slide my hands down until they're settled on his ass, pushing him deeper. Holding him there.

"You feel so good," he murmurs close to my ear, his panting breaths making me shiver. "I can't fucking get enough of you."

I feel the same. The exact same.

"Don't stop," I tell him as he increases his speed, hitting the perfect spot over and over again. The very spot that's going to send me tumbling over the edge. "Please."

"Never," he breathes out, fucking me harder. The steady pace is what eventually pushes me over the cresting wave, and my stomach clenches, tingles sweeping over my skin as the orgasm grips me. I'm moaning, my brain going blank as every single part of me shakes from the force of my climax.

I cling to him, riding out the orgasm as he continues to pound inside me, his breathing becoming more and more ragged, his groans louder. Our sweaty skin sticks together, his hips slapping against mine until he arches against me, a rough moan rumbling from deep in his throat. His hips jerk with one last, rough thrust, and I open my eyes, watching him come, fascinated by the look on his beautiful face. His lips are parted, his eyes half-closed, but they flash open when he catches me watching him.

And when he dips his head, his mouth finding mine once more, I kiss him with everything I've got, breathing him in. Trying my best to absorb him as much as I can.

When he eventually stops shaking, his breaths coming slower, his entire body squashing mine into the mattress—not that I mind—I whisper in his ear, "Can we do it again?"

His deep chuckle ripples along my nerve endings and settles right in between my legs. "What about my slight concussion?"

Oh, now he's using my argument against me. "I think you can handle it."

"Baby, I can fuck you endlessly, and I won't ever stop if that's what you want." His mouth is on my neck, his hand on my breast. "I can guarantee that."

"Prove it," I say, with a laugh that turns into a moan when he gently squeezes me.

"I will," he says, determination filling his voice. "I'm going to prove it to you all night long."

And he does.

The next morning we exit Nico's bedroom together on purpose, entering the kitchen looking like a couple as much as we possibly can. I'm in one of his old Dolphins football T-shirts, which swamps me, hanging just above my knees. He's clad in a pair of gray sweats and nothing else. Both of us are barefoot, our hair is a mess, and we look, as Nico put it only a few minutes ago before he kissed me soundly, "freshly fucked."

I can't deny that I'm loving this look for us.

Coop is at the dining table eating a bowl of Honey Nut Cheerios, his favorite cereal. Frank is sitting across from him, sipping a cup of coffee with too much cream and sugar, a plate of toast crust in front of him. He loves sourdough toast but hates the crust like he's four, but it's also kind of cute? Maybe I'm just weird.

I love that I know these little details about these men. My roommates. My friends.

My family.

"Morning," Nico announces when neither of them looks in our direction to acknowledge us. He sounds vaguely irritated, which almost makes me giggle, but I try my best to keep a straight face.

"Hey." Frank doesn't even turn around.

Coop says nothing. Just keeps shoveling cereal in his mouth, slurping up the milk.

Nico lets out a frustrated growl, releasing my hand so he can curl his arm around my shoulders and tug me into his side. "Just so you guys know, we're together."

Coop finally glances up, his gaze shifting from Nico's to mine. "Duh."

"I mean it's real. Official. We're in love." Nico glances down, his eyes glowing with all that love and aimed right at me. "I'm in love with Everleigh."

"That's sweet." This comes from Frank, who's halfway turned around in his chair and studying us. "But this isn't news, guys. We've been seeing this coming for a while."

"For real," Coop adds.

"Oh." Nico and I share a quick look before he continues speaking. "We just wanted to make sure we have your approval."

"Always," Coop says, Frank nodding his agreement. "You two look disgustingly happy."

Well . . . that's one way to put it.

"We are," Nico says firmly. "She's good for me."

"She's good for all of us," Coop says, his gaze settling on mine. "I'm glad you're here, Ever. And I'm glad you two are happy and in love."

"Me too," Frank adds, and I can hear the sincerity in his voice.

I pull away from Nico's arm and go to Frank first, bending over to give him a hug.

"Thank you," I murmur. "You're a good friend, Frank."

"You, too, Ever." He returns the hug, and when we're done, I check on Nico.

But he's not jealous. He's watching me with those all-seeing dark eyes, looking proud.

Proud of me and the fact that I'm his. That we're in love.

"Where's my hug?" Coop asks as he rises to his full height.

Laughing, I go to him and give him a hug, a whoosh of air escaping me when he gives me a big squeeze. The man is huge, and his hug is all consuming.

"I couldn't have asked for better roommates," I tell them when the hug fest is over and I'm back at Nico's side. "I love you guys."

They all smile, Nico pulling me into his arms, holding me while I stand in front of him.

I think about when I first came to this house. How nervous and scared I was. How alone I felt. I realize as I look around the room, thinking about where I am now, that I will never feel alone again. Not with these men in my life.

Especially the one who's currently got his arms around me.

Acknowledgments

First off, I am so incredibly grateful for my agent and publicist and friend, Georgana. Thank you for believing in me always. And for helping me gain this opportunity with Montlake. This career is a wild ride, and publishing isn't for the faint of heart. I consider myself lucky to have you in my corner.

Thank you to Maria for allowing me to basically write whatever I want. The idea I pitched versus what this book turned into is totally different, and I appreciate you still loving it.

Mackenzie, I'm so glad we're working together again. I've known you a long time! I appreciate the way you make my books so much better.

Shout out to my daughter for all her help and love and for being the perfect travel companion when we go to signings together. Love you, Amy.

To my author friends, especially Devney, Marni, and Laura. Your texts get me through the slog parts of this job.

And finally, to Travis and Taylor and their relationship—the epitome of a sports romance to me. This book doesn't come out until fall 2024, and my fingers are tightly crossed the two of you are still together. Maybe even engaged. I want you two to end up being each other's "End Game." Maybe Ed will perform at the reception and you can sing the song together. UGH, a woman can dream.

About the Author

Monica Murphy is a *New York Times* and *USA Today* bestselling author of over sixty novels. She writes mostly contemporary, new adult, and young adult romance. Both traditionally and independently published, her work has been translated into more than ten languages.

The author lives in central California near Yosemite National Park with her husband, children, one dog, and four cats. When she's not writing, she's thinking about writing. Or reading. Or binge-watching something.